A Monk's Way

A Novel Journey Into Spiritual Awareness

By

Clark Eide

Volume One

The Abbey Chronicles™ Trilogy

CLARK EIDE INC.

Acclaim For *A Monk's Way*

"This engaging, memoir-esque spiritual exploration ultimately raises age-old questions in a fresh format...A thoughtful, engrossing rumination on the relationship between organized religion and personal faith."

Kirkus Reviews

"Impressively well written and consistently compelling from beginning to end, "A Monk's Way" is as thoughtful and thought-provoking as it is unfailingly entertaining."

The Midwest Book Review

"A superb achievement, full of practical wisdom, and, a good read."

Tessa Cason
Spiritual Coach, Teacher and noted Author on EFT.

"This rare book transported me to the world of my inner life and spirituality, connecting me to another dimension. For anyone who seeks to know more about meaning in life, I recommend this book very highly. Everyone can benefit."

Rabbi Yosef Levanon

"…This book describes a unique contemplative journey in rich prose. Clark Eide weaves a fascinating tale about the spiritual path and waking up to Presence in our lives."

Michael R. McVay MD/retired Cardiologist & Practitioner, Teacher – Mindfulness Meditation

Titles Featuring Jean Moreau

Novels

The Abbey Chronicles Trilogy

A Monk's Way
To Everything A Season
Life & Love

Self Help

Little Books of Wisdom Series

Compassion
Patience
Imagination
Gratitude
Humility

Other

The Ecstatic Prayers of Jean Moreau

Author's Note

It is evident that traditional religion, with its tenets, dogma and responses, has not been enough to satisfy a multitude of people in our age. It has left many spiritually unfulfilled. For most people, it is the only formal introduction that they have had to Spirit, and when it has failed them, the choice left to them is either to leave it all behind or look again by embarking alone on a new path of discovery.

This is a story of one who started that journey of discovery — in the very heart of a great religious institution no less — and succeeded in finding his answer — sometimes in spite of his religion. Though his search is non-traditional, he finds what was missing — a direct connection to God — and he discovers ways to activate that connection.

To write about spiritual concepts in a clear and precise way is a very difficult exercise. As exquisite and beautiful as English can be, sometimes words or phrases fail to express an exact meaning. Occasionally, there are no words or phrases that exist to do it; or, sometimes the limitations of a writer's abilities hinder capturing the faithful expression of meaning.

In religious or spiritual instruction, it is not unusual to rely on story-telling — or parable — to give the listener or reader a precise sense of meaning by illustration. This was my intent in creating the personage of Jean Moreau. It is up to him, via his story, to explain concepts and truths that are not only important, but eternal.

Often writers see their characters take on personalities all their own, and Jean Moreau seems to me now an intimate friend. I hope he becomes that kind of friend for you. He and I will continue to work on projects in the future and I am looking forward to that collaboration.

Please note that I reference God as both Mother and Father. Naturally, you are free to see Him or Her as you please. I use the French "abbé" (ah-bay) for the English "abbot". Also, note that the French pronunciation of Jean is equivalent to "zhaw(n)" in English. Finally, I use monastery and abbey interchangeably here.

Now, let's go and meet our friend, Jean Moreau.

Preface

Know thyself.

The Delphi Oracle

My name is Jean Moreau, a monk in the Abbey of Kervennec in Brittany, France, and I have a question for you. In the Western world, how does one judge success? What is it to which most people aspire? What is it that they think they will have, or be, when they finally have or become it? What would you say?

I think often it is connected to the "four Ps" — position, possession, power, and prestige, the world's notion of success. While these are ingrained aspects of modern life, I will submit that they do not contain the seeds that will bear the fruit of real contentment.

Visitors here at the abbey are often very successful. What has made them successful in the world's eyes — a degree, parenthood, business, becoming a leader, teacher or an authority of some kind — might no longer hold its appeal, or, perhaps it no longer plays a principal role for them. While the lives they have led as successful people in the world have brought them some satisfaction, something is still missing. They hunger for more in life. They are not sure what that "more" is, but all evidence tells them that these "four Ps" are not the stuff of happiness — at least not all by themselves. They have yet to find the path to Awareness, to Spirit, which is the only place that one will find real meaning and fulfillment.

As you will see, much of what I will profess in these pages will be what you would expect from a monk, but I assure you that some of it will most certainly surprise you. Mine has hardly been an orthodox path, sometimes pitting myself against my own religion; but, religion and spirit are regrettably often not the same thing. As a monk I have found Awareness through trial and, especially, through error. I have been spared none of what life and the world can deliver, despite being who and where I am.

I'll start my story with a look at how an abbey functions – a mystery to many. Then I'll tell you a little about my origins, family and how I got here, before getting into the meat of my story – a tale of temptations, ups and downs, moments of pure glory as well as moments of near despair. Woven in between, I will share with you tools I use to further my ultimate purpose and ours as humans…our destiny – connecting with the Divine.

By telling my own story, with its conflicts and doubts, with its moments of transcendence and vivid emotion — all that is human — I hope to show that when connected to our Source, life takes on new meaning. All of us are heirs to this astonishing Kingdom of peace and fulfillment. We must only reach out and touch it!

Part One

My Home in the Monastery, My Roots, My Friend

Kervennec and the Rhythm of Abbey Life

I have freed my soul.
– *Abbé Bernard of Clairvaux*, Letter to Abbot Suger

I remember the first time I really noticed the beauty of Kervennec. I hadn't been here very long. It was in the early winter — December, I think. I was walking back to my room after breakfast and the abbey stones had begun to show their golden hue at the dawning of the day. Accompanying first light was some haze, which gave the ancient walls an otherworldly look. I remember smiling to myself and thinking how perfect the moment was and imagining how that scene had repeated itself day after day, season after season — century after century — and here I was, another witness to it, and caught short by it all.

As I continued my walk that morning, what I could not have imagined was what was waiting in the wings for me here — how the love of a woman would bring me to my knees and how my indiscretions nearly had me removed from this place that I love best. But God and my angels never let me fall that far. In fact, it was through that turmoil that I found a more perfect Union with my heavenly Father/Mother. With God's help, my redemption has been complete. That is the story I am about to relate.

Going back in my memory to recall those early days, I remember the first time I really heard the music here, too. I had been so busy trying to learn my parts in each song that until that revelatory instant I had not really heard it. What a moment it was when the chant finally did find its way into my consciousness — a moment that I will never forget.

We were singing one of the Divine Offices. It was Vigils, our first service of the day. On that particular day, instead of just reading and singing my part, something seemed to take hold of me and to distance me from the physical. It was as if I were transported to someplace where I was watching the whole of the proceedings from another vantage point. My ears were suddenly open to the wonder of the unmistakable sound of our chant. It was resonating with the words of the Psalms, words far older than our abbey walls. The chant's purity and sonority and its depth of feeling came home to me, and it has been that way ever since; simple and ancient as those melodies are and as ever-present as they are in our worship, chant still has the power to move me emotionally and to lift me spiritually.

When I sing, I imagine the hundreds, no, the thousands of brothers who have come before me here chanting these very same melodies with their eternal texts. I find myself, as I did that day, readily able to connect to my spiritual ancestors, my spiritual roots. It is a magical feeling and floods me with a wonderful sense of continuity and community.

What is my motivation, my "mission," for being here at Kervennec? I will tell you simply that my mission here in the abbey is to make the effort to know myself — my true self. Why? That true self shares in the divinity of God. Being united to Him is where all true joy lies, so that is the connection that I seek. It is only after I have come to understand my true self and my authentic nature in Spirit that I will be able to know and enjoy a fulfilling relationship with my Father/Mother in heaven. Without that intimate knowledge about myself, I can never have an intimate knowledge of my Creator.

I know that some think that an abbey is just a retreat from the world. I can tell you that it is hardly that. It is, in fact, quite the opposite. It is an embracing of life in all of its depth, in all of its complexities. What can be more difficult for a person than to be alone with him or herself without distraction, hour after hour, day after day? I search for myself and for God in the quiet of prayer and meditation. While I also search for these things in my relationships with my brothers in the abbey, think about what challenges there are in living in close proximity to the same group of men, private and enclosed, for life. I can tell you that there are many — as in any family.

But these challenges, if we do not shy away from them, allow me and my brothers to get to the heart of things; things like self-knowledge, brotherly love — Jesus' second commandment — and understanding. They build character. They are opportunities. Through them, I have come to understand in mini-steps what makes me "tick" and what God wants of me to make His imperfect creature as perfect as he can be in this lifetime. I want to know the emotional man, the rational man, and ultimately, by the grace of God, come to know my eternal self, my spiritual man. When I have accomplished those things, then I can come to know my Creator. In knowing God, I will be complete, wanting for nothing.

Let me tell you more about everyday life here. Our days in the abbey are always busy and productive. It's not all work though. Everyone knows that all work makes us not just dull boys, but not very balanced human beings. None of us want that, so we combine work and prayer with personal and community time in a very satisfying way. This method of living each day has come down to us with very little change from St. Benedict, who conceived it and encoded it in his *Rule*, now known as *The Rule of St. Benedict*, fifteen hundred years ago!

St. Benedict. God raises up the right men at the right time — and the right time was the fifth century, when stability was a disappearing dream after the Pax Romana. He was a man of astounding wisdom, stuck as he was in the abyss of the Dark Ages. The genius of St. Benedict is embedded in the wisdom of the *Rule*. It is comprised of many parts, but perhaps the most enlightened is the concept of the structure of the abbey day. St. Benedict was very specific about how the day and the responsibilities of work and prayer should be organized. We Benedictines have the motto "Work and

Pray." It is anything but an empty credo, that I can tell you, and every year I appreciate its brilliance more and more.

Here is a little about the structure of our day: We start our singing of antiphons (short verses of scripture) and Psalms from the first moment we gather every day. During the whole waking day, we sing six Divine Offices and celebrate a Mass. An Office is a time of prayer and adoration as a community. St. Benedict knew the power of worship as a community, and he also knew the discipline it brings to the contemplative life. In that act of coming together, we strengthen our spiritual resolve and challenge ourselves to grow in brotherly love and patience. In the Offices, we have the prayer structure we need to thrive as men on earth but live with one foot in Paradise.

St. Benedict knew that any life devoted to God had to be practical as well as contemplative. Everyday life as it exists on earth cannot be ignored. The *Rule* lets us immerse ourselves in the work and affairs of the life of the senses, within a structure that gives us ample time for the development of our immortal souls. We need time daily to appreciate who we are, why we are, and Who made us, to worship and commune with our God. We also need to provide for ourselves and our bodies. We are not many of us constructed to be hermits. Thus, our community gives us what we need to thrive on every level.

Each monk is expected to attend all of the Offices and to be on time, but Père Abbé, head of the abbey and our spiritual Father, can grant someone a special leave should one of us have a duty that requires missing an Office. I myself love our rituals so much I feel empty if on occasion I might miss one.

We perform most of the Offices in the abbey church. Vigils is our first Office. Vigils is often sung in the dark or at dawn in our abbey, depending upon the season. It is an especially beautiful service. It is the time of day when the earth seems new and the spirit and its energies most palpable. It is the time of day when the distance between our world of activity, life on earth as it were, and the peace and incisive wisdom of the next world, that of the spirit, is lessened. At that hour, the "veil is thin" between the two worlds.

Following Vigils we have some time for ourselves, individually, or for sharing a cup of coffee and a snack with our brother monks, before heading back to the church to start the next Office, Lauds. The Latin meaning of that word translates into English as "praise." This Office, along with that of Vespers in late afternoon, are my next two favorites. Lauds is full of chanting the praises of God in its selections of Psalms and antiphons. For me it is a second beginning to my day. Lauds is one of the longest services, lasting a half hour or more, but it is a most beautiful one.

If you picture in your mind the "choir" in our church, which is situated on the altar side of the communion rail, you can picture how we gather. We sit in two groups, facing one another. We have nineteen monks on each side. Our iterations of the songs are sung as if by two separate choirs. One choir, or "side," sings a certain number of the verses of a

Psalm. Then the other side continues singing the next few verses, and so on. At certain times, we sing together, usually at the conclusion of the Psalm. This echo effect is very nice and it is also wonderful to be able to face our brothers while chanting. There is a heightened sense of community and intimacy in performing our services like this. We feel as one band, one brotherhood, united there before the Lord enjoying the rapture of these prayers and melodies.

When Lauds is finished, we go to breakfast. Benedictine monks eat well! This was a strong mandate written into the *Rule* by St. Benedict. Men in the abbey need to eat wholesome and filling foods, with as much of it as possible being produced by the men themselves from the farms, orchards, and gardens. Much like an army, a monastery marches on its stomach, and our cooks do their best to give us interesting and tasty meals.

We eat in silence after the abbé sings a prayer, but we always have — or should I say, we usually have — an interesting reading that is chanted by a brother throughout the meal. It can be something written by a monk or saint, books or letters, and it is often quite humorous. We sit on the perimeter of the dining room at long tables in assigned places. The meals in our refectory are for monks and male visitors only, who eat at a table reserved for them. If families or women wish to come and stay with us, we welcome that. We have another nice area where they can be served.

After breakfast we have free time until Mass at ten o'clock. Mass generally lasts about an hour. We follow the Roman Catholic Church's liturgical calendar of feast days and seasons. After that celebration, many of us have specific duties to attend to, such as working at the monastery shop or farm, or administrative duties to perform. Time can go quickly and before we know it we're gathered again in the church for Sext, the short Office that concludes our morning worship and is followed by the next community gathering at lunch. We have another brief Office together after our lunch called None before we breakup to continue our work for the day.

My work has consisted of helping at the shop, general cleaning, and offering help on the farm in season. I have always been good with numbers, so I have also helped on the finance side a little bit.

I mentioned Vespers earlier. It is celebrated in late afternoon. The sung liturgy is exquisite, rivaling Lauds. It is at this time that we see the greatest number of outside visitors of any service. It is a lovely way to wind down the day and prepare for evening, especially in winter. We emerge to a dark world and I find the sense of community heightened then. I also think we are at our finest voice at that time of day, which enhances the liturgy. An hour or so later finds us back at the refectory for dinner, and then we finish the day at about 8:45 p.m. with Compline, our last Divine Office for the day.

People often wonder if we are allowed talk to each other at the abbey. That is a great question, to which I answer, simply, yes, we can talk. Monasteries all differ on how they treat silence, however. At Kervennec, we have certain times reserved for silence — from 8:00 p.m. to 8:00 a.m. and at meals. We have one quiet time after recreation in the afternoon, prior to Vespers. At all other times, the idea is just to not make unnecessary conversation. I don't find these rules difficult to follow.

All in all, it is a most pleasant and efficient organization of the day and allows us to fulfill perfectly St. Benedict's monastic vision "to work and to pray." There is nourishment of the soul, mind, and body, beautifully intertwined. While this kind of life is not for everybody, if the world could take the best parts of our lifestyle — working, praying, and living in peaceful community — wouldn't it be a beautiful world?

My Room

*All men's miseries derive from not being able to sit in a quiet
room alone.*
 — *Blaise Pascal,* Pensées

The idea of being alone is so far separated from being
lonely. I love my time alone. For me, being alone is a
time of reflection and of peace — a time of really
getting to know myself. In the monastery, we are alone
quite often, but we feel a loving community around us,
and that energy comforts us and works to reinforce our
intent to know ourselves and our God.

We monks each have a room in the monastery that
some on the "outside" refer to as a "cell." What a
dreary sounding place — lonely, cramped, and
solitary! Nothing could be further from the truth. It is a
wonderful place — a place of inspiration and prayer
and I never tire of it. Its energetic warmth and its
familiarity constantly nourish and comfort me. It is not
a retreat from the world, but a place to go into myself
and into the midst of the spiritual forces that constantly
and lovingly swirl within and around us.

I have read how the physical space around some
holy men, their lodgings and their places of prayer
particularly, take on the positive energy of that person.
My room possesses a soul — part of mine, certainly,
but also traces of the dozens of others who have lived
in this space in the centuries before me. Anyone can
feel it, though the degree to which its power is

communicated depends upon each person. This kind of energy can be appreciated for what it is by those who can fully comprehend its nature but it can also be appreciated by the uninitiated for its warmth of feeling. I always sense it. I use that energy and benefit from what it has to give me by tapping into it in my meditations.

Sometimes I think it must be so hard to find peace for those who do not have this private luxury — those in the outside world who lead much different lives with their many different kinds of distractions. To have and honor a private place in one's home or in one's mind and to still live in the world can be done, certainly, but the effort is great. He or she who can achieve that is destined for great peace and contentment in this world, and receives a taste of the unimaginable contentment and beauties of the next one. How I admire and continue to pray for those outside who are working to build upon their spiritual leanings.

I like to sit in my room in this old comfy chair of mine and look up at the light passing through my window. It frequently falls into my room as a golden ray with surprising warmth even in the dead of winter. There is a softness but also an intensity about it. I love the contrasting shadows it creates and the specks of dust that seem like contented angels flitting and floating in the air. This light often appears most glorious mid to late morning, depending upon the season. The world seems to slow to a crawl, everything more vivid at those times. I was born just before noon and I've read that all of us are more sensitive to things at the time of day that corresponds to the time of our births. Late morning seems to be a time of greater physical energy for me, so maybe that is true. I have felt my subtler energies, those that I touch in prayer and meditation, to be heightened at this time. It's like the world of the unseen is more near. It is a place of calm, this old room, in a thousand small ways.

It's important to feel that world of the unseen. We all can do it. We only need to stop in the busy-ness of our day or at any other time that suits us and go into the Quiet that is within us all. There we will find it. It is there, in that quiet spot, where we really get to know the truth of all that is around us and within us. With that knowledge comes a serenity not found anywhere else, I can promise you that. I will come back to that whole subject, which is really that of Awareness, very often in this story. It is our goal to become aware, the first step on the way to fulfillment.

One thing that I like to do in my quiet time here is to read or even recite silently from memory any Psalms that come to me. These are, for me, the jewels of religious literature. The Psalmists, in their litanies of "why's" and "thank you's" and "how could you's," state the case for a loving and attentive God even in the face of a deck often stacked against them. They cut to the quick and tell the whole and unvarnished truth of the human condition. How many times have I read or recited them? Thousands? Tens of thousands? It doesn't matter. No matter how many times I have read them or sung them or meditated upon them — season after season, year after year here during the monastery services — they never lose their power to inspire me and to move me.

I now feel like I know personally those writers of old. I am in awe at how my fellow human beings' cries from the heart and shrieks from the soul could be expressed so simply and so effectively in their writings. At nearly every reading there is something — their imploring, their confidence, their remorse, their utter despair, their praise, their sense of ultimate triumph — that moves me and brings me closer to my Creator. The Psalms, in the end, show us how a little grain of faith can flower. Sometimes after I read them or recite them privately, especially early in the morning and just before bed at night, I write down my own prayers and poetry that come from my own heart — my own shrieks from the soul. It helps me clarify how I feel about so many things.

The Psalms remind me so often of the person most dear to me, besides my parents. That was my first abbé, Abbé Paul, a man of great warmth and love who is so often on my mind. He is now enjoying his heavenly reward. He was also a man of much learning and wisdom. It was he who taught me so much about everyday living — how to bring the spirit into my daily life, how to know what Jesus meant with his sayings, how not to judge, how to love myself — well, the list could go on and on. How I miss his presence here in the earthly life…yet I know he watches over me from his celestial home!

One thing he used to tell me, and which he mentioned that the Psalms pointed out repeatedly, was that the Enemy was never far. I often recall the discussion I had with him about that long ago at the beginning of my monastic career. It went something like this:

"Who is the Enemy, the Adversary?" We were walking together after a morning Mass and the question came out of the blue from Abbé Paul.

"The Enemy is Satan," I remember responding.

"Ah, yes, our old friend Satan, my well-trained priest. That's a good answer — at least according to the Catechism. But now I will ask you, my young friend, what does the word Satan mean, other than Adversary? Who or what is Satan? Who or what is the Adversary, and do those terms really get us any closer to who that Enemy really is, what defines him, what his essence is or what it tells us about life, about ourselves, about our spirits? Do you think that it does? Well, I don't.

"What is it that separates us from God?" he then asked.

I remember being afraid to spew back the answer that I had learned in Catholic school and seminary. It was sitting now at the tip of my tongue — sin.

"Mon Père Abbé, I know the answer I would like to give you, but now it seems so inadequate and nondescript. I want to hear what you can tell me, how you can guide my thinking."

Père Abbé chuckled and said, "No doubt you were going to say 'sin.' And you would be right, Jean. Any good Catholic schoolboy would be correct to respond that way. But then again, what is sin? What is it really,

Jean? Give me a good definition. Is it just the list our Heavenly Father is keeping of, shall I say, our less than optimal decisions or attributes?"

Abbé laughed that time as he said that. His joy in life was apparent. I remember that laugh especially. I started to laugh, too, because his laugh was infectious. As he laughed, he put his arm around my shoulder and we walked in the garden for a while. He loved all of his charges, this was true, but there was something special that he saw in me and I knew it.

"I will tell you who the Enemy, Satan, the Adversary, or whatever you want to call him really is. The Enemy is, in a phrase, all things that block one's way from finding or connecting with God and entering the Kingdom of Heaven right here on earth. The Enemy is anything that separates us from God. That is a big list of things! There are lots of opportunities for the mortal blows that he can deliver under many different names and guises.

"Remember those references in the Psalms to an advancing army?" he continued. "They are not to be taken literally because they are nothing more than an action or omission or even a way of life that threatens to obstruct the soul's connection to the Godhead. The more we engage in the untoward, the lower our defenses become going forward. The Psalms are warning us that the Adversary is always advancing and preparing for his attack on the integrity of the soul, and that this Enemy attacks from within. It's a constant battle with him to make the right choice and avoid the destructive choice as we work to advance to an evolved spiritual state.

"You know, Jean," he said, "there is always that choice of advancing or of stepping backwards. But the Enemy — the Adversary, Satan — is very clever. He operates one-on-one, exposing weaknesses, testing, and so often succeeding in separating man from his peace, from God. He can and does also operate within groups, including tribes and nations. Anger and fear are his principal weapons but the Enemy can bring another type of obstacle that is so very difficult to fight — despair. We must never despair. The cries of the Psalmist were desperate, but not despairing; how easy it can be, however, to fall into a feeling of hopelessness, then or now."

I remember how we talked of many things that day but that concept of the Enemy and the definition of his success and our death — being cutoff from our Heavenly Father, from our Source, to be where "His face no longer shines upon us" — is what has stood out for me over time.

Abbé Paul went to his heavenly home many years ago, but I feel his presence and his smile often. I frequently think about what it means to have daily triumphs over the Enemy. A triumph for me is maintaining a connectedness to God and a sense of His presence, particularly in the face of difficulty. Connectedness by its very nature will eventually become Understanding, the recognition first of the possibility and then of the reality of the temporary nature of life on earth and its sufferings and the recognition of another dimension. That is Awareness.

Awareness is that place where Love and Compassion begin. It is the place from which one can really begin to experience the Godhead, Who encompasses those virtues. Under the fire of the Enemy are forged man's noblest characteristics, or greatest failures. The tempering of the earthly man through his many difficulties and challenges is where he can learn to connect to his own soul, his Higher Self, the Divine within. It is this connection to the Divine that gives humanity its only true possibility for happiness in a world incapable of delivering it by itself. We eventually come to realize that earthly life should not be taken too seriously, and that all works for our good.

Divine connection — there cannot be happier or more satisfying moments in any human experience. The peace that pervades us is not of this world. It is a contentedness, a lack of fear or anger, a state of complete satisfaction. It is the prelude, a glimpse of what we can expect in our coming life in Eternity. It is for "those who have ears to hear," the Pearl of Great Price, the one thing that a person should sell or renounce everything to possess. It is nothing less than the Kingdom of Heaven itself and as Jesus said, it is there, available to all of us. We can lose our "gloom and doom" — we can learn to live. That is the promise of the Good News!

Now, I have to tell you about someone. She has been the light of my life, and as you will see, someone who has brought me challenges that wracked me down to my very soul. I love her. You will see why.

Elena

What is a friend? A single soul dwelling in two bodies.
— Aristotle, quoted by Diogenes Laertius

Elena! Where do I begin? I want to tell you everything about her, this kind and blessèd human, my soul mate…and by far my greatest challenge in life to date, which I will describe in much detail in the coming pages.

Elena is a woman who has intrigued me all of my adult life. I can hear you saying to yourself, "A monk with a female soul mate?" It is true. This radiant soul and I had a bond that we felt from the beginning of our acquaintance. We met at university in Brest. She just had that "way," that something that attracted me from the start. It has always been exciting just to see her, anytime — after class, around town, on outings, at the monastery. I can't put it into words, really. The best I can do is to quote a young visiting novice. We were in discussions about sexuality and its lures and attractions, among other things. As he spoke about a woman he had once been very attracted to, he said, "She just rattled my cage." I haven't found a more apt description of the "process" yet! It was an attraction that grew into much more than a physical one. We think the same about things, we enjoy the same things, we love our God the same way, passionately; and, we love each other.

At university, we did not meet until late in our last

year. But it took just those few months for us to learn so much about each other and to come to know each other's intimate thoughts like we had been lifelong friends. It was a very sad day when we parted, me for the monastic life, eventually, and her for her artist's dream. But, we knew our choices were the correct ones, no matter how painful it might be for each of us for a while, and painful it was for some time. I had the sense that I had lost the one person in whom I could confide, and I was starting on a path in life that could be quite lonely at times. I didn't enter the monastery right away, but took a job as a salesperson with a travel agency in Angers, still not quite convinced about my vocation. Elena was based in Brest but traveled quite a bit in Europe for her inspiration.

We knew, of course, that we could write to each other. But I had a premonition that that would not last with our respective careers developing. I was right and our correspondence soon petered out. Writing could not replace what we had experienced in person during those intense few months. We never became intimate but it was on my mind and I am sure that it was on hers. She didn't need to say it. I could see the longing on her face; and I could make no secret of my physical desires. Still, I knew it was for the best to leave that as it was, knowing that my life might soon change. And if I had pressed it, she would have resisted, I believe, to spare me the task of confessing it when I would commence my priestly training. She was, and is, so unselfish.

A lot of our time together we spent out of doors.

She is a lover of nature, as am I. It is there we feel God really resides on the physical plane. Nature offers us a chance to get back to our roots, no pun intended! There is no pressure from others or from daily life, no interruptions in our thinking or our meditating about things, just a sense of oneness and unity that is hard to experience anywhere else. I wish sometimes that I had made a fastidious record of all that we discussed. Some of it, in light of life's experiences, would now seem trite, I am sure; but there were bits of wisdom here and there that would be fun to see now. Such a diary would serve, if nothing else, as a history of a friendship, with its serious side, its inanities, its insights, its humor, and mostly, its connection.

Our story recommenced a little more than a year ago. Out of the blue she contacted me. What a surprise it was! She had written to me and asked if she could come and see me: Would I be available one day so that we might catch up on things, talk about old times, and get reacquainted? I was delighted to have heard from her so I naturally said yes. We quickly fixed a rendezvous for later that same week. She would come to the abbey to meet me. I had decided that if the weather were nice, we could have a walk around the grounds and maybe take a sandwich and have a picnic.

The day arrived and fortunately it was a beautiful Breton day. The wind was fresh and bright clouds were rapidly pushing past high in the azure sky. Elena arrived right on time. As she approached the *accueil*, or welcome center for the abbey, I could make out the familiar shape of her face and her tall, slim body. She cut a lovely figure. As she approached, it seemed to me that she had hardly aged. Tall and angular, with only a hint of gray now invading her long dark hair, she was still striking in appearance. I remember that I suddenly became conscious of my own appearance — something that hadn't concerned me in quite that way for years! I let that thought go — fortunately, my cassock hides a multitude of sins!

I met her enthusiastically and gave her kisses on each cheek. She responded in like fashion and smiled warmly.

"Hello, Jean! Or, should I say, 'Father'?"

I smiled and then chuckled a little. "No, Elena, I think I'll always be 'Jean' to you!"

As I was speaking, I couldn't help but stare at my beautiful friend. In fact, I couldn't take my eyes off of her — all of those years, and now, here she was, here we were, together again.

"How did you find me, hermit that I am?" I asked, trying not to be nervous.

She smiled that big smile and responded, "Well, I'll tell you. I was reading one of our university newsletters last week and you came into my mind. It got me to thinking more about you. To be honest, I have thought of you so many, many times over the years. We were so close and I missed you, but I knew that you were otherwise 'occupied'! But after getting that newsletter and with you fresh on my mind, I became more and more curious about where you had ended up. I wasn't sure if you were still in this area, so I decided to call around a few parishes in Brest a couple of weeks ago. One priest there said that he recognized your name and thought you were here at Kervennec.

"I had come out here a month or so ago to get some ideas for a project I am looking at doing, and also just to visit the place. Of course, I had no idea that you were here. Funny, but I hadn't ever been to Kervennec before, even though it's not that far. I had a nice walk around and toured the church and the other buildings. Crazy to think now that you were here so near to me.

"Anyway, I wrote to you and, voilà, here you are, an hour from Brest — not quite as 'hermity' as you'd like to think!"

There it was — that sassy sense of humor. How I had missed it!

"Well, okay, you got me there — I'm not quite a hermit," I admitted. "But it must have been your feeling my vibrations here during your first visit that aroused your curiosity!"

"No doubt!"

Back and forth we went like that for a while. I remember how I enjoyed gazing at her thoughtfully as she brought me up to date on common friends and other happenings. She seemed calm and confident to me. She had a look in her eyes, in her regard, that was very peaceful. There is something about her face and eyes that has always conferred a softness about her. She also has what appears to be a sort of perpetual half-smile on her mouth that gives her a look of approachability.

After a bit, we decided to take a long stroll around the monastery grounds and we continued to talk. She was a little reluctant to speak too much of herself at the start but she asked me lots of questions about my lifestyle now and what had transpired for me over the last twenty-plus years. I told her things of a general nature — how I feel here, what a typical day is like, a little about some of my brother monks…things rather banal. We were sitting in one of the monastery's public gardens when she decided to open up a little more about her own life those past two decades. Her story was like many others these days, full of hope and then disappointment, a modern world sometimes grown cruel.

"I got married at twenty-five. Not too long after university, really," she explained. "I had lost contact with you then, Jean. You must have been here already. Those years were a sad time for me. I was only married for four years before divorcing."

I was curious how someone so mature and assured could be linked to that kind of personal disappointment, even failure, as I know it seemed to her.

"What do you think happened?" I asked her.

She sighed and said, "During the last two years or so of our marriage, I sensed a great change coming through me. I realized that I had a real need to explore my existence, my spirituality, my whole sense of who I am and where I come from. I think I had a midlife crisis!" she said, lightening her tone just a bit. "But seriously, I started to read a lot and attended many talks and gatherings in the city attached to things spiritual. I found myself opening up to new thinking and exposed to new and different ideas, and I liked it."

"That is wonderful, Elena. It sounds like a real awakening. That does change a person. What did your husband think of all of this — didn't like it too much?"

"That's just it, Jean. Julian found the 'new' me very disquieting and he even tried to forbid me from continuing to attend things that he considered threatening to him or 'evil.' But, you know, Jean, by then I had gone much too far and I was not about to stop the one thing that was fulfilling me and that was bringing me to another level of awareness. Our marriage had never been a strong one, so I left. At the end, I didn't think there was any hope."

"Wow, Elena, that had to be tough."

"That's not the half of it," she continued. "I felt very bad, of course, as you can imagine, but he was distraught. We had no kids and thus no reason to keep seeing each other, and I wanted a fresh start and really didn't want to talk to him anymore about any of it or even to see him. There was no point. It was finished. Then the other shoe dropped. Julian died two years later — a rare form of cancer. It was all so sudden, so quick. It really stunned me. But, he was gone and the finality of it all struck me. I thought, 'I really am on my own.' I got used to it eventually but it was hard to live through."

"I am sorry you had all of that sadness, Elena." I could see a touch of that sadness was still there all these years later — it had crept into those lovely eyes.

"Thank you, Jean," she said. "It's okay now. It's been a long time, more than fifteen years. It gave me a chance to redefine who I am. And also to continue my studies of the spirit and the energetic world around us…how it all manifests. That continues to be exciting to me."

As usual that afternoon we were on the same wavelength about so many things. I was happy to hear that part about her spiritual self. Everyone's journey to that place is different, but all of us can get to that place where we become seekers, regardless of our situation in life or the point of view we may have been taught or have developed, whatever life throws at us.

I then wanted to break the spell of that sad story and change the topic a bit — there was still a lot I wanted to know about my dear friend.

"What do you do for fun?" I decided to ask.

"I visit priests in old abbeys."

"BORING!" I shot back.

"Oh, it's not that bad. It depends on the priest! Some are very interesting, I know, and very good-looking."

"Present company excluded, no doubt!"

"Oh, you always were handsome, Jean, and you know it! There were some broken hearts in Brittany when you entered the seminary…"

"Too bad I didn't know about it — I might have been swayed!"

It was after saying this that some uncomfortable thoughts started to reveal themselves to me. Maybe it was more uncomfortable feelings than thoughts. I was smiling outwardly as if taken in by my own funny remark, but I knew in an instant looking at Elena how much my last words might contain a truth that I didn't want to own at this time.

"I don't think so — you are happy here, I can see it," she replied.

I was listening but not concentrating, still aware of those new feelings I was experiencing.

After a little hesitation, I replied. "You always had a brilliant mind, Elena. You hit the nail on the head. I couldn't have chosen better." Suddenly that statement felt a little forced with the state of mind I was in.

I went on anyway, though a little off-balance. "But you still haven't answered my question — what's fun for you? It's about time you tell me about what YOU do all day!"

"Yes, I do have a real life…" she replied.

"Then tell me all about it. I'd be shocked if someone of your talent and charm did not have a 'real life' and an interesting one at that. By the way, how do you fight the guys off?"

As I said this, I wasn't convinced I was asking only out of polite interest — I realized that perhaps I was more invested in her answer than I should have been. A spark of jealousy came out of nowhere before she even spoke. I wasn't sure I even wanted to hear what she had to say.

"Jean…whoa…sorry, but men – who needs them!" She let out that hearty laugh of hers. Then she quickly added, "Just kidding — I know there are some really good ones out there. I'm talking to one."

I felt pleased. But the feelings wanted to know more. What if I had followed up on this wonderful relationship with Elena? What if I hadn't gone to become a priest, but instead shared my life with her? I remember the unmistakable thrill of goose bumps running up my spine and down my arms as those thoughts materialized.

It had all passed through my mind in a millisecond and I gave her a look like she was a naughty girl and said, "Let's not talk about me anymore, you charmer. Tell me more about your 'real life.'" I wanted to move on.

"Well, I am an artist, or didn't you know?" she replied with some energy.

"I knew you liked painting…but, pray tell, what have you been doing with your talent?" I tried to stay light and loose.

"Something close to your heart as a priest I am sure — stained glass!"

"Ufff, I don't like a lot of stained glass. It makes me think of sad old dark churches with a heavy, heavy feeling and saints being chopped up into bitty pieces as martyrs, and…"

"Stop, already, Jean, for heaven's sake! You're making me hate it, too!" she laughed. "But, you know, my dear prelate, there are some motifs running through stained glass that are a bit lighter. And, believe it or not, my fine churchman, some stained glass is not for religious consumption!"

"Well, I'd have to see it to believe it!"

"Stop up and see some of my etchings sometime,"

Elena teased me.

When I heard her say that, I must confess that my feelings got the better of me. I felt things in a sexual way I had not felt for years. I found a lot of enjoyment in it, and, unfortunately, I didn't try to stop it. There were warning bells ringing in my head. I recovered as best as I could by saying, "You haven't changed a bit, Elena!"

She smiled and continued. "I don't know if you even knew that, besides my painting, I had started some stained glass work towards the end of university. I probably never mentioned it as I really didn't get heavily involved in it until after graduation. Anyway, I really liked it and continued that while I was doing odd jobs and studying painting. I really love doing it now and consider it my dream job. I have been able to launch a career in stained glass. I am even getting commissions now!"

"Commissions…that's great, Elena!"

"Yes, and maybe even a big one," she went on. "The nuns at the Abbey of St. Michel are looking for someone to redesign their church windows in stained glass. They've asked me to make a presentation."

"Aha, they'll have you enlisted in their abbey before you know it! Sister Mary Elena, resident saint…and artist!"

That broke the mounting tension for a moment.

"I'd be a tough nut to crack, Jean. Of course, I am sure they'd never have me — with my checkered past!" She laughed again. "But, you know, having said that, the peace and the quality of the people I have met at abbeys makes me think and feel that something great is going on with that lifestyle."

"And now you've met me and I've spoiled it all for you!" I said, starting to feel a little more like my normal self.

"You're such a goofball," she replied. "I love that about you. But, yes, you're right!"

After that we decided to take another long walk through some of the orchards and gardens. The time went quickly. I wanted the afternoon to go on and on but when Elena glanced at her watch and saw how late it had gotten, it was time for her to think about leaving, so we walked back. We stopped just before the abbey gate.

"Elena, I want to tell you how glad I am that you took the trouble to find me and to come visit today. It was great fun to see you again and talk of so much."

I remember then adding, as much more than just a polite gesture, "I hope we can do it again soon."

"Me, too," she responded.

I was thrilled in one sense to hear that. In my other ear, I could hear my guardian angel whispering a little warning. We walked to her car.

"I'll see you soon, Padre," she said with a warm smile and a kiss on the cheek.

Then she left.

That's how it all got started once more.

I realized as I walked back to my room that Elena's type of feminine presence was exactly complementary to my masculine energy. I missed it. Our meeting that day was the thing that started a chain of events I shall relate that brought me so much pain — but it also brought me much wisdom. It all seems to go together. We need the one to kick-start the other; and so it has always been for man on this beautiful planet. I can tell you that those events forced me to deal with things brought up very rudely from my subconscious to my conscious mind that needed my attention. Though I hardly would wish to experience a challenge like that again, with God's help and love I am the better for it now, this I know. She was the catalyst for that growth — and how grateful I am to her for that.

I remember also on that walk back to my room feeling exhilarated yet befuddled. I was feeling a kind of excitement about life that I had not felt in some time…and I was feeling the stirrings of desire. Being with Elena once more had evoked these things.

I had time after she left before the Office of Vespers, so I sat in my beloved chair in my room and closed my eyes, trying to understand my real self and its needs and desires, but also, I confess, savoring the feeling of her. I certainly then hoped that we would see each other again soon — little did I realize then what complications lay ahead for us.

But more on that as my story unfolds.

My Mother

Mother is the name for God in the lips and hearts of children.
  — *William Makepeace Thackeray,* Vanity Fair

My story cannot really go any further without at least a brief encounter with the two people who brought me into the world, who nurtured and loved me and did their very best to make me a person of whom they could be proud.

I am an only child. I was able to spend a lot of time with my parents without interruption. With that communal time, and being of a sensitive nature, I was able to perceive and come to understand many of their beliefs, both stated and unstated, in a world grown increasingly complex. My mother was much more transparent than my father. I could connect with her. My father remained much more of a mystery due to his emotional armor which was very difficult to penetrate. Let me take some time to describe them. I will start with my mother.

In many ways, as I have alluded, she was less complicated than my father. I know that females are often considered the more complicated or mysterious, but unlike my father, my mother was direct and always let me know her feelings. She never tried to hide her emotions from me. My emotions run deep, too, but I am not as good as she was at handling them. I do not have her strength. I am still trying to learn from her example to not over-react. But my mother also had a very tender side that has stayed with me in the image I carry of her. She was incapable of hurting anyone on purpose, but was by no means a pushover.

She and I would discuss so many different topics, and I respected very much her insight and the passion she felt for her points of view. She also loved to cook and we had some of our best times there in the kitchen. I always fancied myself a good cook due to her mentoring. Certain kitchen smells bring her back to me instantly if they waft my way. Those were certainly some of our closest moments, affording us time to talk about anything that came to mind.

We talked about religion and spirituality a lot in those discussions. She never distinguished between the two. Without religion, there could be no spirituality for her. It was one area where our thinking came to differ. She was passionate about the Church and the authority of its teachings. I certainly did not always share her lockstep approach to Catholic doctrine, like many my age, but both of us believed strongly in a loving and very present God. We both believed in the importance of that relationship. What differed between us were our ideas of the extent of the role our own Church played in enhancing and maintaining that Divine relationship. She was one who took every word that came out of Rome as the Gospel, while I, then and even now as a priest, might question or possibly reject in my heart of hearts some of those teachings.

As a younger man, I was quite happy to accompany her and participate in all of the rites and ceremonies of our Church — especially the sacraments. My father usually abstained from going. In Brittany, most villages have a day when its citizens perform a ritual called a "pardon." On that particular day, villagers form a procession and carry an effigy, usually a statue of their patron saint taken from the local church, on a parade route around the town. It was notable to me to see women and men, a few of them very important persons in the village, lowering their heads and marching one with the other on this pilgrimage of sorts, at least by appearance devotedly following our statue. Small to medium-sized towns often have huge divides in social classes and ours was no exception, but all of that was forgotten for a few hours to serve a higher cause, to praise and thank God. I will always remember how it was a time of unity and cooperation in the village.

It was also a festive time and as a young man these processions and the festivals that followed were huge occasions. I remember my mother enjoying so much working with the other townswomen, dressed as they were in their traditional costumes with their elaborate *coiffes* or lace head coverings unique to each village, some a foot high. These festivals attached to our religious life were fun and memorable. They were also, quite frankly, for a number of us, an added opportunity to accumulate some good marks on that scorecard most of us believed God was keeping of our actions and omissions here on earth.

Like most kids I pretty much did and believed as I was told. I didn't think much about religious beliefs until I was about fourteen. It was at that time that my comfort with some of my Church's views began to subside. I started to see some beliefs as fantastic or at best unimportant, if not unbelievable. I will tell you more about that relationship with my Church, a very personal and deeply important subject, a bit later. For now, my purpose is more to explain the relationship between myself and my mother, in which religion played an important part, at first uniting and then dividing us. That division, though, never became a rupture.

Her views, as I mentioned, were very conservative, but my mother was hardly the kind of woman whose opinions one could dismiss lightly. She was very intelligent, not at all loud or boisterous, and she possessed this inner strength and conviction that impressed others, especially my father. Like many mothers the world has known, she was a rock, the most stable influence in the family. My father was the titular head, but I don't think anything important was ever decided in the family without at least her tacit consent. I know she did give my Dad lots of leeway and support and was generous in her recognition of some of his sterner and, for her, unpopular beliefs. The important thing that she demonstrated to me as I grew older and could discern more about what made that relationship tick was her unconditional love for my father — and for me. Never did I doubt her support and it was only later that I appreciated how much giving up her only child to the monastery meant to her.

I remember well the subject over which our first religious conflicts were brought into view. After attending university for a year, it was a little awkward fitting myself back into the family rhythm on our long summer *"grandes vacances."* Time moved slowly during those months and although I had a job I had become accustomed to being on my own schedule, satisfying my own needs, and making up my own mind about things. One of the first days that I was back at home was a Sunday. My mother was preparing for church and said we were leaving in five minutes. By this time, I had left the Sunday ritual behind, seeing it as drab and pointless. I had forgotten all about it, in fact, until my mother gave me notice. For a moment I didn't know what to do. I didn't want to go but didn't want to hurt her, as I believed it would. Finally, I decided to tell her I was ill. That bought me time for a week, but when confronted with the same situation the following Sunday, I changed course. I had thought about it during that week and decided to let her know the truth. When that moment came, my heart was thumping and my hands were sweating. After my rather shallow excuses, she said nothing, but with two jerks yanked on her gloves, looked at me one more moment and left. I felt the fool — why would I not consent to go just to make her happy? — yet, that was not me, and although it was very difficult, I had to take the course of action that I did.

Occasionally thereafter she would make some sarcastic reference to the "silliness" of going to church or this or that Catholic precept we may have discussed and I had dismissed, but those occasions were rare and mercifully of short duration. Still, it put a wrench in the works of our daily repartee as it had changed something on a fundamental level. I respected her beliefs but I don't think she ever respected mine to the same degree. Why should she? She, as a practicing and faithful Catholic, had a religion that worked well for her. She thought the Church was right and that was that. There is a practicality in that — whether one is Catholic, Jewish, Muslim or another religion — as it gives a structure to life that can be so useful and comforting. We humans love the familiar and when it promises a route to eternal happiness, it can become almost irresistible.

I remember one day some years later when she invited me to sit beside her as she lounged in her favorite chair — a rocker — just knitting. I was home after graduating from university. I had in those four years developed many of the nascent stirrings of what I now feel about the world and about God. The priesthood began to attract me, funnily enough, at university, where I had developed my very un-Catholic philosophies. In those deep recesses from which our true selves emerge, if we let them, I knew that despite all of the Church's "flaws," I was a once and future Christian and a Catholic. The place I still felt the best to "be spiritual" was the Catholic Church. It was my only real experience of religion; and, at that time, religion was what I associated with being spiritual. I knew deep inside that I was a man of Spirit, and it needed to be expressed. That last spring at school I had started thinking of enrolling in a seminary. It had been a recurring thought. I began thinking that the life of a monk might be the perfect spiritual expression I sought. I had told no one and I was still several years away from that decision.

As I came into the room that day, my mother put her handiwork down and I sat by her. She had a certain look in her eye that I not seen before. It was a look, it seemed to me at the time, of seeing something in the distance while at the same time being present for me. As I sat there, she looked at me with eyes that became softer and full of love. I was completely taken in by that look. She was beautiful — like a young girl. I had an overwhelming feeling, suddenly, that this was to be an important moment. Her smile and face slowly relaxed and she began to speak.

"Jean, I know that we have had our disagreements about things religious. I have tried not to interfere, though I have been worried about your lack of religion. I want to tell you that whatever you believe, I will always love you, and that I've always just wanted the best for you. Part of that 'wanting' is wanting you to embrace not just a religion but a morality, which, to me, the world needs."

She stopped for a moment, now with another reflective look. "I have watched you grow and become a man, and even though you have not been with us very much these last few years, I have watched you become a wonderful young man. Both your father and I are so happy with you and I want you to know that we are proud of your accomplishments — yes; but, I really want to tell you that we are most proud of the kind of person that you have become, and we thank

God for that."

Then, with a twinkle in those Celtic eyes she added, "I can't help but feel that our prayers had something to do with that, despite your resistance!"

She laughed deeply and I laughed with her. Any tension that had been between us up to that point seemed to break completely, and so it was until the end of her days some nineteen years later. I know that she passed away a happy and satisfied soul. I saw that peace, too, with a few in her generation who followed a strict Catholic path. What has stayed with me for all of these years is simply, "Who am I to question their personal beliefs?" Though I may see some of them as rigid and impractical, I have no right. Many of these people can and have lighted up my day and I admire them despite what negativity I see in their view of the eternal — so much doom and gloom within its complicated theology. It simply works for them. I wish I could say the same for many priests I have seen sharing their beliefs — but without the joy! But that is yet another story.

After my mother died, I found some letters in her personal effects. She had made copies of some of her correspondences. There were many to her sister who lived in Châteauneuf-du-Faou, a market town in the Department of Finistère in Brittany. There were others addressed to friends and relatives. One was even to the President of the Republic. Then, towards the bottom of the pile, I was startled to see many letters addressed to me. They were letters that I had never seen, and in fact, were still in their sealed envelopes ready to be mailed, but never sent.

I sat there just looking at them for a while, stunned at having found them and also by the fact that she had taken the time to write but had never mailed them. It was a fantastic discovery. It was like finding the key to a magic door that led to a place where I could be with my mother again. These letters were conversations with her that we never had. She was there again in that room, and my hands were trembling as I gently lifted the pile and put it on my lap. My instinct was to open them all and devour the contents, but a part of me was also reluctant. Whatever these letters would say was final. I would have to take them as they were, as the last word, and I knew that those words could certainly bring me a lot of joy, but they could also hurt. There would be no going back to her to get a further explanation about something or to ease the blow of her truth, so I was a little afraid as I opened the first one, but I must say that deep inside of me I felt more confident and I was so excited to think that mom was here with me anew — with fresh thoughts waiting — than worried about any of the contents the letters may harbor.

I saw after opening the first few that they were in a sort of chronological order. The first was dated about the time I left for university. It was touching. It was the letter of a mother letting go — profound in its sadness at seeing her life's work leave, never to come back. It was a lament, of that there was no doubt; but, it was tender and full of a mother's love. It gripped my heart. For just a moment, no longer, I remember thinking with great sadness how I would never know that feeling of parenthood. Tears were welling as my emotions took over, and my heart was full to breaking with love for this kind and powerful woman who had given me my earthly life. So much she had to give, and so much lay inside this woman. I have mentioned how intelligent she was, but as I read the letters, she showed me a side of her, a complexity really, that I had never fully appreciated before in its true depth. She talked of her love for God, her love of the classics written by Catholic saints, especially St. Teresa, and they revealed her wide-ranging knowledge of theological thought. I saw then, too, how I had been selfish in just thinking of my own philosophy of life, my own needs and convictions, and how I had chosen to go no further with hers than to consider them to be old-fashioned and out of step with reality. Even then in my insolence, if I had examined my inner notions and let the truth come out, I would have readily admitted that we had much in common, and that here was a woman of great substance and consideration, not an automaton of Church belief. I didn't want to do that then. Yes, she took those beliefs seriously, but she was no sheep, no simpleton or rustic, as I am now ashamed I had thought about her in the context of her beliefs, God forgive me! Strange how I still need to make this supplication to a stern God for forgiveness, when I know beyond a doubt that my mother would already have forgiven me… How far I have yet to go to convert my interior man to the man I want to be…a man seeing a loving and forgiving God only. Perhaps I am pandering still at some level to those ancient beliefs I so detest!

In addition to baring her soul about her religion and her hopes for me, much of what she wrote was about day -to-day things, the things we might have discussed had I been home with her. There were always some instructions for life and her cautions to, in effect, "be a good boy," but there was much in them about our village, the latest news of comings and goings, and who had made the news for any reason. Reading them was so fun and moving at the same time. I sat there for some hours, mesmerized, still aching with love for this woman who had taught me more that I would ever realize. I suppose in some sense she was the quintessential mother. I thank God for giving me this beautiful gift, this incomparable start in life. She gave me faith but she also gave me room to grow and express my own truth. How proud she was at my ordination; and how happy I was to be able to give her such a gift that was precious for her and only mine to give. Somehow any worries she may have had over my immortal soul were gone, I felt. We never again really discussed the differences of our beliefs in our common religion. It didn't really matter, nor should it have then or even now were she still with us in body. What mattered was the love that flowered between us.

What matters to us all is only the love we express one to another. That is the message that Jesus taught us. Is it really so hard a thing?

When my mother died, I must admit I was nearly inconsolable. I had come to know and already appreciate her so much by then. My father had already passed. Mom was my last connection to family. I was comforted only in knowing that she was now enjoying the rich prize for which she had toiled so hard. I was left here alone to continue my journey, but I know that I have it quite good. I believe in the fraternity of men that forms my new family. It is now here, in that family, that I can take my strength and my consolation in earthly matters.

I feel her presence less now than I did before, as I know she has other things to do, to accomplish, but she remains firmly implanted always in the back of my mind. My father, well, he is more distant to me: still with me but in my mind a bit fuzzy and not often prominent in my thinking. Though I loved him, that relationship was nothing like the one with my mother, and I would like to tell you about it now.

My Father

For rarely are sons similar to their fathers…
— Homer, The Odyssey

As complex as the relationship between mother and son has the reputation to be, in my mind we often underestimate the complexity of the father-son relationship. There is something palpable about the male energy, and that something is surely activated around other males. No doubt it was designed to keep other males at a distance. We see it so often in the animal kingdom as each young male seeks a mate or mates, but, notably, we see it frequently between the males of two generations. We humans have not been spared this tendency in our makeup, and I have felt it often. We monks are certainly not immune to it here! It goes a long way in teaching us humility, as you will come to see in my personal story.

My father, like many of his contemporaries and the generations before him, was not in touch with the emotional aspects of himself. In my case, this whole competitive response to the generation before was made more complicated by my father's inability to express feelings, especially tender ones. They were locked tight inside. Denial or repression was the order of the day, particularly the latter. In addition to his natural bent, the effort to keep his emotions in check, the "good" as well as the "bad," gave him the appearance of being distant. It wasn't quite the same as being aloof; it was more as though he were just disinterested in whatever it was I was trying to show or tell him. He traveled alone quite a bit for his job and was not used to having people around him for long periods; or, at least, that served as the explanation that I used to give myself when he would come home and show little interest in me. It was my excuse to lessen the impact of his remoteness towards me.

In one of my mother's last posthumous letters, she did allude to the fact that it had been difficult to talk about certain things with him, and how happy she was that she could have some of those conversations with me. In fact, I became at a very young age her surrogate confidante. It was too late to respond after reading that letter that the subject matter of those conversations was a little too much for me emotionally. It is true that I was the only other person around her most of the time, and certainly the only other male; but I believe that she treated me emotionally like an adult since I had that type of mature façade, but I found it troubling when she gave me too much intimate detail about her feelings on some subjects, most markedly on her relationship with my father. I learned a lot about him that way, however. His distance was thus not limited to me. She was rarely privy to his thoughts. He had few intimate friends and I often wondered if he had anyone with whom he might share his innermost thoughts. I doubt it now.

My father was not a religious person and rarely went to church. I was always curious how my mother could have picked such an opposite as far as faith was concerned, but she was certainly not alone in that regard. Many women went to church unaccompanied by their spouses, though I think less so here in Brittany than in other parts of France. This is not to say by any means that he wasn't a good man nor do I mean it as a judgment of any kind. He was, quite simply, a man of his time in his emotional makeup, less open to the contemplation of religious matters and affairs of the heart, and not really available for a discussion of those affairs. I am sure this was an important factor contributing to his early death by heart attack. I firmly believe that the body's maladies are simply reflections of our inner turmoil — emotional and spiritual. That turmoil, I am convinced, is always there at the root of these maladies.

When I was five years old, we moved across the Atlantic to the province of Quebec, not far from Montreal, where he had a chance to sell farm machinery. He was very gifted for language, picked up English quickly and soon we moved to the little town of Milton in Ontario. I went to school there until I was eleven when we returned to Brittany for an opportunity for him to own part of an office products company. Living in Canada those years was a blessing for me as I became fluent in a second language and learned a little more about the big world outside of my tiny province in France.

My father had the knack for quickly connecting with people, despite all. He was a good actor. He was successful in his job because he made friends easily — not what you would call deep personal friendships, but good, solid customer relationships. I had seen him in action when I was a younger man. There were times when he would host customers at home. He had a completely different persona and was really quite likeable and very open in that context. I could see why customers would trust him and relate to him and why they would buy from him. This only made him more complex to me — a man who could talk to anyone, except his own family. In his business life, he was not the man of conflicted emotions I knew him to be as an everyday person. I know that it was one reason he so enjoyed his work — he could be at ease and "forget" who he was while meeting people on the job. That constant positive feedback from work was very important.

My mother was very supportive, but the weight of what I now know to be his own emotional distress would eventually overpower whatever she could give. As for my father and me, our competitive male energies, accentuated as I matured, didn't make it any easier for us to communicate. We were both strong-willed by nature. We didn't mix too well and I wanted to break free. Ashamedly I say now, I wanted to beat him in everything that we did — to win and to reaffirm my independence — and my superiority. After a while, we could only talk about the most banal of things — some sports and some politics. Frankly, at the time, that was enough for me. Being around him was not enjoyable. I was much too immature to even attempt to normalize our relationship. The competitive forces within me, the male hierarchy of nature, and his sullenness were too strong a mixture for me to fight off successfully until much later. On the other hand, had he been more open, more confident in himself, more aware and accountable, I think that we could have had more quality time together. I might have relented somewhat. It is water over the dam now but it is important that I, too, acknowledge my contribution to our failure to connect well. Our actions and reactions were unconscious at the time, but my father never attained an awareness of these negative energies, and quite naturally remained victimized by them, too.

We were very solid middle-class citizens. He was a good provider and we always had plenty of what we needed. I know that he was proud of that, as he rightly should have been. He spent long hours on the road. He brought work home with him. He put in whatever effort was necessary to get the job done right, and this is one great characteristic that I learned from him and have always appreciated. He taught me by example to never give in, to get the job done, and to do one's best. This was a great set of lessons for life and it was he that instilled them in me. It was and continues to be one way that I can put my competitive juices to fruitful work.

There is one particular incident that I want to tell you about concerning my father. It is engraved in my memory, and it gave me a new respect for him. It also taught me quite a bit more about those male energies.

One evening when I was about twenty-one and home from school on a weekend, Dad came home from an outing with one of his few good friends. He appeared to be much shaken. It seemed odd to me at the time because it was a casual Saturday night and he had been friends with this man for years, a man who would one day be elected mayor of our town. The two of them would often talk late into the night discussing the issues of the day in France, politics or other topics, but particularly the former and usually with opposing or at least very differing viewpoints. Some of those discussions naturally revolved around economics. My father was a rather conservative man in that regard, an individualist, and the future mayor was on the other side of the spectrum, a socialist. Neither would have been able to convince the other to change a position from which the other would clearly never budge, and the subject would normally change when one or the other sensed it had gone as far as it could. My father carried his convictions privately, revealing them to my mother sometimes and only occasionally to his few friends, like the future mayor, if the opportunity lent itself. I knew how very passionately he felt about these things, but one would never have known it from his demeanor. It was part of his emotional armor.

At that time he had been greatly distressed by the nationalization of the French banking system by the new government. I knew this because I had heard him speaking unguardedly to my mother about it — a rare occurrence for my ears. He could not understand how the government suddenly had the right to be so embedded in the very fabric of its citizens' lives; how any well-meaning government that practiced democracy could so insinuate itself into such a private sphere. One's money was a private affair. When government had control of that, personal liberty was at risk. He would talk to me about it on other occasions — it was one of the few areas where we could have an open and frank discussion. I didn't have enough experience to have much of an opinion about economics at the time, but he was certainly on target and prescient about privacy issues, as we often now see.

On that night, my father had come home a changed man. His face was distorted, his color ashen, his manner so calm yet strained. I remember how he wandered blankly over to the kitchen sink to get a glass of water. I caught a look at my mom's face. She had said nothing but clearly she too was shaken by what she saw. It was then that he turned and, unusually for him, began to relate his story to her, with me still in the room.

He said that his future-mayor friend, his name was Henri, had run into him on the main street that evening. After a little chat, Henri suggested they go to a nearby bar for a drink to have more time to talk together. My dad said that it started innocently enough, but that Henri had seemed to him to be noticeably ill at ease and different. Aggressive was the word that had come to mind at the time, he said. After a little more idle conversation, Henri had asked him if he had heard the big news about the banks, knowing, of course, that he would have. Henri started to take the conversation there, and became more and more vehement in his manner. Henri was cognizant of my father's views, the antithesis of his own, but continued to rail at those, my father included, who might be opposed to this latest government move or who might try to thwart that action, which would have been futile anyway. He had indicated that those who opposed this move had better learn — it was now a *fait accompli*. My father then said that Henri began to cast anyone opposed to the developments as the socialist party's "enemy," in whose numbers he knew my father was counted.

Dad said he had attempted twice to dismiss the subject and end the conversation with Henri, but the latter was not to be stopped or dissuaded from continuing his attacks. The diatribe, for that was what it now had become to my dad, had even degenerated to name-calling by Henri. My father had had no wish to participate further, particularly at the level to which the discourse had descended.

He then paused for a while after another sip of water, and he was looking very sad. He continued his story after a few more moments of silence and another drink of water, talking quite softly to me and my mom. He told us that Henri had showed himself quite simply a completely different person. He had never seen this side of him before. "A man possessed" is how my father described him. What had begun as a normal conversation had become one man's tirade. It was as if Henri were gloating and releasing many long-held hostilities. In a rare moment of introspection, my father said quietly, "It was a complete unmasking of the real Henri." Those were his words exactly. When my father got up to leave Henri's table, he was further castigated and ridiculed in a loud and unforgiving manner. Henri had severely damaged and perhaps even destroyed in one fell swoop the deep threads of friendship that had existed for many years.

After that, in fact, Henri had become a bitter enemy to my father, though I know he felt himself not so much a party to that as Henri did. He rather felt the sadness and the setback of losing a friend. Seeing him like that and hearing the story during a rare moment of paternal openness registered strongly with me that night. It was a big lesson, too. It had taught me something about human beings and their behavior that I have never forgotten. Never again will I be surprised at anything anyone does or says. I have seen many times since the lack of good judgment and singular unfairness that can be the result of the politics or egos of groups or individuals. And never will I underestimate the power and the obsession that an idea can generate. That rings true on matters of my faith and my Church as well, more of which I shall relate.

I have not as a result of all of this become less trusting of people or institutions, but rather more particular and cautious with them. I will err always on the side of generosity in my assessment — there is far more to be gained by being trusting at first glance than by being overly cautious — but I will never be naïve. One must be circumspect from time to time, and, if the situation calls for it, protective. Being trusting for the most part has paid many dividends for me as it has opened friendships and deepened relationships, providing far more positives than negatives.

I believe we are all good by nature. Events and pressures, however, can make us act in unseemly ways, not at all our better selves, when we let our darker side emerge; and, there is a dark side, let there be no mistake about it. It is very much a part of ourselves. Some people have been pushed to the brink so young and so often that the dark side's emergence becomes quick and normalized. Others, by burying it so deeply and never confronting it, have great difficulty accepting themselves and others when it does emerge. But it is a reactive part of our inherited instinct, primitive, and for most of us only revealed when pressures become too great for our "normal" loving side. It can be used for fuel and, of course, can actually feel good and empowering. The classic example is revenge, but it is a trap destined to bring the perpetrator far away from the joys and happiness of goodness, a quality for which he may have nothing but ridicule in his ignorance. To be attached to that mentality is to be trapped in the emotional, where no long-term happiness can hope to penetrate. It is important for us to admit that our dark side exists and that it is up to us to see it and recognize it for what it is and make friends with it, to ultimately not be afraid of it, to incorporate it and not to judge it. This we can do — we must do.

In the case of my father, this explosion of the darker side of Henri had its positive side for me. I became more loving of my father, more empathetic of him with this expression of emotion of his, despite how subdued it may have been. I respected very much what it took for him to display true regret and sorrow. I drew closer to him with this unmasking of himself and his admission of his sadness and disappointment. Seeing the frailty of the man encapsulated in that moment filled me with compassion. I had sometimes judged my father and I was worse for it. That was a valuable lesson.

This change in my father, or rather the change in my opinion of him also helped me understand a very important principle: when I recognize myself being judgmental, the discomfort I invariably feel is a signal to me that there is still some work to do. It is an opportunity for growth. To see our weaknesses and to be able to work to correct them is a gift from God. It is a way to better ourselves as human beings. "Judge not lest you be judged" were the words of Our Lord. It was He who forgave His torturers on the cross, knowing that their lives, their situations, and their ignorance had brought them to that point of cruelty. He did not judge them.

When I think of my father now in my private time or my prayer time, I often think of this vulnerable side of him that I was privileged to see. I think how he never reacted with bitterness or revenge, just sadness; in his own way, he acted with compassion. My early judgments and my competition with him are now long forgotten — most disappeared that very night and how lucky I was to have that experience when I did. He had gained my respect, and I know he appreciated the change in my behavior towards him. That change pleased me very much then and much more now that he is gone.

I do miss him. He was a good man and I am sure he is enjoying his eternity in peace. What beauty lies potentially within each human's soul.

I am proud to be his son.

Part Two

What Religion Is... and What It Is Not...

Connectedness

Thou art Peter, and upon this rock I will build my Church.
— *Jesus,* Matthew 16:18

Before I begin to talk of the challenges I have been through recently in the monastery, I need to give you a little background about the monastery's relationship to the Catholic Church, and, more to the point, my own.

As a group of Benedictine monks, however, we fall out of the normal Church hierarchical structure. We consult with the local bishops in the dioceses where our abbeys and monasteries are located on any abbey matters that may affect the diocese, but our allegiance is directly to the pope. Each monastery also belongs to one of a number of Benedictine "congregations," organized to help audit and regulate each of the abbeys within that congregation — a type of checks and balances, if you will — including supervisory capacities at the election of new abbés. Abbés here in France occupy their offices for life. This fact has great relevance to my story as you shall see. It is an office of great importance.

At base, it is always the Catholic religion that ties us together — congregations, hierarchy, clerics, and the laity. It is this religion that I love, but...it is a complicated love. My Church: Founded on the love of Christ and His example: yes. An institution: assuredly. A beacon in the night of the human drama: it should be. But has it always been? No, like any earthly institution, it has fallen short frequently. I have experienced many beautiful moments, both emotionally and spiritually, as a part of its ways and beliefs. Christ is the greatest spiritual teacher that I have found — though I am under no illusions as to the beauty, truth, and spiritual realization of other great Masters. His Church can continue to be a teacher of great import who can lead us Home…it has that potential. But, perhaps it has lost its way in some important fashions and that is sad to me. I have chosen a spiritual path within its structure, under its wings as it were; but I am not so much a member of a religion per se as a man seeking the Spirit. The Church has given me a wonderful opportunity to develop that search within its structure, living in the serenity of my Benedictine monastery, though my views may not always coincide. Am I ungrateful?

Some believers today denigrate the idea that religion and spirit can be separate things. They state that to profess that one is spiritual, but not religious, is "à la mode," a fashion, and is a flight from responsibility. The other extreme insists religion is often spiritually dead, a shell of rules and regulations and prohibitions whose meanings have been lost in the sands of time. Can one be a spiritual being and not subscribe to a particular religion? Yes, of course. Neither my religion nor any other confers automatic spiritual wisdom or the desire to obtain it — that is something that is personally driven. It is there to instruct and unite worshippers in its particular theology and in acts of praise in pursuit of the Spirit, to make available to members a path that it believes leads to Spirit. But that is the confusion. There are many organized (religious) paths; many profess that their religion represents the only way to Spirit. Others are open to less rigid views. Then there are individual (nonreligious, in this sense) paths for the intentioned searcher. There is no rule saying that one has to be part of a religious organization to seek spirituality, though I may get some argument from more fundamental religious practitioners, and certainly from most leaders of my Church. I believe that one can even be both; I can be a very spiritual person within the "confines" of my religion.

I do believe it is more difficult to be a nonreligious spiritual searcher in what is often a lonely quest, than to be a simple follower. It takes a good deal more effort and persistence and, to a certain extent, both courage and faith, to search one's spiritual roots outside of or in addition to the acceptance of certain religious dogma. Blind obedience by those who think they have the only Way, and their scorn of those who disagree, can have no appeal to the serious seeker. While the individual search may only appear to be a "fashion" to those in religions who are satisfied with doing and believing what they are told, to me it is a fashion whose time has come. We need the fresh air of that type of thinking. I certainly will not exclude or exonerate my own Church from that need.

To remain members of an organized religion, there must be for each of us at some level a resonance in beliefs. The movement today away from the great religions gains further impetus when educated people see how those great religions have departed from the paths their teachers laid out, a casualty of our human involvement.

The search itself has always been a part of the human psyche, but the individual search has been accentuated with the maturity of society. This individual approach on the path to Spirit, which is the reality for many in our modern world, has been adopted by many very sincere and often holy people. I have met them here in the abbey. We who work primarily through formal religion must face the challenge — no, the opportunity — of becoming whole spiritual beings by also using the wisdom of our personal experience, which may not coincide exactly with our traditional instruction. We must work to inculcate a broader and more inclusive view. We must try always to "practice the right as we see the right" and leave the rest to God. This can be a very difficult path.

I have introduced to you the fact that I have my doubts about my Church and its formal ways, but in fairness, I'd like to show the possibilities and opportunities for greatness that it has, by relating an episode that has stayed with me for some time. I remember it rather particularly for the force it had in demonstrating good, and because the moment was closely shared by one of my best companions in the abbey, Brother Herman, an American with whom I often speak.

We had just celebrated Mass at the abbey one morning several years ago. It had been a solemn High Mass, the pinnacle rite of our Catholic worship observance. It was filled with glorious music, and, at least this time, had conveyed a message of joy in its readings that took our minds away from the morose and reiterated pain and judgment of our Church's all-too-common Vale of Tears spirituality. There were many visitors with heads buried in their prayer books, following each expected step of the service, content with the ritual itself, comforted by its unswerving predictability. But for some in attendance, and I count myself in that number, I can report that the effects of the service had been very different this day. Instead of the rote and staid and sad, my Church's worship had wandered into a fertile landscape of joy and compassion. Those who took notice felt blessed by the experience. For us few it was a time of celebration with a God that one could deeply love — and by whom we could enjoy being loved.

I had had the privilege of concelebrating this Mass with my brother priests. That day, while I was speaking the holy words, I had marveled again at the beauty of the readings, seeing that beauty unfold before me as a spectator would have seen and heard it. The reading from Jesus' final discourse to his apostles from the gospel of John was perfectly placed. Everything else seemed just right, too. What was it today, I wondered, that caused me to be almost dumbstruck by the majesty of the Mass' constituent parts, so perfectly juxtaposed, the liturgy, the music, the scripture, the commentary, the light beaming into the sacristy; in short, its sanctity? It had been a long time since a service had imprinted itself on my psyche as this celebration had.

I felt again very close to my Church. I remember thinking to myself how sad it was that it had been unusual for me to feel that connected. The experience of connectedness I felt to all that was good and marvelous, these things that that service had brought and rekindled, had filled me many times before — but other than in chant it had been rare in this formal setting. It was usually a result of my private prayer and meditation. This service, however, had brought that connection. The Mass that day had struck a chord of harmony with my "connected" self — that part of me connected to the Divine, the connection I long to have abide with me continuously. That a ceremony so emphatically and routinely a part of my formal religion could still do this truly made me feel grateful.

As I was pondering all of this after Mass and leaving to go to my room, Brother Herman caught up with me.

"Good morning, Father Jean," Herman said with a lightheartedness in his voice. He is a happy soul and a delight to be around. I wondered what might be up his sleeve.

"Good morning, Brother Herman. How goes the battle?"

Herman smiled for a second and then, looking as dignified as possible, launched into a response in a mock-serious tone, saying, "I am winning on all fronts. Never will you see a more perfect monk in your presence; rich in spirit, exemplary in prayer, bewitching as orator and teacher, strong of limb, youthful…"

"Et cetera, et cetera, Herman. How in the heck were we lucky enough to attract you to our most humble monastic home?" I had to laugh — like many of the monks, he has a delicious sense of humor.

With a face and a manner worthy of an Oscar nomination, Herman looked momentarily hurt. "You didn't let me finish."

"Oh, I think I heard quite enough…and all true, of course!"

"Well, I should say so. Monks can't lie," replied Herman.

"No, but there may be one or two prone to slight exaggeration…"

Herman appeared to give that a great deal of thought. "Yes, one or two, perhaps. But none that I know personally!"

He giggled and touched my shoulder as we were walking toward the abbey shop.

"Have you got a minute, Jean?" he then asked, this time in a much more serious tone.

I knew he must have something very important on his mind to be asking that.

"Yes, of course, *mon ami*. I'm not due at work for another twenty-three minutes, in fact."

Herman took me aside.

"Well," he began, "I just have to say that today's service was really different for me somehow. There was a satisfying 'something' about it that is difficult to describe."

"How do you mean?" I asked, curious that he had also felt that way.

"I don't know. It's hard to put into words, Jean. Today's Mass was just special to me in a deep, really spiritual way; can't put my finger on it. Just wondering if you thought there was anything special about it, too."

There it was — the same notion that I had had about that day's worship, now being expressed by Brother Herman.

"There did seem to be something about it, Herman, I agree with you," I replied. "I can't tell you what or why. It just all seemed to come together differently…more profoundly today. It 'worked.'"

"Did you talk to anyone else about it?" I asked.

"Yes. On the way out I said something briefly to Father Guinot about how special I thought it had been, and he looked at me like I had two heads. I came directly to you then to make sure that I didn't."

I laughed. "Rest assured, Herman, you still have only that one goofy one that I can see!"

"That's some kind of reassurance. Thank you…I think."

After a few more steps he said, "Maybe it was just me and you today about that Mass. Funny how that works."

We detoured away from the shop and walked on past the public gardens and into the private orchard. It wasn't the first time we had been on the same page about something. We appreciated that in one another. Herman had been touched by the service. He was curious to see if others had experienced it the same way that he had; and, I sensed that he really wanted to share that special moment that he had felt. "A pleasure shared is a pleasure doubled," goes that old adage.

Herman continued. "What do you think causes those feelings, that satisfaction with something we see often but rarely in the way we did today? There must be something, some power or energy coming from somewhere. We both felt it. The fact is, we both felt something profound — maybe something just holy."

I remember we stopped walking after that, thinking about what that certain element might be. Brother Herman, daft as he could be at times, was on to something and I was intrigued by this whole connection to what I felt was Spirit that both of us had felt.

He continued his line of thinking. "I know, Jean, we have a great connection as good friends, and we have similar ideas and values. Maybe that's involved somehow, but, this power or energy or whatever it was we both felt must have come from outside me and you — outside ourselves and yet connected to both of us. It is very wonderful and a little mysterious — that's how I feel."

Nor could I, at that moment, give it a rational explanation or name it as something tangible and concrete. It was something that did appear to come from the outside, at least at first glance, and I did feel it as something sacred — a sacred and loving connection. I felt we could define it as something from the realm of Spirit at least — something involving the spiritual level energetically. I was convinced that that "outside" feeling to it was only part of the story. It was a perception of subtle energy that seemed in some way to enter us from "outside," but which in truth might only be a manifestation of our connection to the Higher Self, and in turn, its connectedness to the Whole. Is that Whole outside us, inside us? To me, that Whole to which we feel connected is both exterior to our being and within it. It is God wrapping Himself around His creation, getting to know Himself from another angle, from the point of view of one of His creations, and we in that deep connection enjoying the benefits of that as sentient beings. It was my Church that helped create that experience that day. It is a marvelous thing and an example of how it could still be very much relevant in our world.

In addition to our Lord Jesus, I have read many of the great connected spirits, men and women of very diverse backgrounds and belief structures: Paramahansa Yogananda, the Buddha, Mary Baker Eddy, Walt Whitman, Madame Blavatsky, Bernard of Clairvaux, and Lao Tzu, for example, among others. I have discovered with age and openness and with their help and God's that the Whole contains the Realm of all Possibilities. In that realm, it is energy that is the key player. The energetic vibration is full of life. It is thought, it is intention, and ultimately Awareness, a type of intuitive perception, the great teacher. The energetic is integrated into every thing and into every thought. It is cause and effect. Its moves are discernible in the visible world, but most of it remains hidden to that material world. This vibration, this Word of God, Spirit, is accessible to all and any who wish to go deeper, to those who wish to explore their own innate ability to perceive. We all have the power, active or latent within, to discern. It is just a matter of degree. That day at the Catholic Mass, I knew that some level of my discernment had been tapped and had grown, and I knew my friend's was evolving too, though Herman might not know how to define or understand completely the energy he was picking up. The world is now moving undeniably towards recognition of this essence of the Spirit in its many manifestations. It is a fact that I not only deeply appreciate but love with all my heart.

I wanted to try to explain my feelings about this to him that day. I sat down on a bench and asked him to join me. The sun was high in the sky but the air had a touch of frost. It contrasted with the warmth of the midday sun. The afterglow of the service was being reflected for me in the beauty of nature all around us.

"Herman, what we experience together in moments like that I am convinced is a type of energy. We feel it often in each other's presence, more like a subtle force radiating from the other. To me, even though at first this energy feels like a power emanating from without, I believe that that is only partially true. I see it as the energy of love originating with God and accessed by and connected to our inner selves…that part we call the spiritual self, or what I call the Higher Self. It is that special aspect of ourselves, all of us, that makes us One. What we feel is that union, that oneness with God and His creation. Such oneness is an emanation of the Eternal One. I believe that we two, Herman, are both built in such a way that we can now detect it. Upon sensing it we drop our psychic defenses, our egos, and we become totally open; and, it is there — in openness and love — that our true brotherhood, our shared Source, emerges."

Herman nodded and I could see the wheels turning. He looked at me and said quite simply, "Jean, I feel like that's it. I love the beauty and connectedness contained in that argument. It's a notion of how a loving God would do things, how He shares."

I then leaned over to my friend on the bench and said, "Herman, sometimes, like now, these things make perfect sense. But try as I might, I can't seem to stay there in that state of understanding for a long period of time."

"What's a long period of time?" he asked me.

"I hate to say it, but maybe ten minutes on average. One hour total on a good day! That is where much of my contemplative energy has gone. I have wanted to stay in that state of knowing the Truth…complete and whole and undeniable…to stay connected, to be Aware. But, the more I work to attain it and then keep it a part of me, the more I realize I cannot corral it. It is a gift, not something to be summoned at will, but presented to me as I prepare myself for it and given when I need it. The more open to it I am consciously, the more it is available. Being open is the same as asking, and we will not be disappointed. I have only recently begun to understand it for what it is. All I can really do myself is to keep working to be open to it. I like the fact that this clear-sightedness is bestowed, not acquired. I like humbling myself to the Great Mystery and His or Her love. It feels right."

That day had started with a sacred service organized by my sometimes overly rigid Church, yet there, in one of its principal services at least two of us had found what we cherish — direct connection to Spirit. It showed how my Church's as well as others' rituals and prayers can have great power when they emphasize the positive about the universe and about God's people. Let's leave it to God to judge and let's concentrate our energies on being open to His wisdom, and that energy.

I'll tell you now about another experience I had at a service here, when I was a younger monk some time ago. This had quite a different feel to it, and will serve to further illustrate the sometimes contentious bond I have with my Mother Church. While I treasure moments like I have described above, in my opinion we still have a lot left to do to rehabilitate our organized religions…as you shall see next.

A Death

The hour of departure has arrived and we go our ways; I to die,
and you to live. Which is better? Only God knows.
                    – *Socrates,* The Apology of Socrates - Plato

Not long after I had entered the monastery, I had a far different type of experience in a church service. It tested me and my faith — but in the end it served to transform me in a fundamental way, a change for the good as I see it now. My memory of its every detail rests clearly in my mind.

One night, somewhere between deep sleep and dream, I was awakened in my cell. I looked over lazily and saw it was too early for Vigils. Then, disturbing the habitual quiet of my room, I became conscious of a muffled but rhythmic sound. I recognized it as one of the monastery's church bells, and I soon enough also recognized its measured cadence. Its toll was a slow deliberate gonging, a pace and sound familiar to our centuries-old abbey. This bell was breaking the news to the community that one of our brothers had left his temporary earthly home for his true abode in Spirit.

The death of a brother is always a bit of a shock, even when one is not so long for this life. It is, of course, an emotional time at the abbey as ours is an intimate community and we naturally have a great feeling of loss. But, somber as the bell sounds, there is accompanying it a certain joy in the news for most of us. It is quite simply the fact that a brother has been released from this material world and has been reborn in Heaven. He has finally entered Paradise, the place of rest and of indescribable joy promised by Our Lord to those pure in spirit.

I wondered who it might have been who had given us cause for this joy and this sadness, and who even now was making his way Home. It had been happening all too often at Kervennec, though, as our members were growing elderly and departing at an alarming rate. Now that trend is reversing, and thank goodness, we have young men here again, eager to serve God in our way. But I digress.

I dressed in my cassock and overcoat for that chilly spring morning. It was about 3:00 a.m. when I headed out my door and felt the damp, cool air of the corridor strike me rudely on my face. I ventured out into the passageway to the church, peering out one of the large windows. I could vaguely make out the church, whose bell tower's outline was just visible in the darkness. I watched the dark clouds file past the tower in the brisk wind, revealing luminous patches of stars brightly visible here and there in the moonless night. I remember thinking, "Isn't it strange how this parting of the spirit so often occurs before sunrise, in the bleakest part of the night?" Is there some correlation there, a man departing for his eternal rest at a time when other men were enjoying their earthly rest? Perhaps the dawn is a symbol for the dawning of a New Day that the liberated spirit was about to enjoy. What better time to pass from the old to the new?

When I reached the church, I started thinking

about things I had read about persons who had had a near-death experience and how they wrote of having seen themselves — their lifeless bodies — from "above." The stories are always the same. All of these "dead" persons, their consciousnesses at least, felt themselves floating, suspended above their "deathbed." Remarkably, they had been conscious of everything that was going on around them. They can recall conversations word for word that caregivers had said next to their bodies after they had been pronounced dead. Many have reported a feeling of great discomfort as they saw all the sadness surrounding their "deaths." They did not have the means to let those grieving below know that all was well. The pain and discomfort of their disused bodies was gone, and they felt a lightness and peace that gave them an indescribable joy, fulfilling them. The thought of those experiences came to my mind particularly strongly that morning. I remember welcoming such rumination. It was a joyous reminder to me of what I already professed to believe: never to worry — in death there is Life.

Upon entering the nave of our church, I couldn't help but then wonder if my dead brother, Father Garrard, might be even now closely present, observing the ancient rituals surrounding his passing. Did he see the tributes of his friends congregating for him "below"? I caught myself unconsciously searching high above the place where Father's body was now lying, instinctively looking for any evidence of the energy of the dead priest as he was readying himself for his new life.

What must it be like? What sorts of joys or fears might attend the flight to the next world? I felt a thrill as I thought of him metaphorically sitting near the throne of the Father, his race run, victory his.

I remember how there was an echo of a feeling, a faint longing rising up in me, which grew in amplitude until I decided to arrest it — I realized that, for that moment, I envied the man in that spot. And why not? Why feel sadness for one who is now loosed of the shackles that have bound him to a cumbersome body and to that prison of incessant activity and emotion, the mind? Why not feel some envy of those who have lived good lives and were now enjoying the fruits of their labors? So I then reconsidered and allowed myself to continue to indulge in that thought. Wouldn't it be a strange religion if — after all of those years of practicing it, a religion whose Glory was the promise of Eternal Life — one could not feel happy for, and, yes, even envious of one who had gone before and received his Prize? Eternal Life is the reward to those who are faithful! Not a life resembling anything like this life of difficulty and of suffering, of endless ups and downs. Eternal Life is to be a life of peace, joy, and fulfillment — in Spirit — a life of eternal bliss through union with All There Is. There was a Promise given, the Good News of Jesus Christ. Isn't it simply a wonderful progression — a passing — from life to Life?

It has always been a comfort to see the wistful looks and occasionally the smiles on the faces of many of my brothers at the time of a passing. That is why that day at Father Garrard's funeral was so memorable. It got me to thinking about my faith's view of death in a way I had not really thought about it before. Never have I thought about it the same way since. What a contrast I see between those hopeful sentiments at the funeral of a brother monk and the funeral proceedings that I attended in my pre-monastic days, and do still occasionally attend in Brittany. There is, unfortunately, rarely the hint of Eternal Life hovering around the latter's obsequies…outside of the abbey, the atmosphere at a funeral or visitation is predictably solemn. During those ceremonies, I haven't seen that spark of optimism that their faith should be giving these mourners. Why is it not there?

One can certainly understand deep sadness at the loss of a friend or family member on our earthly level — to no more see nor hear, nor laugh nor speak with that person in this life — especially so when children and young people pass. When those who have departed have lived normal and fruitful lives, however, the sadness in people the majority of the time seems an embedded sadness in the concept of death – not as a passing but as an end, an end to life. There is no evidence of the joy reflecting that Great Promise that Jesus made us, no hint of relief. Most unfortunate to me is how the clergy, too, have been complicit, and thus my point. This deeply rooted melancholic atmosphere has a source other than the obvious one of losing a loved one or friend. This way of looking at death, at life — this mentality — completely reflects the views and the mentality of my own Church. We have been rooted in the medieval, unable or unwilling to look at the Good News for what it is. We have obsessed over the subjects of inescapable guilt and damnation — shameful, destructive teachings. I know from my life in the outside world that many laypeople in Brittany, good Catholics all, are anything but comforted by their religion. That tells me quite simply that the Church has failed them.

This troubled and morbid view was not what Jesus taught His followers. Why have we clung to this doleful vision of life...and death? I've looked at it from many different angles. Historically, we clergy were jealously guarding our flocks in very demanding times, from the early practice of Christianity right through the Dark and Middle Ages, and perhaps our comportment, with its emphasis on eternal damnation and the control that that exerts, was necessary then for an illiterate and simple people. But things have changed! We are now a very literate and sophisticated society in much of the world and we can think and choose and decide things for ourselves. We as a people can still benefit from guidance in how we look at our Christian beliefs — a presentation of what those beliefs mean and why they make sense — but that presentation must take on its original colors of hope and love. No institution based on love, hope, and charity should try to scare its adherents out of their wits.

Perhaps there is even another subtle, subconscious idea at play concerning us clergy and the Church. Perhaps those adherents, should we get off of the eternal damnation bandwagon, might begin to think that they just don't need us, that they can commune with a loving God directly; that we and our trappings of rank and ceremony might not be necessary for their personal salvation, if salvation is really what is required. Perhaps, just perhaps, they will come to see, correctly, that direct connection with the Godhead is all that they will need. It is we, the clergy, who will find it difficult — or unacceptable — to tolerate such tenets of belief after these centuries of power.

I am a monk — a priest of God. I cannot tell you how much this emphasis on an all-punishing God, as is frequently taught by my Church with all of its unhealthy consequences, has frustrated me and unnecessarily frightened people. It is destructive to believers, and, to the extent that it removes compassion from the lexicon of the priests, as it often does — the very shepherds left here to guide the faithful (at least according to us clergy) — it then destroys the charity and love within them as they assume such postures. We sow destruction instead of love and forgiveness with this barbarous teaching of eternal hellfire. I tell you again, people are neither comforted in life nor in death by our religion. Many, if not most Christians, not just Catholics, are afraid of death. It is because of their religion's preoccupation with sin and eternal punishment, an area in which we Catholics excel.

It seems true that power and control are recurring themes in ours and other churches, but surely they can and should remedy this and return their emphasis to the Good News and all that it promises. Without the control that the pernicious teaching of the loss of

Eternal Life imposes, an unfettered people would be free to celebrate life on its own terms. I imagine that that would be difficult for some of our trained clerics to accept. Where, in fact, would this leave the authority of the institution, its power? Many churchmen that I know are emphatic that their role is to strictly and unquestionably support moral law as interpreted by the Church only, under pain of loss of their own souls. But let's face it, everything I have discussed above, from the role of the people determining their personal beliefs to the interpretation of the canon and its enforcement by the clergy, has at its heart one thing: judgment. It is this continual judgment that saps the life out of people — the ready judgment of souls by the Church itself, via its own interpretation of laws, etched in stone. What results is too often the destructive power of the judgment of self.

In this word — judgment — is something personal, subtle, and immensely powerful. As exercised by so many organized religions, not just we Catholics, judgment takes an insidious form. It is a ruthless, continuous judgment acting both subconsciously and consciously. While it is important, of course, to examine our behavior and to acknowledge when we fall short of our goal of living in the way of the Good News, to be continuously looking for the dark side of ourselves and to evaluate ourselves only in the light of an unreachable perfection is wrong. We can never be pleased with ourselves. We can never develop a healthy self and worldview. We mustn't forget: We are to love others as we love ourselves! We must be good to ourselves!

The unhealthy self-judgment and ensuing self-condemnation that I often see in my work with those inside and outside Kervennec has no place in our faith. Its power literally brings good people, millions and millions of adherents, to their knees — but not in the way that it should. We must see God for the loving Father that He is.

An excruciating and scrupulous self-judgment certainly was not a foreign feeling to me as a young man, but now I have seen it for what it is and dismissed it as in no way representing the way of my God. But if I had been feeling its ponderous weight and joy-robbing effects at one time, then I know others have and are still feeling that way, too. How many of them have been able to see through it, to survive its withering attacks? This type of judgment so often overshadows and even repudiates the good that one does, or the fact that one has even tried. It speaks to man of his abject unworthiness, his guilt, starting with the "stain" of an undeserved original sin at birth right through to the uncertainty of his salvation at death.

And speaking about the notion of salvation, or "happy death," I note sadly, and a little sarcastically, that the uncertainty connected to the state of one's soul near death for Catholic believers can only be ameliorated by a priest and one of three of the sacraments possessed by that institution: baptism, confession, and the last rites. These, and only these, uniquely dispensed by and under the auspices of the clergy of my Church, have the awesome power to confer (or, by their absence, deny) the certainty of Eternal Life. So here is my Church, and others like it in these modern times, telling good men and women that they are all horribly imperfect, that they were already guilty the day they were born, and that even though they have been born imperfect and are thus imperfect by nature, they are somehow responsible and accountable for making their way to perfection — to sainthood! Never mind that "flawed" is how the Creator made us; we must somehow be free of any blemish to gain Eternal Life, and my Church, according to itself, holds the only solutions. Hardly a Christ like sentiment. Inexcusable, in fact.

Christian churches must act out of love and compassion. They insinuate themselves into every aspect of true believers' lives with a power that is, for most believers, both total and unyielding. My Church has assumed the role of supreme judge of its people, whether it be in the books they read, the movies they see, the political attitudes they adopt, even the views they harbor about other religions, which, unfortunately cause me to wince. (They are often ungenerous at best, other faiths considered nothing more than "quasi" by my Church.)

Unfortunately, I still find that all too often there are no "gray areas" in mine and other churches when it comes to morality and salvation, even though life itself is full of gray areas. For me, it is always intent that matters. There is no book written, no checklist possible, to describe and judge a man's conscience. It is most distressing to me, however, to see how often my Church's right to judge is insinuated or expressed, and then to see the resulting effects on its people. We must change if we are to effectively bring the Good News of Christ to so many who desperately need it.

I have never worried if my unorthodox views on this subject make me unfit as a priest in my religion. I look at it this way: All organized religions carry the effects of human intervention. Thus, by their very natures, they will be touched with error and miscalculation, especially if they are two millennia in age. I am not putting myself before the doctors of the Church. I believe simply that the prime relationship to be developed in the spiritual quest is that relationship between a man or woman and God, not the relationship between one and one's Church or its clergy. I believe it is up to each of us individually, where possible, to take on the great personal responsibility necessary to pursue that quest, and to thoughtfully manage our moral lives.

Some will err with that freedom. Some, though sincere, may engage in behaviors or pursue actions that most of us find incorrect. That is a risk we must take if we are to be a free and enlightened people. Freedom of will is our birthright. We may, as individuals, see truth in many shades — but usually our differences are minimal on the essentials. The Church is there to offer us guidance but it should not be micromanaging our lives. I turn to the Man Who founded my Church. How many laws did He give us? Two. He said, simply, "Love God with your whole Mind, your whole Heart, and your whole Soul…and your neighbor as yourself." Everything else is secondary. Everything else is details. The Awakened man sees this. He thanks his Church for its help, its support, for preserving the words of the Master, for creating a community of believers and offering a system of communal worship. The Man of Discernment does not ask his Church to direct his life — that is his own responsibility. He is no longer the illiterate serf of the Middle Ages. He is a modern man, looking to love God with his whole Mind, his whole Heart, and his whole Soul.

Father Garrard's funeral is etched in my mind. Now you know why. I could say it was a day of anger for me as these unsavory things about my faith flooded my brain. But it was also a reconciliation of sorts. From the discharge of these emotions came a new platform on which I could rebuild my relationship, not just with death but with my Church. I could look at the glass half-full now. As difficult as Father's funeral was with the thoughts surrounding it, in many ways I could say then and I can say still that my Faith is a great faith. It has directed men at their most defining moments in life and it has given them the strength to make incredibly hard choices. It has marked out a pathway on an extremely rocky and perilous passage. In Western civilization's darkest hour, however, I am proud to say it was we monks who kept the flame of faith and knowledge alive…Irish monks, Celtic people like we Bretons. Without that reintroduction of the accumulated wisdom of the West at that time, how much further would we have been set back in our still often herky-jerky march to progress? It can be a Rock, truly; and, for this I am and will always be eternally grateful. There is, however, still some work to be done to make it the spiritual Mother that lovingly embraces all of her children.

There is no greater methodology or religion, or better demonstration of the potential of the human towards greatness, than to be motivated by love and selflessness. This is the message of my Jesus. This Man embodies all that I love about our Faith — about man and his potential. He was a man of action. What is our Faith other than Love in Action? It is love in action that redeems us, makes us holy, pure and simple. To dedicate ourselves to that is to dedicate ourselves to God and His Way — this is what our true Christian faith asks. It is this God of love that we must turn to. It is He to Whom we must give ourselves in total. What we really find when we do that, when we give up the Ego before God — the Ego's notion of who it thinks it is, its pride and self-importance — what is left is the Me and the You of Spirit, the persons we really are and have always been from the beginning. The return on that "investment" of surrender vastly outweighs any short-term discomforts, and the gift of Life through our surrender of who we thought we were remains one of the greatest of paradoxes.

It is essential to our spiritual evolution that we develop this direct relationship with God. Prayer is a wonderful way. Yet, there is more that we can do. There is a constant give-and-take between God and man. It involves a subtle energy that all of us possess and any can cultivate. It is direct soul contact with God. When we learn to consciously access it, we know that we are touching the Divine. It is through what I call our Higher Self. I'd like to write to you more about that now.

The Higher Self

To see the world in a grain of sand and to see heaven in a wild
flower,
To hold infinity in the palm of your hands, and eternity in an hour.
—William Blake, "Auguries of Innocence"

Deep in our psyches we yearn for something deep and mysterious, a kind of ultimate satisfaction. We know intuitively or experientially, consciously or unconsciously, that it exists. After some experience, if we are bold enough to look more closely, we discover that the commonly sought-after things that the world can bestow — riches and pleasures — are transitory. That discovery reveals to us that the satisfaction which we seek is not something that the world is capable of giving us. We come to know that what the world touts as something to bring us fulfillment really cannot. Those things don't satisfy our deepest parts, our essences. They don't reach the place that aches. Investigating still further, we can begin to sense what it might be that will satisfy us. Becoming conscious and aware, we then discover what we really yearn for is completion.

Where does it come from then, this possibility of completion? The answer is that there is but one place, one Source, from which we can procure it. It comes from our unfettered connection with All There Is, our Source. It comes from God.

There is in each of us a place — or a state —

where we can entertain the Holy Spirit of God. It is a place where we greet Him and welcome him into our innermost parts, the parlor of our soul. This is the state of direct interaction between our Creator, in the aspect of His Holy Spirit, the Advocate and Helper, and us, His creation. All of us are privileged to access this place. I call that part of me my Higher Self. I didn't always know about it. But now that I have experienced it, I know it is there. My friends and family and even my monastic brothers have never referred to such a place in my presence, yet I know it is there, and if available to me, it is to all.

What is the nature of this Higher Self? It is a part of us that differs greatly from the thinking or intellectual self. The Higher Self is that part that is always in touch with the eternal spiritual realm. The Higher Self is a dimension of ourselves separate from the material self. The latter is always living and grounded in the material dimension. The Higher Self is not a part of that dimension, but of Spirit. The Higher Self is the integral part of us, our eternal and unchanging Self, a fragment of the Creator. Like so many sages of old have written, it is ultimately a vehicle of communion, nothing less than God-communion, a conscious extension and reception of God's spirit into our own life. It is a thoroughly different state of being, more profound and ethereal than the sensory. It is a curious mix of eternity, ecstasy, love, and complete satisfaction in one swoop. Nothing that we can feel or buy or gain here in our temporal lives bears any relation to the satisfaction, fulfillment, and happiness that the Higher Self brings. It is the gateway to the Kingdom of Heaven, that spiritual and mystical place to which Jesus so often referred, where one accesses the Living God. It is the part of the soul bathed in the Eternal Holy Spirit. When we can sustain our cognizance of this Higher Self, or at least remain constant in our attempt to touch it, then we can enter the gates of the Kingdom even during this lifetime and be resident in the Promised Land. It is where we already touch the Divine. Those who enter the Kingdom never die. That is the Good News. It can already be a reality for us in the here and now.

To know the Kingdom of Heaven intimately is to become the Man of Discernment, a Man of God, a spiritual man who understands his place in God's universe. The Higher Self is the one component, the one part of myself, with which I wish to remain in contact as much as possible. Personally, I believe it was Michelangelo's inspiration for his famous painting in the Sistine Chapel, where the Father is reaching out to touch Adam. Our relationship to the Father, the Creator, is that close. On the other hand, to be disconnected from our spirit and our Creator is to be floundering. To live in that state of emptiness and nihilism eventually becomes Hell. That is where Hell resides — not in some distant inferno as depicted in our medieval art, but in our disconnection from God, from all that is Good and Giving and Loving and Compassionate.

Its discovery starts, like all spiritual growth, with that state to which I have and will refer many times:

Awareness. The description of someone becoming cognizant and alive in the Spirit is a description of someone having awakened…awakened from the slumber of not knowing, of unawareness. The unawakened state is not a fault, not something for which to blame oneself; it is rather an undeveloped aspect of self seeking a new maturity, an end to spiritual adolescence.

When Awareness does arrive, it is often described as the experience of being "born again." Its arrival changes one's viewpoint entirely. We read about its nature in the New Testament, in the story of Nicodemus coming to Jesus by night. Jesus tells him that to live forever he must be "born again," not of a woman, but of Spirit. This is what Jesus was referring to, the act of awakening, a type of rebirth in coming to know and live in the Spirit — Awareness.

On occasion, we can be jolted out of unawareness through some traumatic event, and we come to experience its arrival. One reads of these transformations regularly in the lives of the saints, and there are many examples of how these important events change people and give them peace. In the Higher Self–God connection, we don't "find" it. Make no mistake, it finds us, through the grace of God. We become aware and begin our search for completion, and though its arrival can be rude, ultimately it is a gift from our loving Creator. Its essence humbles us and fills us with gratitude at the same time. It comes when we are ready to receive it, when we can best realize its value and existence in our lives. That moment is already in place when we are prescient enough to ask, when we are aware enough to ask. Many of us are already asking for grace on an unconscious level as we advance in our progress towards Awareness.

To become Aware is an experience like none other. It is a peaceful feeling. It is a sudden confidence in things, in life. It is clarity. It brings joy when it arrives, and it can come and wrap us like a luxurious blanket, warming us, influencing us for the good even in the midst of all of the distractions of our sensory experiences. This connection to our Higher Self can come when we least expect it, startlingly, like a flash from out of the blue, bringing an instant of perception, almost like a memory reawakened.

What triggers our receptiveness? Willingness, of course, and perhaps it's prayer that helps or perhaps we reach this game-changing moment through the accumulation of past-life experiences; it may be due to a growing feeling that this spiritual dimension exists or on the aforementioned unconscious level in a fit of depression or anxiety. I do not know for sure. What I do know is that we are ready for it on some level and that God always responds to our demands.

Once we are "born again," we are open to the Higher Self in our lives. Jesus said: "Watch!…The wind blows where it wills, and you hear the sound thereof, but cannot tell from where it came, and where it goes: so is everyone that is born of the Spirit." Like the wind in Christ's explanation, the Higher Self, our spiritual connection to the Kingdom of Heaven, comes when it chooses from wherever it chooses. When it comes, it is up to us to cultivate it, to make it welcome, and invite it to stay.

If you think on a conscious level that you are ready to meet the Higher Self and you have not yet felt its dramatic impact, ask forthrightly. There is no point in meekly coming to God feebly mumbling some request, hat in hand. Don't come like a beggar. That's medieval thinking. God does not listen to or act upon that. God respects those who put forward their agendas, who approach Him in a way that reflects their true standing as a blessed inheritor of all that He has prepared including, naturally, His Kingdom. Ask confidently. He does respond and Jesus has told us this many times.

Look at what was promised in Matthew 7:7–11:

"And I say to you, ask, and it shall be given you; seek, and you shall find; knock, and it shall be opened to you. For everyone that asks receives; and he that seeks finds; and to him that knocks it shall be opened. If a son shall ask bread of any of you that is a father, will he give him a stone? Or if he ask a fish, will he for a fish give him a serpent? Or if he shall ask an egg, will he offer him a scorpion? If you then, being evil, know how to give good gifts to your children: how much more shall your heavenly Father give the Holy Spirit to them that ask him?"

And again in Mark 11:24:

"Therefore I say to you, all things for which you pray and ask, believe that you have received them, and they will be granted you."

And *again* in John 14:23:"And I will do whatever

you ask in my name, so that the Father may be glorified in the Son."

God's presence, God's Peace, is a gift. He comes to us. It is via His Grace. The best thing that we can do is ready ourselves for that moment. Recognizing God's answer, His response to our demand, is not difficult. It will arrive. It may not come as a lightning bolt, but it will always arrive as a new awareness.

How do we ready ourselves for it? That is the task of mindfulness and meditation. Mindfulness and meditation keep the mind focused and still, creating a space where He can enter. We should not wait for lightning bolts that may never come. Via mindfulness or meditation I have sometimes entered into that state of awareness and union where grace is providentially provided. Wow! Just a split-second in that state of consciousness, that dimension, and its effects are amazing. In that split-second, I reach a consciousness from which I can see and feel and understand the true nature of things on a level that is far beyond the "normal" and everyday understanding of things. I feel almost omniscient. It is my Higher Self activated. It's a wonderful place, this Higher Self. Wouldn't that be great if you or I could make that our new "normal"?

Remember that mindfulness is the act or state of being completely in present time in its purest and most rewarding form. The mindful self leads to an evolved self — more experienced and wise in matters of the soul dimension and the material dimension, confident and unpressured. Mindfulness helps us understand and incorporate the higher aspect of self into our lives. In mindfulness, we are neither in the past nor the future, but fully aware of what is transpiring within us in the present. It is essential for Awareness. Mindfulness is a quiet mind, an aware mind. We see more and understand more truths in a mindful state. We can take the little things that we see in our lives and gain great lessons and insight from them. Gaining wisdom via God's grace comes mostly in little steps, with new little gifts of Awareness. Mindfulness itself is not about "arriving," but about being.

Meditation is another tool and takes many forms. It works hand-in-glove with mindfulness. Both are preparatory and both are intertwined. A meditation on an intention is one type of practice; a meditation on becoming aware of God's connection to us is another type. There are more. Let me give an example: I have been to Thich Nhat Hanh's Plum Village here in France. He is a writer and monk in the Buddhist tradition with wonderful powers of expression in his many books dealing with mindfulness. At Plum Village, it is walking meditation that centers each person to mindfulness. Step by mindful step, one enters into that connection. It is quite beautiful. In all meditation we plow the ground and make preparations for the arrival of the Higher Self. It is through this preparation and through our demand, on some level, that by the grace of God we connect. Think now, those of you who might know it, of the parable of the "Treasure Hidden in a Field," which Christ told us. It is our connection to God that animates this parable. It is that valuable "treasure" found. It is the Kingdom of

Heaven found, never to be forsaken. As the parable elucidates, it is worth whatever earthly treasures one has and much more to possess it. There is nothing remotely so satisfying to be experienced and enjoyed here on earth than His Kingdom.

In my everyday consciousness, as I do my usual things — responding to situations, working, cleaning, and even sometimes while praying — I find I am often on autopilot. I am not particularly good at concentrating on the present moment. Being "present" in mindfulness in whatever I am pursuing mentally or physically is a practice to which I have to give a lot of effort, a lot of awareness. I am always working at it. If for any reason I am not being in the "Now," however, I don't let it trouble me. I just know that I have to keep trying harder. It might take a lifetime of the practice of mindfulness to become a totally mindful person; but the effort to be that kind of person gives me so much, even in my very imperfect state, that it is well worth the effort. I can see the results. I know that when I am unhappy, I am that way because I am disconnected from my Father/Mother God — my Source. I practice to be especially aware in those moments, once I take note of my feelings. All is as it should be and my petty worrying and doubts are needless. That type of mindfulness will bring me around quickly. That peace will stay with me as long as I practice being right where I am — which means as long as I stay in the present moment and do not take life too seriously. One foot on earth, one foot in the Kingdom. That is where fulfillment and satisfaction lie.

God is ever-near, though not ever-apparent. It is an important lesson. That dichotomy has caused a lot of problems for mankind. Sometimes it seems, at the most difficult times in our lives, like God is deliberately trying to be difficult to find. We know about the great saints who have written about "the dark night of the soul," that feeling of being abandoned by God. Is it our expectation that our communication with Him should suddenly be different because we will it so — faster, more profound, more obvious? Sometimes we need to show some faith and some perseverance, show Him we mean what we say. God wants us to knock on the door a second or third time if He doesn't answer right away. Remember the parable of the "Importunate Widow," she who demanded justice so often from a judge that he finally acted, giving her what she demanded. See what Christ says this about perseverance in Luke 18:7:

"And will not God bring about justice for his chosen ones, who cry out to him day and night? Will he keep putting them off?"

My goal in the end is simply to be more mindful and more aware of my Higher Self every day. When I do that, I am in a position to receive the grace of touching my Higher Self more often. I hope someday to experience everything about me from the point of view of a man complete, a man taking everything possible from the moment, a man connected to his Source, the man I call the Man of Discernment.

I do have a little plan I can tell you about that I have put together to remain more mindful. It is simple in design, yet surprisingly difficult to effectuate. Here is what I try to do. I try to refocus and become aware of mindfulness with every pealing of the bells at Kervennec. Sounds easy, doesn't it? It isn't! They come and go like clouds in the sky, without me noticing. I am too busy focusing on the "important" things like where I put my clean cassock, what we are doing after lunch, or of who I have slotted in to work at the abbey shop! But I keep trying.

Do I talk about this much here in the abbey? I have from time to time. Some know exactly what I mean. Others don't and I think are mildly suspicious. To them, that's what happens to great saints, not to fellow monks. But I believe that the true Man of Spirit, the Man of Discernment, possesses at all times the opportunity to receive and become the Higher Self, to dig into his own reservoir of spiritual sustenance. It is a state of allowing and permitting, much like the "Tao Te Ching" reminds us.

Whether or not I succeed in touching that blessed state of union with the Higher Self through any particular effort of mindfulness or meditation, I know that with each act of opening I am readying myself for the untold benefits of God's grace. I am evolving. This evolution will take me off of the roller-coaster ride of emotional responses to everything. It will give me a method to develop an inner calm and a compassionate view of life and of all people. With it, I have the power to enjoy all of the richness and fullness and insight that life can offer. With it I have the power of the universe behind me because the Great Creator is directing things. "If God is for us, who can be against us?" So it was written, and so it is.

It is my definition of Reality.

Part Three

A Challenging Time, a Time of Trouble...

A Return Visit

Summer afternoon — summer afternoon; to me those have always been the two most beautiful words in the English language.
— Henry James, An International Episode

It was about a month later that I received another note from Elena saying that she would like to stop by and see me. Naturally, I was delighted. I had found myself thinking of her so often since that first visit. She had brought me something, I can only call it an energy, that was different than any other I knew. I missed that whatever-it-was.

We decided that we would meet one afternoon the following week at Kervennec. The prospect was very exciting for me. I remember that day well. The morning services and meditations seemed to drag on a bit. Lunch was perfunctory, and I found its reading particularly stodgy. It was a series of letters written by a cardinal from Italy to various people in the 1930s. Not too inspiring. By dessert, I found myself deep in my own thoughts, anticipating the afternoon to come with Elena.

At two o'clock, I was at the welcome center to meet her. She was right on time, having driven from Brest in her snappy little white Renault. She looked great, dressed modestly in a business suit, but still so very lovely and feminine. She had a big smile on her face as she gently embraced me. After a short chat, we walked slowly over to the public garden area. As we approached the same bench we had used the last time, Elena stopped me and asked if we could just keep walking, maybe down through the orchard. So off we went, finding another bench much further away, near the end of the orchard.

"I love being outside here. The beauty of nature just seems to burst into my head and senses. Everything about it seems more intense. I'm not sure why — the place just has that effect on me," Elena declared.

"Oh, it's probably really the company," I remember joking.

She rolled her eyes appropriately at my bad joke as we sat down together.

I noticed her happy look as she gazed out across the deserted orchard. There was a peace that I could feel emanating from her person. I was able to relax with it and enjoy its flow and the beautiful surroundings. We sat there quietly for several minutes, each in our own thoughts, not really needing to speak.

Elena was the first to break the silence. "I haven't called you Father Jean yet — it would sound funny. I've hardly called you Jean or anything else either, for what, twenty years?" She sounded wistful and then she added, "Is it really okay, or would you prefer Father?"

"Elena, you can call me anything you'd like. I don't care. It would get a little tiresome, though, to always hear 'Father.' Weird, actually. Like I said the last time you were here, I feel like I will always be Jean to you."

We were quiet again some moments.

"You know how pleased I am you have come to visit again, don't you?" I asked.

"Me, too, Jean. I had hoped you would be," she assured me, softly.

Again nothing more was said for a few minutes.

"Do you remember Sylvie from school?" She had been a girl I had dated my third year at university. Why I was bringing this up, I really wasn't sure.

"Sylvie Martin? Yes, I do. She was really pretty as I remember. I didn't know her well, though. You mentioned her once or twice to me at school."

"I wonder what she's doing now…" I said.

Elena looked surprised, and said innocently enough, "It never occurred to me that you might be interested in a woman!"

I smiled to myself when she said that. I could tell then she felt a bit embarrassed at her statement and she tried to soften it.

"I mean, you were certainly very attractive at university…" she stopped again, suddenly seeming very self-conscious. She turned a slight shade of red as she looked for a way to exit what was for her a precarious conversation topic.

"Well, I mean you still are, Jean, you know…" she said, in her attempt to right herself. She stopped then again, obviously not quite knowing where to go from there. As her old friend, and one who teased her a lot back in the day, I watched and grinned sadistically, trying to contain the mirth I felt at her attempts to extricate herself from the discomfort she was feeling with her comments. Then I gave out a hearty laugh and she raised her purse in mock pose as if to strike before breaking out and laughing.

"You're mean!" she said holding down her voice only because of where we were. "I can't go around calling mature priests attractive, even if they are!" she said, as she feigned offense. I enjoyed hearing that comment very much.

I touched her hand and said to her in mock sympathy, "You just can't help it!"

I knew that she was enjoying it just as much as I was. Whatever distance that might have been created by our twenty years apart was gone. We were the close friends that we always were. That's the amazing thing about true friendship.

After a few more quiet moments, Elena spoke to me again.

"Jean, tell me what you were going to tell me about Sylvie."

I felt hesitant all of a sudden. Still, I owed her an explanation, and in so telling might find out what had brought this on this sudden memory of a woman.

"Oh, yeah," I replied, as my mind reverted back to that time and place. "I'm not sure why she came into my head. I can tell you about what happened, though. I had thought Sylvie and I were going steady back then — you know, seeing each other exclusively. I know I was, even though nothing had really been said."

I remember speaking slowly, feeling the emotions rise again within me.

"One night, I went over to my friend Jules' house — you know, the rich guy who drove that Mercedes coupe even at university. He wasn't a bad guy. In fact, he was one of my good friends; and, that was a cool car, I must say. I wonder where he is now? But I digress."

"I thought he was kind of cute!" said Elena.

"Great, a cute guy with money coming back to haunt me again. Well, I went over to see him, you see, and I thought I saw a light on at his place, but nobody came to the door when I knocked. So, peeking into a window, I saw Sylvie in a very compromising position with Jules. I don't think I'll ever forget that sight. It didn't put me off women…just drove me to the monastery…"

I started to laugh through the memory, though it was still quite unpleasant to think of it. Having a sensation like that come up again in life means to me that there is still some work to be done to resolve it, or to let it go. I know now that it was about trust and my feelings for Elena coming to the fore had triggered something unresolved.

Elena looked serious and put her hand on mine.

"I'm sorry," she said softly to me. "I really am. You, of all people, didn't deserve that."

I smiled at her and felt her warmth and compassion. Strange what a relief it was to deal with this emotional scar, not quite healed, and particularly to be able to talk to a woman about it.

"I was sad…and very disappointed. But let me tell you one thing I did learn. I learned the role of victim then and there, and I played it well, until I finally figured out that that role was hurting me a lot more than I was punishing anyone else. I had had a strong inkling during that period anyway that the religious life was for me. Not being involved with a woman helped. It all kind of worked out."

I felt relieved but still awkward. It was clear that being with Elena triggered something deep down within me, and that only some of it was about Sylvie. In recollection, I realized that perhaps I had had the need to convince myself subconsciously that any relationship that might have continued between Elena and me after university would not have worked out. I had come to realize that I felt much more strongly about Elena than I had wanted to admit.

"Yes, it did. It really did," Elena responded with some feeling. "And I'm so glad we have reconnected."

I heard that last remark but I was distant. She noticed and I could tell that she was looking to change the subject. An animated look started to brighten her face.

"I didn't tell you, Jean, but that I do have another job. I call it a job, but for me, it's not really like work. I enjoy it so much and it is so different to my stained glass work, though they are both a bit intuitive. It involves healing. It has really come to fascinate me."

"That sounds interesting, Elena. Tell me more," I replied, breaking out of that unpleasant reverie. "Votive candles?" I half joked.

"Ha! Good guess! I happen to love votive candles — especially when they are sitting in some beautiful colored glass holders! But that's not it. Here's what happened. As I started to become more fascinated with spiritual things, I began to read a lot of the classic spiritual literature. I read some Christian classics like *The Spiritual Exercises of St. Ignatius Loyola* and St. Augustine's *Confessions*; but, I also really enjoyed reading and thinking outside my Christian upbringing and reading other spiritual classics that maybe you've heard of or read, like *Cosmic Consciousness* by Richard Bucke and the *Tao Te Ching* by Lao-Tzu — I just love that one. I also love some of the Hindu literature like the Bhagavad Gita, and discovered its wonderful interpretation by Paramahansa Yogananda. Magic. There was also a novel that I read at that time. It was called *The Shoes of the Fisherman* by Morris West, a Christian author from Australia, and it intimated things about spirit in the context of the modern world. I don't know why, but it was the perfect thing for me to read at the time. Then, I reread the four Gospels several times.

"Surprising, as least to me, was how much I then began to appreciate them. I'll bet you, Jean, like me, remember going to church all those Sundays with our parents as kids and adolescents and hearing the Gospel readings time and again. I didn't get much out of it at the time and I must admit that I wasn't very interested in any of that after school. Well, I decided to reread them.

"One thing I really noticed as I reread them was

that so much in the Gospels concerns Jesus' acts of healing. I had never registered much about that aspect of Jesus. I was just fascinated with how often He was healing someone or He was talking about healing. I found it remarkable and somehow consoling. It also came at a time when the concept of healing and my involvement in it was growing stronger inside of me."

She had a point. Healing plays a most important role in the Gospels. It was something that I had thought about quite a bit over the years, too. Why hadn't the Church put that aspect of Christ's life more to the forefront? I'm not sure. The Church may have been more interested in emphasizing the fact that He performed miracles — perhaps to establish Christ's divinity — than what the miracles accomplished. Often, they were acts of healing.

Elena continued with her history.

"I began to feel more and more drawn to healing. I really loved the idea of being able to do that for others. And I have always felt, right from the beginning until this very day, that aiding in the healing of another person helps the 'healer' in untold ways, too. We receive by giving and by being the conduit for healing. I know now because that is the other job I was telling you about. I practice a healing technique called applied kinesiology. I get paid to do it and that helps me support my art and live a 'normal' life, but honestly, Jean, I think I would do it for free. One day, if I'm ever in a position to do that, I will."

Her enthusiasm for this was contagious. I think my interest in what she was doing showed, as did my surprise at what she had learned. As a man of the cloth, I could not have said any of it better than she did about Jesus. She had indeed come a long way since our college days.

"I really didn't expect to hear anything like that from you, Elena," I told her, my surprise no doubt showing, "but I think it is fantastic! Your healing does seem to be like another art. They do talk about the 'healing arts.' I've only heard about kinesiology from Brother Luc here, but I must say that I really am ignorant on the subject. Can you tell me what it is all about?"

"Well, Jean, in a nutshell, applied kinesiology is a therapy based on interrogating the body about the truths it holds about a person. The idea is that the body registers and stores what happens to a person emotionally. Emotional energies can, however, become locked or 'blocked' in the body, which ultimately affects a person physically or mentally or emotionally and it manifests often in damaging ways. With applied kinesiology, we uncover and explore all of those held long-held emotions, unblocking and unlocking them, as it were. This brings a release, which helps a person rid himself of any difficulties he has experienced as a result of them.

"The body's energy system is a complicated one, but there's a flow to it," she continued. "If something blocks that flow of energy, it can cause a dis-ease. The energy systems we work with are the chakra system that you may have heard of, which is a series of energy centers in the body identified by the early Indian savants, and the meridians, the paths of energy up and down the body that are such a part of Chinese medicine and treatment, like acupuncture.

"For example," she continued, "you know all of those old expressions we've grown up with like red with rage, green with envy, yellow with cowardice? That's where it gets interesting. Each chakra corresponds to a color, and it's amazing how they in turn correspond to those various emotional energies, like the ones I just mentioned."

While this therapy was pretty new to me, the idea that illness is derived from our emotional *"points de faiblesse"*, fragilities and stresses in our outlooks and our attitudes that become transmuted into our bodies, made sense to me. I think we can all see time and time again where that has been in evidence, within ourselves or with others.

"It often seems that a lot of that 'primitive' wisdom is loaded with insight," I added. "How often do you practice?"

"I can see up to five people in a day, but usually it is about eight or nine a week, at least for right now. And that is probably enough with the stained glass."

"I wouldn't mind trying this sometime with you. You might be really disappointed, though, with what you find there!" I joked.

"Yeah — I've always wanted to get into the head of a priest! You'd be a great subject. Just off the wall enough to be very interesting!"

I rolled my eyes and then we got up to take another stroll around the orchard. I could see that she continued to enjoy just soaking in the atmosphere of the place and the beauty of the grounds.

"I have become very attached to Kervennec," she said. "There seems to be a palpable feeling of peace here."

She then told me that her sensitivity to the various energies around her had grown dramatically as she had developed her applied kinesiology skills.

We took a seat again as we found another bench further on and she closed her eyes. I thought of the connection we had had and now felt once again. Even with all the changes we had had since university, our relationship had picked up right where it had left off. We could talk about anything. I kept thinking, too, about how Elena had evolved so much in these intervening years. Hers had not been an easy path.

I was feeling things that I hadn't felt in years. I liked it, but I also felt an unease, one that I did not try to ignore, but to reason with. I could reason that it was right for me to be interested in and enjoy the company of a dear friend who happened to be a lovely woman, one whose multifaceted personality was complementary to my own, but I was still uneasy in some way. I sensed there might be some thin ice out there somewhere, waiting for me, that I was rushing towards and choosing to ignore.

Elena opened her eyes eventually and then turned to me with what I can only describe as a very affectionate look, a look of friendship, yes, but also a look that said more than that, a look of tender feeling. She was radiant. It was then that I suspected that there was something beginning to stir in her as well.

We sat quietly for several more minutes and then Elena took out her phone. She didn't have a lot of time, I knew.

"Jean, sorry, I'm going to have to go. I have an appointment to keep and I know that you have your things to do, too. But I loved coming back here to see you again. I promise to come back soon, if you'll have me!"

We stood and I gave her a little hug around the shoulders.

"I'll take that as a 'yes'!" she exclaimed.

We soon reached the abbey gate leading towards her car. Time had flown. I couldn't help but watch her motions, feminine but very assured. "What a wonderful person" was the thought that went through my mind.

"Thank you for your time, Jean. This was such a lovely visit. I know that your time is precious and you welcoming me here means a lot to me. I do appreciate you and your friendship so much."

She gave me a kiss on the cheek and got in behind the wheel. I remember that lovely fresh smell as she brushed up against me. As she backed out, she gave a little wave through the window. Then, she was gone.

I felt her leaving keenly. Something was happening inside of me. Feelings were growing. I was getting into trouble my intuition was telling me — would I listen?

Intuition, Our Quantum Consciousness

Indeed, it is not intellect, but intuition which advances humanity.
— *Albert Einstein,* Interviews with William Hermanns

The short answer to the question I posed at the end of the preceding chapter about listening to my intuition was "No." A big mistake.

What is intuition? Intuition is the ability to simply sense a right answer or a right course of action — to be able to see what is correct to do or to believe in a situation, without the intervention of the intellect. It is an essential element on one's journey down the spiritual path to Awareness. The beauty of intuition is that it gives us not only insight into the "nonrational" within us, but also much needed aid in our everyday lives with decision making. It is, in a way, a sort of refined hunch. It operates at a level completely removed from intellect and the reasoning mind and can be developed when discovered.

With intuition we arrive at the right "answer" in a way substantially different from the way we arrive at an answer for a mathematical proof, for example. Both of these methods, reasoning and intuition, can deliver a right answer, but in completely different ways and by completely different means. Reason is intellectual; intuition works in the energetic realm. It is a message that is not intellectual, but perceptual. Intuitional answers or direction seem to involve a "sixth sense." It is akin to a "feeling," but it is more than that. It is a type of knowledge, knowing which course of action or nonaction is most correct. In those cases, reasoning is clearly not involved, nor would it be practical. There appear to be some things that only intuition can answer, and there are some phenomena that can only be explained by the energy it represents.

Empirical facts have very limited application or use with intuition. Intuitive answers do not have universal application nor objective attributes, but are always supportive, specific, complete, and correct for one's own benefit. Intuitive answers are tailor-made. Somewhere along the line intuition connects us to another place outside of space and time, perhaps even to another dimension. (We don't talk about dimensions too much, but I do firmly believe they exist. Ask any cosmologist.) Is it a physical or spiritual dimension? By its nature and the fact that it is always supportive – for my own good – I label it spiritual. The intuitive dimension contains a reservoir of knowledge and wisdom with which we can tap into a universal storehouse of Truth. It can come as an urge or a hunch, and I find most often the intuitive side engages when I am considering whether or not to act. I can know things to be true in areas where empirical facts are not available or not relevant. Sometimes it even flies in the face of facts. It gives all of us something rather like an insider's knowledge that enables us to understand a thing when that information or answer is otherwise unobtainable. By its nature, it helps formulate personal applications of universal truth tailor-made for the individual.

An interesting thing for me now is the realization that my intuition has played a prominent, if not an essential role throughout my life. When I was younger, I thought nothing of it, as I was really not aware of the process. It was a normal part of decision-making. Later, I saw that I made decisions differently than a lot of people. When I became more aware and appreciative of intuition, I then started to understand it and its applications. I cannot think of a time in my adult life when I haven't depended on it for my everyday decision-making. I use it now quite unawares — it's second nature, and its use is not limited to critical or spiritual decisions. It is a very practical tool in everyday life, giving direction and maximizing use of time.

I can try to purposely summon it up, but I don't trust that as much as when it arrives on its own and makes itself known to me. Most of my intuitive truths arrive in that way — they "bubble up" from somewhere below the conscious level, just at the right time. I need always to be aware, however, that my intuitive self can be mimicked by my emotional self from time to time. The emotional part of me can subconsciously "will" a certain action or outcome, and that can take some experience to understand and differentiate from true intuitive messages.

Let me give you two examples of instances of intuition in my life, the first perhaps life-saving, the second expanding on a story I have already told. I was about twenty years old at the time of the first example. The weekend was approaching. I had nothing planned and I didn't like that. At that time of my life, I always wanted an option to do something or other, even if I wasn't sure that I really would. It was a little psychological game, I suppose, to avoid being lonely. Usually, it worked. This time I had that antsy feeling again as Friday night approached — I wanted an option. A friend of mine had called that morning and asked if I would like to go along with him to a club that night and see a new band. That sounded like a good offer and just as I was about to say yes, I got a very uncomfortable feeling…a feeling that told me very clearly not to go. I watched myself as I declined the offer and wish my friend a fun evening. I was a little miffed about it, especially when later that evening I was sitting in my room, all by myself, watching TV. At about eleven o'clock, I received a call from a mutual friend telling me that the bar hosting the new band had burned to the ground and that several people were injured. Thankfully, my friend was only slightly hurt. I have never forgotten that message delivered by that part of me, the intuitive part.

The second example was the story about Sylvie Martin I had brought up with Elena. You may remember how I wasn't busy one night and I decided that I wanted to visit my good friend, Jules. As I got my car keys to go I received what I can only describe as a sharp interior "warning message" that clearly was telling me that I should not go. There was no specific reason "given" nor any alternative activity suggested to me; it was only this message that I shouldn't go. I decided to go anyway and there I saw Sylvie, the woman that I had thought was my girlfriend, with Jules in that compromising position.

It served as a touchstone moment for me — not because I lost a girl, a girl whom, in all sincerity, I felt even then would not have been right for me. There would be other times and other girls. No, it was the fact that I "knew," in the complete sense of that word, that I should not have made that trip at that particular time to my friend's house; that ended up as the most significant point about that event for me. This episode was simply an important lesson in following one's truth. That truth had "bypassed" my intellectual processes, but my decision to take the car that memorable night also showed how warning signals can be overruled by an emotional filter. I had received the warning from my source; but my heart overruled my gut. I could have saved myself some searing pain had I listened and acted on that intuitive information that I already possessed. The very fact that I had also already "felt" that Sylvie had not been right for me was still another example of this phenomenon, though it had been less urgent in its expression. Intuition will always demand of one adherence to its message with full faith and confidence in what it has to say. Now, I enjoy and look forward to those moments of intuitive guidance.

As I have come to realize, there are three different methods for me to arrive at a decision to proceed or not to proceed in a situation: by the normal thinking processes; by conclusions colored by emotions; or by intuitive response. I can easily tell the difference between reason and intuition. When intuition is involved, there are rarely any data to consider or facts to evaluate to reach a conclusion, so I can often eliminate the rational mind. Conclusions colored by emotions are sometimes more difficult to isolate and distinguish from intuition. In matters touching more sensitive areas, I need to subject my truths to intuitive testing very carefully. These are often the areas where these very emotions are being challenged, and I must be attentive to which emotions may be making headway in my decision making. I need to identify the personal filters I have put into place. But there is a benefit to that: it helps put a spotlight on my own prejudices, which I want to eliminate as best I can. The more insight I gain into these emotional filters, the less likely they are to intrude and attempt to sway my answer or course of action. As I have grown more experienced with this source of wisdom and with my emotional filters, the process has also become quicker and more assured; but I can never stop subjecting certain conclusions to an examination. I never doubt the legitimacy of the intuitive process; there are just times when it has strong competition so I am tenacious about verifying that it is actually intuition appearing in its subtle form and not wishful, emotional, or self-directed thinking.

I sometimes refer to this sixth sense as "Quantum Consciousness," existing here and now when it taps me on the shoulder but existing somewhere else or perhaps even nonexistent when I don't need it. It seems to fly in and out of existence like the quanta in physics. Most of the time, intuition comes through with such force that it is unnecessary for me to question the source. A powerful, unadulterated intuitional moment, a moment of Quantum Consciousness, requires no thought. This type of experience is also clearly delineated from the emotions and certainly to thought and to rationalizing. It just is.

Intuition and its recognition is an essential early step toward Awareness. I firmly believe that this sense, this intuitive blessing, is within reach of everyone. It is only a question of degree. It is an unconscious part of oneself until it decides to break through into consciousness and communicate. It is an integral part of our normal processes, like our rational processes or unconscious physical processes, if we will only listen. I also believe that we can develop it like any spiritual gift. When it appears to be true, it sometimes requires abandoning the "sensible" and accepting the unknown and the unfamiliar. Reason has to be left on the sidelines on those occasions. I know that many in our age are in the process of cultivating intuition and becoming aware, but too many let it go and are terribly afraid or skeptical of it.

We can improve our sense of it by consciously and carefully tending the soil where it will grow. We should consider the gut feeling or the tiny voice in the mind as something important, and listen to what it is saying to us. When it manifests, we need to separate ourselves as much as possible from the rational thinking with which we are accustomed to living, so that we can feel it and permit it to express itself unfettered and unaffected by the conventional. It is only then that we can begin to benefit from it as a separate "power." To get to that point, many pieces of mental and spiritual furniture might have to first be removed or rearranged to make a passageway for the new interior possibilities, a space free of accumulated doubt or misbelief, free of impediment. Further development then comes from practice after we see its truth.

Sometimes the emotions can be a most powerful adversary. We sometimes fail to listen to this essential personal guide, our intuition, and I was not listening to mine with Elena.

It didn't bode well for the future.

Troubling Feelings

Those who do not observe the movements of their own minds must of necessity be unhappy.
— *Marcus Aurelius, Emperor of Rome,* Meditations

Sometimes there doesn't seem to be any rhyme or reason to what happens in life. My own faith in the Eternal has taught me a lot and I know that events are tailored to my needs but there is no mandate that says what is good for me will be sent by the universe in an orderly or expected (or pleasant) fashion! And, of course, we often need a "test" in order to grow, particularly in the face of the big issues that may make up a large part of our life's purpose. One must go with the flow and be spontaneous. There is not much use in fighting it. Otherwise, it is like to trying to hold back the tide with a sword and buckler — pointless. It serves only to rob us of our precious energy, no matter what our desperate egos may think. It seems like I really thought I could face off against my intuition and win! These next few chapters will illustrate well what it is to try to fight our intuition, and what suffering we put ourselves through if we attempt also to ignore or circumvent it.

How did I feel now after this second visit of my soul mate, whose reappearance into my life was so unexpected? A little bit helpless, a little bit euphoric, a little bit guilty, and a lot energized. In the days after that second meeting, frequent thoughts of Elena continued to enter my mind. It was such a novel experience for me, both lovely and disquieting. For over twenty years I had been habituated to having two things on my mind: my relationship with my Divine Father/Mother and my daily monastic routine, with its prayers, duties, and relationships within the abbey walls. Now, I had another place to go with my thoughts, a new and very different place. It wasn't forbidden by any means, but I have to tell you that there was always a vague discomfort shadowing my mind whenever I thought of Elena, and it took away some of the pleasure of that pursuit. Looking back, rightfully so. I was at a loss at the time, however, to say whether or not those vague feelings constituted valid warning signs, pointing out who I was and who she was, or whether they were just active remnants of my strict Catholic upbringing. That message was always to err on the side of conservatism — or worse, self-recrimination. Maybe those remnants were again being triggered and were starting to engage themselves in their familiar and obtrusive way. I vowed not to accept that. I couldn't let that happen. In any event, I was out of practice — thoughts of a woman had not been active in me for most of my adult life.

I knew that I was very attracted to Elena, certainly. That in itself was not an issue in a general sense. She was an accomplished, elegant woman with whom I shared like interests and tastes and with whom I had a shared history. But somewhere inside, as I have just written, I knew I could be unwisely dallying a bit in my mind with these thoughts, and it most certainly occurred to me that perhaps I should be a little more careful in dealing with them. But time and again I firmly resolved to myself that if this were the recommencement of an erstwhile type of useless, antiquated, and overly rigid reaction to things sexual, the way I had been instructed in the extreme by my Church in my youth, I would not let it enter and toy with my conscience — at least not without a fair fight. I no longer had the time or the patience for that extremist viewpoint and I would deal with it as I should.

Elena came to visit a couple more times in the next two months. Each visit seemed to be better than the last. We had fun, and I loved being around her. I found myself always very excited about the prospects of her coming, and was always so fulfilled by our time together. Sometimes, she would look at me in a queer way — like she was trying to analyze my thoughts or see through me. Other times, she would have a distant look on her face as if she were somewhere else, lost in thought. I must say that each of those looks was very fetching to me, and I sometimes longed to know what she might be thinking. I know she enjoyed the peace and the atmosphere that Kervennec provided. She said as much many times. Inside, I fought the idea that there was more to her thoughts than that.

A short time after Elena's most recent visit, I attended a meeting of the committee in charge of the abbey's long-term economic and building plans. I was second-ranked on that committee. I have always had a facility with numbers and I liked being the numbers person on the committee, though I felt the committee itself was next to useless, unfortunately. It was chaired by Father Benedikt, an urbane middle-aged monk from just over the border in Germany. He was a practical man but his communication skills left something to be desired. He was, however, trying very hard with a group of men not accustomed to working in this way and I did not find him difficult to work with, so the committee work was tolerable.

On that day the agenda was more interesting than usual, as it was concerned with the first submissions by a subcommittee charged with finding ways to fund the completion of the cloister. The existing cloister structure was, oddly enough, only finished on three sides, so it was not really a cloister at all. Abbé Rénard, our current abbé who had replaced Abbé Raymond, my second abbé, seven years prior had felt that this arrangement was not well-suited to encouraging meditative prayer or a sense of the sacred, and I think that he was right. It was very little used. Abbé also felt that such a "monstrosity," as he termed it, did not befit an institution like this meant to praise God and "show Him off" to those who might be drawn to the abbey to explore the world of Spirit or to pray from time to time. The cloister itself was off-limits to visitors but it was easily visible in publicity pictures of the abbey and from various vantage points on the grounds. Abbé Rénard was very direct, especially as he aged, and it was obvious that he meant it and that he sincerely was offended by the sorry "sort-of" cloister.

A fourth wall would need to be built to finish it,

but therein lay the problem. The cloister was formed by our dormitory/living quarters on the one side and the great hall on the other. The front of the church with its corridor then formed a third wall. There was a large creek not far from where the fourth wall should have been. It would be quite a project to construct a fourth wall with the existing slope and the rivulet. It would be hard to get to for construction, but it could be done at great expense.

The meeting had had the potential to be interesting, but as it worked out it had been humdrum. No new ideas were really exchanged. Despite the importance of the subject to Abbé Rénard and the subcommittee's charge to find solutions, Father Benedickt did not get much response from the committee members, whose duty was to look at revenue sources. There were again the same old tired ideas of expanding the abbey shop or the shop's internet sales or increasing sales of our music with our admittedly very good choir of monks, but the process of locating and tapping new revenue sources was foundering. The great majority of the committee members were strictly "men of the cloth" and were out of their element in things financial. There were hardly any "fund-raisers" among us. The issue was again pushed to the next meeting, some four weeks away.

As I left the meeting and the building, I walked past the fountain to one of my favorite benches, the one to which I had taken Elena during our first visit at the abbey. I found my mind back on the subject of her immediately. I would have loved to have spoken to her at that moment. She would have had something wise to tell me on the subject of meetings. Whereas before I might have gone strictly to God with these thoughts or problems, more and more I was thinking of her and what she might say or think on a topic. She was beginning to share my thoughts and I was comforted by it. It was peaceful and, I admit now, exciting, whenever thoughts of her entered my head.

I sat for a minute. The meeting had drained me and not in a good way. It had been tedious and a bit depressing. But there was one other thing about that meeting that had remained on my mind. It had to do with Abbé Rénard. He had stopped by during the meeting, as he often did. He seemed much different this time — much less involved and less "competent," for lack of a better word, than I had seen him in other meetings. I had noticed something different this last couple of weeks. There had been a big change in him. I had seen it in these types of everyday administrative functions and I had seen it in the way he communicated, too, particularly his listlessness during the Offices in church. He seemed so very tired, and he was starting to treat us more and more like children. Something was wrong but I really didn't have a clue what it was. He was not himself and looked every day of his seventy-eight years.

The abbé is the heart and the head of an abbey. His importance to it cannot be overestimated, so I found this very disconcerting. I wasn't yet comfortable discussing this with fellow monks. All of them had to notice, though. I could tell by their quizzical looks at meals or even during Offices. In his new comportment, I sensed that I was beginning to see a failure of leadership at the abbey. One never knows who might be a friend or foe in such matters, so I decided the best thing would be to write Elena a letter. I could bring up these matters and get my concerns off my chest. I felt secure and confident writing her.

I keep copies of most of my letters and here is what I wrote that day to her:

Dear Elena,

You have been on my mind lately. I enjoy our back-and-forth on so many topics very much — as I am sure you have guessed. I have just emerged from another boring financial planning meeting. I'm afraid these men don't have a clue when it comes to financial matters. I'm sure when I explain it to you next time I see you, you'll have some ideas. At least I'll feel better talking to someone! I am praying daily for some resolution and I know something will come along.

There is also another issue. It is potentially much more serious than my committee work. The climate in the abbey is a bit stormy right now. There is an undercurrent of tension. I'd even call it dissatisfaction. It is becoming more obvious what the problem is. Abbé Rénard is getting on and he seems increasingly out of step with the needs and spirit of the men. He looks terrible — certainly his physical health has deteriorated, and he seems not able to keep attentive in services and in public places.

Nothing ever seems to get done — like our finance meeting today. It's frustrating. It's the same with recruitment — Abbé says God will find a way, but there are many more things we can do to get young men to visit here. He doesn't support "going out into the community to fish," as he puts it. Abbé has become so demanding of the silence here, too. The "laxity" that has developed lately needs to end, he says. Quite frankly, I think he is imagining things on that point, as that has not been the case as I see it. We are not now nor have we ever been lax around here, I can say that categorically. At any rate, I hardly see things getting better with him.

Now, there was a rumor around here this morning that the abbé will go on leave of absence soon and that our prieur, Fr. Guinot, will be the acting abbé for a period of time. Considering the abbé's health, it well may turn out that his coming back and staying on the job will be out of the question, too, and a change will come. But the whole thought of change puts the men under stress — a change of abbé, even having our prieur in charge temporarily, is a big change potentially to their way of life as they know it now, and change is feared even if things are not perfect here under Abbé Rénard. We have good men who could eventually take on the job. Father Guinot is the one most often mentioned, but he wouldn't be my first choice at all. I find him shallow and a bit puffed up. So, it is a little frustrating here.

I thought I would write and get a few things off my chest. Thanks for "listening" and I hope we are still on for another visit here at the abbey in a couple weeks' time.

Yours affectionately,
Jean

I dropped that note into an envelope a little later and then into the mail pouch managed by Father

Guillaume.

Two days later I received a short letter from Elena asking if she could come to the abbey in a week's time instead of the two as we had planned, as she had business not far away. I felt a little surge of what I can only guess was adrenaline. And maybe I shouldn't say a "little surge" — it was a big surge — and I responded in the affirmative.

My mind was beginning to feel more muddled. The tension in the abbey was one thing, but increasingly coming to my mind were my thoughts of Elena and my continuing "fascination" with her, as I stealthily termed it inwardly. It wasn't something, at least at first, that I willed or sought after. I would find myself sometimes stopping what I was doing just to think of her. Of course, I would tell myself that she was a good friend and a wonderfully "solid" person who could offer me an equally solid friendship; and, all of that was true. But, I knew deep inside that it was getting more complicated than that.

And there was another thing. Women friends were not an everyday item in the abbey. Mothers and sisters, cousins and aunts, occasional female visitors, pilgrims, and workers were not unusual to see. Those were taken for granted and welcomed. But women friends who visited frequently were very rare. They were not encouraged. Perhaps there were good reasons for that. But my case was surely different, I told myself. My case I saw as a "gray area" at worst and I certainly wasn't ready to exclude Elena. I needed to be careful, though, I knew. Regular visits could become an issue.

A monastic community of men was closed off to women by its essential nature. Women friends didn't fit well into the overall picture. There was no doubt that that was one of the strategies to relieve monks of the burden of the temptations of the flesh. So far, so good on that score, I knew, but her visits might become a concern in some circles.

To my detriment, in retrospect, I continued to downplay my fascination with her and I decided just to consider myself lucky to have such an interesting, supportive, and engaging friend, which, of course, was true. I wasn't going to look for trouble where there was none to be found. I would certainly include the topic in my prayers, and continue to believe that if any clarification were truly needed, it would be forthcoming. With that type of reasoning, I would close the subject, at least for the moment, but I always had a nagging suspicion that my thoughts of her would soon surface again, along with the persistent question of propriety. I was afraid, in the recesses of my mind, that those thoughts might return with even more power.

Unfortunately, I was right. Return they did — time and again. I still wouldn't acknowledge that they were beginning to be a problem. I deflected my unease by blaming it in that old feeling of guilt mounting to the surface and unfairly causing my disquiet. The unease was similar to the guilty feeling that I had endured so often as a youth when justifying my thoughts and behavior. It was triggered this time, of course, by my having a legitimate "friend" who, it said, was taking me places where maybe a monk ought not to go. That wasn't all. Aside from crowding out my thoughts of God and Spirit, thoughts of Elena had the potential to bring me face-to-face with an aspect of myself that I thought I had well regulated and robbed of any potency — my sexuality. But to go back to dealing with that subject would be tiresome and clearly a reversion, and in truth, a little scary. Naively, I said to myself that I wouldn't.

It was not as easy as all of that, however. One cannot just "want to" when such a tenacious energy like attraction to the opposite sex is involved. It is a magnificent power and woe to those who leave their feelings and approaches to it unsorted. It must be confronted with an equal energy. Engaging with this fundamental power and to savor its allure without being overwhelmed by it would not be child's play. Continuing down any path connected with it, especially in my position in life, was playing with fire. The result would be inevitable — it could only lead to one being burnt. I wasn't ready to acknowledge that, however. I liked it too much.

I got into still more game-playing with the uncomfortable feelings. I purposely left open the question of whether or not my visits with Elena were good for me by saying that they were good for *her*, as a seeker needing guidance. This gave them an air of legitimacy, in addition to supporting my assertions that this uncomfortable sensation was just a remnant of my guilt-ridden self of old, not a real thing worth listening to. I continued to half-sell myself on the premise that this internal warning to stop was just the vestige of those outmoded beliefs of mine, and that, importantly, she needed me in her search. It remained essential to me at the time to not be victimized by my former scrupulousness — to never again revert to that young, uninformed, and overly conscientious Jean. That truly was a point of concern — and confusion — for me. There was some legitimacy in my questioning these feelings; just enough in my mind to at least justify my actions. If I had wished to look ever closer, however, I might not have been so convinced. In retrospect, I see that I was clinging desperately to certain notions. I well realized on many levels how difficult and distasteful it would be to give up this friendship, not to mention, regrettably, those feelings that they aroused in me. I was desperate to find a palatable solution, one that could even convince my intuitive self. Even if I had admitted to myself that Elena made things difficult, I was not about to give up that friendship. I would under no circumstances accept that course of action as inevitable, as my only solution.

My ultimate response to this self-questioning came to take still another turn. I began to think and act as if it were possible to sidestep potential difficulties by relying on my extensive training in things moral as a priest. I could certainly resist anything sinful or damaging to me. It would take care of itself that way and I could trust myself to continue the road I was on. I could take care of myself and I could deal with my fears and feelings. Surely a man in my position, with my experience in things of the mind and soul, could find a ready and acceptable solution to these feelings and remain beyond repute. I also felt that I had to be good to myself, and not judge too harshly. I felt that I should talk to myself with encouragement and not rancor, advising myself as I would advise my best friend. These things I was determined to do. Above all, I should not become frustrated. "Pride goeth before the fall…"

There was one other thing I was determined to do: I vowed never to let on or give her even the tiniest notion of what was happening to me deep inside.

What a fool I was to think I could do any of it.

An Interim Abbé

"Do I contradict myself? Very well, then, I contradict myself; I am large — I contain multitudes."
— *Walt Whitman, "Song of Myself"*

Abbé Rénard had been rushed to the hospital. It had all happened suddenly — in the middle of the night a few days after our committee meeting. He had fallen while getting up to go to the bathroom. He had cried out and the noise had been heard in an adjacent cell. We didn't know the extent of the injury at first, but we found out it was not the injury from his fall that was so serious. The fall had been but the effect of a rapidly growing cancerous tumor in his lung that had weakened him dramatically. It would require immediate surgery.

It was not clear at first how long he might be away. Some reports, just rumors really, suggested it was to be a matter of weeks, others a matter of months. There was some question about whether or not he would return at all. Within a couple of days it had been settled: Abbé Rénard was to have a long rest. His prognosis was not particularly good, but if he could resume his duties in three months, he would be back at the helm. If not, an election would be held and a new permanent abbé installed. It would be our second in command, the prieur, Father Guinot, who would become our acting abbé. All eyes now turned to him. The ceremony for the elevation of Father Guinot as temporary abbé would take place immediately after

Mass in three days. Though only for the office of interim abbé, the ceremony of installation would include the pledging of obedience by each monk to his new earthly Father.

This was to be a major change in the abbey and that fact required much attention now. The idea had had very little time to settle in for any of us. But for me, the most troubling thought brewing in the back of my mind was that Guinot would now be my Father, head of the abbey, due all of the respect and obedience that that office commanded. I really could not believe that he was the right man to be head of an abbey. But then again, we did have a history.

We had never hit it off. We had come into the abbey at about the same time but from very different circumstances. He was from a wealthy family in Saint-Malo — very respected and powerful. He carried with him, and perhaps I'm not very charitable in my viewpoint, an attitude that looked and felt a lot like arrogance to me. I searched my soul often to make sure it wasn't just a case of good old-fashioned jealousy or something, but clearly it was not. He did not have a lot of close friends within the abbey, but was respected for his intelligence and held in awe by some due to his family history and attitude.

I had always had the impression, confirmed for me by an intimate of mine who knew him well, that Guinot considered me a rival. We are similar in age, and as I said, we had started more or less together and were both equally respected in the abbey, if for different reasons. He made no effort of any kind to befriend me, though I had tried to treat him as a special friend in the beginning because of our nearly simultaneous entrance at Kervennec. He just wasn't interested, and things had never really improved. Making friends is not my *raison d'être* as a monk and I, in turn, have not made any more attempts to join in any social or other activities with Guinot, though I do not avoid him. He has just been a hard person for me to like and engage with, for the reasons I have written, and it has been clear that he has not been eager for my company.

Another thing that I found difficult to deal with was his penchant for being very traditional and by-the-book Catholic in his view of things. That is his prerogative, but it should not be hard for you to see why this would be an area where we would be like oil and water. I also knew from conversations with others that he had always seen me as far too liberal in my thinking, particularly as I have from time to time openly expressed positive views about other religions in front of him, Eastern religions in particular. As he was so old-school, or should I say, rigid school, I had a feeling that to entrust him with the power possessed by an abbé would be a huge mistake. The thought that he might even become abbé permanently here — that is, for life — was very worrying to me. I had not had the time yet to put that whole concept into perspective, what it might mean to me personally or for the abbey, but it scared me on the surface of it. I did hope that I was making more trouble than was necessary in my prejudgment and my thinking, so I tried to back off in all of that and let God do His work. God tests us every day and relations with others may bring us the biggest tests of all, but I knew that I could handle myself in my daily interactions with him if I avoided judgment and was patient.

For a little while before his installation a happier thought did play within my mind: perhaps things will be different between the two of us when Guinot feels the mantle of responsibility. Maybe he will soften a bit and take his position of abbé in the right spirit; not as a judge and overlord but rather like a loving and concerned spiritual mentor. My hopes were not high for this, however, I must confess.

The installation went about as expected. There was curiosity mixed with excitement in the men, but fear was also an emotion that was no stranger to them that day. I remember the second day of the interim abbé's "reign" very well. Father, now Abbé, Guinot took his seat in the chair reserved for the abbé at lunch. His countenance was beaming, though he continued to be tight-lipped there were hints of severity in his look. I said a silent prayer that I would be given the strength, and more importantly the will, to make that devotional commitment to him as abbé, even if his was only a temporary appointment. I was sure that I could do it and would do it, but I wanted it done in the right spirit, that of meekness and humility on my part. I knew that that would be pleasing to God and the right thing to do.

He had not said anything to me since he began presiding. He had made out his lists of responsibilities in the monastery, however. I was surprised to see what far-reaching changes he had made. For someone in a caretaker role, I though it quite odd — overboard to tell you the truth. I was really hoping that he would know his limits and exercise his powers judiciously. This was not a good sign.

For example, he set up a committee to look at permanent abbey outreach in neighboring communities. He said plainly that it was up to us to evangelize locally, something we had never done in an active way. In the monastic tradition, we felt our role was as a private spiritual community. Spiritual good could be accomplished through our Divine Offices, open to all, as well as through our duty of hospitality for seekers and our spiritual presence and clerical assistance for neighboring communities, not to mention our obvious role of prayer for all. Guinot said it was a large part of our responsibility to reinforce traditional Catholic beliefs in those communities. This was not our role, of that I was convinced. He decided to set up teaching "groups" — more like a buddy system — with two of us paired to go into these communities and spread the gospel, like the disciples in the New Testament. He gave us a copy of what we were to use and say — the only authorized teaching allowed us — sort of like a personal catechism. Needless to say, it was in its tone and content more of a "do what the Church says, and don't ask questions, or else" manual of his own making for the abbey army. The cherry on the sundae was the fact that he made me the head of that new outreach, knowing full well that I was not the best representative for some of our traditional teachings. He was testing me. I was not amused.

I worked hard to feel love in my heart, the love I would and should feel for any fellow man. This feeling of extending your heart, of extending love, can put all of us in a sort of perfect world, a satisfied place. It was a place I had been many times before in my prayer and meditative life. It is the right and Godly place to be with one's consciousness, anyway, so I used it to make peace with my emotional self regarding Guinot. It worked well enough and I was more or less happy with the outcome, though I had planned to stall the community outreach as long as I could.

There was nothing more to do now but let the future reveal itself, hour by hour and day by day, in the new administration of Abbé Guinot. After his taking charge, it was as if the abbey took a long exhalation, fatigued as it was by all it had just gone through, yet curious about what the next weeks and months might bring. It seemed that all of the residents were too tired now to worry about details and about the new atmosphere of the place, and about all of the uncertainties going forward. I had my doubts that that calm would last. It was, however, now time to leave it all alone and to put it and keep it where it belonged — in God's hands. That evening, I recall, there was even a starry sky; the clouds of the previous few days had dispersed.

It wouldn't take long, though, for time to reveal the ravages and the destructive effects of this change, which would come to divide us and threaten our very existence as a family. But, innocent of what was to come, all of my brothers slept well that night. My own thoughts shifted between the week's events and my friendship with Elena. In the end, however, weariness was the victor, and thus I, too, had a deep and dreamless repose.

There would be less of that in the months to come.

Obsession

A god implants in mortal guilt whenever he wants utterly to confound a house.
— *Aeschylus*, Fragments, l. 151

In the abbey, it is always a good thing to get major events behind us to make way again for the peace and certainty that our abbey life typically offers the men. The abbey did begin to find its own rhythm during what would turn out to be a very short honeymoon for Guinot's administration. I was feeling a great sense of unease, as I have explained, with our new abbé at the helm. I quickly learned it was a feeling shared by others, all of which was greatly accentuated by the fact that in just three months, he could become our Father for life. That really depressed me when I let that thought surface. I so hoped that somehow Abbé Rénard would make a surprise recovery, but the way things sounded I knew the chances were remote.

A couple of days after I received the letter from Elena asking if she could come visit sooner, I was returning to my room after Lauds hoping to get in a little nap. As I opened my door, I saw an envelope lying on the floor. I hadn't been expecting anything. I noticed the handwriting and I thought it looked a lot like Elena's. I felt a rush of excitement as I slid my index finger under the flap of the envelope. Upon opening it, however, I found it was just a short note from my aunt on my mother's side, telling me about a proposed family reunion for the following year, and inquiring generally about me and sending good wishes.

"It's not from Elena," I remember thinking to myself.

I realized that I was profoundly disappointed. Why should I be? There was no reason for her to write…she was coming in a few days. Thoughts again entered my mind, uncomfortable thoughts. Was I being warned — or should I say condemned — by the old Jean? I tried to put that out of my mind, but it wasn't just that. Now there seemed to be something new in the mix. I was starting to sense a real lack of something in my life. Not having her available when I wanted her was dispiriting and beginning to frustrate me. I was only disturbed the more because of all of this. I let it go as best I could but these thoughts of her persisted, nagging at me, and I wasn't sure why they were coming so frequently now. What was it all about? A part of me did not want to go there at all. There was something there that scared me and I had this constant pressure of something cautioning me. It was all residing just below the surface of my conscious mind, and was probably quite accessible, I knew, if I would make any effort to uncover it. But I didn't want to go there, to investigate further. I might not like what I found. So I continued to attempt to bat those thoughts away like any other intruding or uninvited thought or feeling. Usually I would try to reason with my thoughts of her, implementing my usually effective tactic of taking a position outside of myself and observing the emotion pass harmlessly away, deflecting its power. However, I was not meeting with much success with that tactic now.

It became very wearing on me. These thoughts, with their yearnings for her, involved me at such a very deep level emotionally. They were striking unexpectedly, too, often in the middle of something completely unrelated — like during one of our two "acceptable" Benedictine obsessions, work and prayer. To top it off, they were appearing with what was becoming an increasing ferocity. My scruples were characterizing them as illicit, and offering no quarter, but my heart saw it differently, so the difficulty for me lay not just in the frequency of my dealing with such uncomfortable emotions on such a fundamental level, but also in the indecision in my emotional self as to whether I really wanted them to go away.

I must say, though, that those emotions and thoughts also brought me a lot of pleasure. I wanted to be around Elena, and the heart would not be so easily dealt with or dismissed. I felt she complemented me on many levels. She was vibrant, worldly, and intensely artistic, in love with life, the life of the here and now, a life bursting in all of its senses. I told myself there was no reason to think I could not have both worlds — the world of the monk and the world of the loving friend. But my efforts to reason with the situation rarely brought comfort. I had a fear in my heart of hearts that all of that was just lip service, though I would not admit it. Those nagging doubts continued, and those doubts were what were punishing me.

Which was the genuine Jean? Could both lay

claim to be a part of me — one part with a very human and primitive desire for a soul mate, in this case a woman, and the other consumed with the desire to live a life dedicated to honoring and loving a gracious God? Is one more "genuine" than the other? I can even remember raising the possibility that such emotions and their resulting thoughts were holy. The argument went something like this: Isn't it our core, our essential self, where our deepest feelings come from? Isn't this where God resides, in the deepest places of our existence? Are these feelings not, then, by nature, Godlike? I had written that out one evening when I was particularly bothered.

This battle started to take a toll on me physically. I wasn't sleeping well. I lacked concentration. I let things slide, like my walks and some of my garden work. I was seeking answers to it all, of course — but answers that would permit me to continue on this uncharted course into potentially deadly waters. I wanted to believe that I could keep a cool head while I continued to turn it over in my mind. I didn't think that I needed to speak to anyone about it, or that I needed any outside help. I would tell myself over and over that it was right not to rush to conclusions. I had those years of training, didn't I? Then, in the middle of coolly evaluating my motives, those old accusations would intrude like a recurring nightmare: How could I trust myself to make a fair judgment when it came to a woman?

I felt those pangs intensely and I loathed them. My mind was made up, however, that this time it would be different. I was resolved to err on the side of liberality in my judgment of my own conduct. I was absolutely determined not to let those doubts intervene and make me unhappy. That was that. Each time I decided that this was the way I would move forward, I would be calm for a time. I would feel good — and powerful. I felt brave and imbued with a new energy, like a revolutionary at the beginning of his rebellion. But it was always short-lived. Soon I would hear them again — the voices of scruples murmuring unrestrained in my mind like an obnoxious tune. I would do something about that one way or another.

The opportunity for that something came quicker than I ever could have imagined.

A Fateful Day

And Jesus said unto her, neither do I condemn thee: go, and sin no more.

—John 8:11

Once in a great while, a single day, a single minute of a single day, changes everything. That day had arrived for me. That fateful day at lunch, I remember I would have preferred to have withdrawn to a table by myself at meal time had it been possible, just to be alone with my problem. I had a sense that others might suspect my treachery to my vocation. This vocation does not allow even the tiniest desire for a woman to enter in. But I meant to hold on to my position. After all, my scruples were usually undeserved.

That day, as I ate and the guilt returned, I felt that I could do the usual thing and for the thousandth time attempt to reason with it, or, I could take the hard tack and stick up for myself, feeling righteous anger and then letting it go. But why should I have to? I didn't feel like it this time. I was sick of it — sick of this situation, sick of this feeling, sick of rigid little laws, sick of my response to it all, sick of always feeling pain and fear and doubt, sick of wondering where it all came from. I was slowly losing my perspective, the one thing I could not afford to lose.

After the meal that day, I walked briskly back to the welcome center and the shop and put on my work habit. I was looking forward to escaping into my work.

In the shop I took a quick look around. There was a stack of boxes of books in the back that needed marking and sorting. I would appreciate that today. Quiet, silent, mindless work was just what I needed.

As I got settled in, the shop was opening and there were a few visitors trickling in. I was caressing the thought of her when it happened.

"Father Jean," came a voice from the vestibule.

It was Father François.

I walked out of the storage room and responded, "Yes, Father?"

"Hi, Father Jean. There's a woman here to see you."

I looked over François' shoulder.

I was ill prepared for what came next.

"Hi, Jean!"

It was Elena.

She was standing there at the shop's cash register. She had seen me right away and waved as I had come forward, a big smile crossing her pretty face. I was not expecting her for another five days. I could have been pushed over by a feather as I came to the front and stood there just looking at her, stunned as I was. I felt lightheaded — I needed time to get my mental and emotional house in order. I was accustomed to having time to "ready" myself for her visits. But there was no time, no place to hide. She who had eaten up a great deal of my thoughts was standing in front of me, in the flesh. She had been there way too often in my imaginary world, and now I was finding it so very difficult to deal with her right here, right now, with no notice. The juxtaposition had put me completely off-balance. I knew that I needed to right my ship and to do it quickly. I was hoping that she wouldn't notice anything. I went over to greet her as enthusiastically as I could, though it was necessarily feigned.

I kissed her and gave her a big smile, completely befuddled inside. I remember how we stood looking at each other, both a little nervous, with me trying so hard not to show it. Our relationship, among other things, had been built on spontaneity of conversation and relaxed expression, so it would soon be apparent if these ingredients were missing today with me in my state.

"Wow, what a surprise!"

"I hope a good one — I know you are busy," she blurted out.

Father François, seeing that the shop was fairly quiet, signaled to me that it would be okay if I wanted to spend some time outside with my visitor. It was a relief. François is a very decent man and a friend. I pulled off my work vest and placed it behind the counter and then mustered up a cheery voice as I said to Elena,

"Why don't we go outside to the garden?"

Nodding my thanks again to Father François I took my coat and we walked out into the late morning sunshine. I was working hard to act "natural" — I knew how that could be the most difficult of tasks. I carried it off pretty well though, I thought.

We walked over to our accustomed bench in the garden almost by rote. I was playing over in my mind frantically what to say, how to be, how to act. I felt like a first-grader and I was afraid I would be tongue-tied. I knew I had to speak.

"I have been thinking about you and even wrote you a letter this week."

I heard myself speak, but it was as if I were in a dream, my mind elsewhere. As I started to speak, I felt the shock of deep discomfort flow through me. Immediately I knew what it was. It was my scrupulous self mocking me. "Who are you kidding? Thinking about you! How about 'wanting you, desiring you,' you weak little man!" The conscience can be cruel.

I ignored these words peppering my thoughts as best I could.

Elena replied, "Yes, I got it, and thanks! I did so appreciate you telling me all that you did, and all about your feelings. I hope we can talk about that some more. You are such a sweet man."

I remember another surge of something running up my spine when she said that.

"And do I have some good news!" she continued, now more relaxed. "I am so happy that I get to tell you in person! I really want you to be the first to know. I couldn't wait to share this news with you!"

These words excited parts of me that had been dormant these many years. Sharing, intimacy — exactly what I had been thinking about. I knew with those words that I was out of control emotionally. I instinctively tried to cover that up with enthusiasm.

"Boy, you really are excited. What kind of good news is this — did you win the lottery?!"

"Better! Oh, Jean, I am so excited. I am actually going to do the stained glass replacement project I had told you about for the Abbey of St. Michel! The nuns told me yesterday that they have accepted my designs and it has finally hit me. I am so motivated and energized! I love it! Can you stand it?!"

Could I stand it? "You are so ridiculously happy that she is here — of course you can 'stand it'!" the little voice shouted obnoxiously in the back of my mind.

Ignoring the voice as best I could, I responded, trying hard to concentrate.

"Elena, I couldn't be happier for you!"

I was doing better. I was beginning to feel more myself, more natural, but still I was woefully unprepared for this visit…and that look of excitement on her face. I had been in a world of fantasy. Elena had become the central part of the fantasy world that I had enthusiastically constructed, brick by brick. That world was now causing me a lot of pain — and pleasure. It was a private place where I had wrapped up so many of my personal thoughts, and, regrettably, so much of my energy, and now this "intrusion" of Elena, the central aspect of that world, here and in the flesh, with no time for transition, had shocked me profoundly. Still, I felt that I could mask it fairly well. I continued my attempts to act natural. For a moment, I had nothing more to say, however. It wasn't exactly awkward, but it wasn't exactly me. Elena knew me well enough now to notice the difference in my manner.

"Jean, are you okay? Maybe I should not have dropped in on you like this. I am really sorry if I disturbed your routine. I keep forgetting that you are a monk…"

I just smiled. I was desperate to reassure her that nothing pleased me more than her coming. I didn't know exactly how to express it without inviting my demons back for a longer stay.

"Elena, you say the goofiest things. We're friends. I love seeing you and listening to you and your enthusiastic way, and what could be a better time than now so that you can share your joy. I am soaking it in! I am feeling so proud. How about that?"

I could see that Elena was listening closely while I spoke these sentences and how she observed me carefully. I wasn't sure what it meant.

Her face then suddenly looked more serious. She touched my arm and said, "Jean, I didn't like hearing about the problems you told me about in your last letter. It was another one of the reasons that I wanted to be sure to come and see you as soon as I could. It was selfish of me to arrive here and just talk about myself. I know that this situation at the abbey cannot be pleasant for you. I don't feel much like a person who can give you too much advice on those things, but I'll try. Is it really that bad here now?"

Glad to have another subject to occupy me, I responded, "I wasn't in a great mood when I wrote that letter. Frustrated is the best word, and very, very anxious over the abbé situation. And, yes, we're a little short on practicality around here in those finance meetings. I've simply got to deal with it. Not much will change for the moment. The thing with Abbé Rénard, however, has been really hard on the men. We just found out this morning that he is going to begin treatments tomorrow, and it has been indicated that he will need to be away for quite a while. Father Guinot, our prieur, has become acting abbé. The change has ruffled some of the men, me included."

I was trying hard to be more matter-of-fact with Elena, pleasant but not overly affectionate — rather more businesslike. I was also happy to talk about the Guinot situation with her because it was easier to be serious, and I could express some of my misgivings.

"Well, keep writing me about it if it makes you feel better. I care about you. Maybe I can be of more help to you in the future. That spark of wisdom may yet ignite!" Elena said that smilingly to help lighten the mood.

I smiled, too, and added, "Send some my way when that moment comes."

We got up and walked through the garden and then to the end of the apple orchard where we again stopped for awhile. Neither of us said anything for the moment. The freshness of the Breton air blowing in off of the vast Atlantic was bracing, I recall that very well. Out of the corner of my eye, I could see Elena looking at me with what I can only describe as a wistful gaze.

I had thought a lot lately about how things might have been different if I had paid more attention to her at university. We were not the same people then. Our destinies were yet to unfold. We had made the right choices to follow our stars, hadn't we? Me, to a life I loved, and she to her art. The two of us were now here at this place and at this time, destinies still unfolding, the future always developing and evolving, nudging us and pushing us on. In retrospect, I can see now that I was still not yet concerned enough about where it was pushing us.

She gave a sigh and then slowly leaned her head on my left shoulder. I found the action totally unexpected, but I did nothing to impede her. I felt the warmth of the gesture go through me, the physical contact with a woman a distant then a familiar feeling recalled now from decades before as a younger man. I was able to catch wafts of the agreeable scent of her hair as the wind rustled it onto my face. There was a fresh smell on her cheeks. We were quiet. It was a moment of silent communication and intimacy. I let my arm rest lightly on her back; then her arm found its way around my waist. I was telling myself it was the touch of friendship, a touch shared by two sensitive people, friends forever. I savored it.

I felt her hold on me tighten. I turned to look at her and she was turning to look at me at that same moment. I looked into her eyes and saw a look that could only mean one thing. I felt her grip suddenly tighten still further and her other arm coming to embrace me lovingly, and before I knew it, she kissed me, and I did nothing to stop it. On the contrary, I enjoyed it. It was passionate. I wanted her so much. I held her close…and then I kissed her, sensually.

I didn't want to stop — so I didn't. I found my hands running over her beautiful breasts and down her hips. I grabbed her buttocks and pulled it to me, hard. She was gasping with the intensity of my affections, looking to find my mouth and kiss me passionately over and over. I felt the sexual energy rampaging through me. This affection, this love, whatever it was…it felt so powerful and consuming. But then, just as I had started to place my hand between her thighs, a voice entered my head, shouting, "What are you doing!?" It was like being hit with a bucket of cold water. I pulled my hand back and turned my head away. Elena looked at me passionately and then inquiringly as she felt my sudden release of her. She soon guessed what had struck me and she, in turn, pulled away. I looked again at her, and when our eyes met, I could see the shame in hers. Mine must have told the same story.

I wasn't sure what to do next. Both of us remained frozen. She was looking up at me the whole time, her vulnerability so evident. The sadness in those eyes pierced me. I turned away once more and surveyed the orchard. There was nobody around — or was there? I thought I heard a noise, but then my nerves were hyper-sensitive. I didn't know for sure. Everything would be all right, I told myself. I was trying to be confident, but I was shaken.

After another few moments, we turned and slowly started to walk back in the direction of the welcome center. We did so with no conversation. The gravity of what had occurred started to assault my mind.

On our route back, I saw something moving in the distance. Getting a better look, I saw it was a monk working in one of the fruit trees. I recognized Father Michel as we approached. He had been pruning. He was older than me by at least fifteen years, and was a very private person. A question momentarily raced through my mind: Had he had just arrived? I wasn't sure, but I had not seen him earlier when we had passed on the other side. We were not close. He was old-school — extremely rigid in his views — and strictly compliant to the Rule of Silence. Reaching him, he stopped his work and peered over his glasses as he heard our footfalls approaching. He recognized me with a simple nod, but ignored Elena. I nodded back without saying anything, and we moved on, reaching the front end of the orchard again, not far from the public garden, which was empty of visitors. We then continued in silence to the parking area, stopping at her car.

Elena turned to me with a sad face and said, "I'm at a loss for words, Jean."

Her look of dismay changed into a look of almost helplessness. I, too, was at a loss, but I wanted to remain confident in her eyes. I could see plainly that she wanted to speak, to somehow gain relief and also to comfort me.

"I…if I…if I have hurt you in any way…if I have done anything today to make your life more difficult here, Jean, I…I don't know what I'd do," she said. "I would hate myself for that— forever. Oh, Jean, I'm so confused. It's like I'm between a rock and a hard place with you. Your tenderness and your goodness, but especially your friendship is so precious. Maybe it is more than that, though."

She started to cry. I looked at her tenderly. She spoke through her sobs. "I want to be able to see you but now I don't think that I should. I would be wretched if you were to disappear now from my life, though, wretched," she repeated, tears running down her face.

She looked away as she opened her purse. "I think I'd better go."

She took her keys out and then wiped her eyes with a tissue as she got into her car. I could think of nothing to say. I just stood and watched her depart. I remained there motionless. I was numb.

I knew deep down that I could not emerge completely unscathed from what had happened, and I certainly would not remain the man I was just an hour before. My playing with fire — rationalizing, disputing, arguing with myself, and ultimately getting too close — had finally exacted its retribution. I had let it go way too far. I had done nothing to stop the growing affection between us. I had a strong feeling then that my day of reckoning was to come.

I turned away, summoning up only the strength to take a deep breath, before shuffling back to the shop, totally unnerved.

There would be consequences. Of that there was no doubt.

But what those consequences might be, for me and for the abbey, remained to be seen.

The Emotional Me

*Rather than being your thoughts and emotions, be the awareness
behind them.*
– *Eckhart Tolle,* The New Earth – Awakening to Your Life's
Purpose

We are body, mind and soul, and if we examine ourselves a little further, we find that we are very much something else which helps to distinguish us as human. I am speaking of the "emotional self." It is the part, for most of us, that rules so much of our thinking and our everyday actions, or, I should say, reactions. The emotional self resides within us all; within this emotional "self" we find the places that hurt or frighten us, but we also find our fondest loves, joys, and our deepest feelings.

As I grow older, one thing stands out to me. I see that one of our biggest roadblocks to holiness is not being able to properly handle our emotions. Emotions affect us constantly and in a myriad of ways. They come in all shapes and sizes, from depression to fear and anger, to ecstatic moments of joy. They can be seen as innate, intractable, and constant; and, unfortunately, more often than not in their extreme, enemies to self-happiness and brotherly love.

What are we, most of us most of the time, in our relation to our inner voice and our many feelings? How many of us are really cognizant of the interplay of our two realities, the inner "us" and things outside of us?

Are we truly understanding the interplay? Are we oblivious or unconcerned, or possibly obsessively concerned? Are we rational, if in fact we can distinguish?

To be totally caught up in any emotion is to be weakened. It coops our personal power, removes us from our calm and peaceful self and often destroys our balance. We humans like to categorize, and we tend to characterize emotions as "good" or "bad," "positive" or "negative." I have found that to be unjust. It is our *reaction* to any emotion, "good" or "bad," that determines its energy: useful or destructive. In my experience, the emotion that wounds easily is also the emotion that is there to teach us something, if we are ready to be taught.

What is it about an emotion that can take away our equanimity? Again, it is all in our reaction, or our lack of reaction to it. For the spiritual man I want to be, the man I like to call the Man of Discernment, it is important to know how to relate to emotions. There are many things that interest me about the topic.

If we make the effort to review our emotional states, we will find a long list of differing ones. The painful ones and the fearful and angry ones are generally the first to appear in that examination. They tend to dominate the emotional part of our interior world. We look for solutions to the discomfort they bring. There is no shortage of "solutions" offered for the pain, often no more than diversions. Palliatives for their "relief" are thrown at us every day from various media. We are easy marks for we all have suffered.

Some treatments are good examples of how the cure is worse than the disease. The abuse of pharmaceutical drugs comes to mind first. Addictions of every sort can easily become the palliative.

There are, however, more useful, more positive solutions available to us when we are confronted by a raging emotion. "Count to ten slowly before responding" is a particularly good one for me when dealing with angry feelings. I have seen, though, in myself and others, that unfortunately solutions are not eagerly utilized, if sought at all. Most of us feel the emotion and immediately just get into it, react to it, and then continue to be affected by it, unconscious of being trapped within it. There is usually not much thinking at all about the emotion, just about that person or deed or situation that is at the source of the emotion, embroiled as we are in the emotion itself. Perversely, some of us are attracted to that feeling and become attached to it, habituated, even if it is harmful. Repeating self-destructive behavior or other emotional patterns can make us sad, but many of us continue to do it. We can't change others, but we can change ourselves and our reactions.

"I'm really angry at him!" As we say this to ourselves, what are we thinking? About solutions? No. Far more time is spent feeling and fueling the emotion than trying to let it go. Particularly problematic is the fact that emotions can sometimes strike seemingly "out of nowhere"; then, because we have not prepared ourselves for those moments, there is no chance to be wise and to think, and there the emotions are in control. Most of us do not even realize at that moment that there is a choice — hanging on or letting go. The key there is a "chance to think." That is what the counting to ten is all about for me, when feeling anger. Ultimately, a solution arises only when I have given it a chance to arise, and that solution begins with an awareness, the awareness of the emotions themselves. Only then can we show the emotions that they are not the boss.

Ultimately, in my life, and I believe in the lives of all, everything we see, do, and think resides in and has a connection with Spirit. This is a most important aspect of the emotions for me. Why? When anger or some other emotion threatens to contaminate or dominate my consciousness, even the so-called "positive" emotions, what is really happening is that I am getting a message. What is that message?

The answer is relatively straightforward. If I were living life in the Spirit, that is, connected to our loving Creator in the way I was meant to be, I would not experience emotions in quite the same way. They would continue to surface and be felt, but they would always remain at the periphery, unable to penetrate my serenity, and therefore my wisdom. I would see them simply as unruly children in the backseat of my mental vehicle, with me as the driver in complete control, should I choose to exercise it. I could even, if I chose, be amused by them, by their honesty and innocence. I could choose to smile at them. I could choose to keep the peace and serenity that is mine to claim — or not. An unarticulated or a dominating emotion is telling me that there is work to do. My connection to God, to Wisdom, is not complete.

The exceptions to the rule of emotions I have described are unconditional love and compassion. These are the two greatest emotions, in a sense, but they are different. They are more than just emotional states. They are imbued with life. They are states of being. They are energies emanating from the Spirit. They are the essence of Spirit. We don't feel these two things, we are these two things. We become stronger spiritual beings the more we embrace these two energies. We are elevated by them. We become our true selves and live our true nature as spiritual beings when we let them dictate our thoughts, words, and deeds.

When emotions arise, my job is clear. I simply need to observe them, and recognize them not as the enemy, but as a friendly warning, and let them go. I look to them for growth and answers, not to fight with them or be overwhelmed by them or see them as problematic. When I find the emotion behind the feelings, I can get a clue to not only my spiritual condition at that moment but frequently I can then see something specific I need to work on.

Emotions must be handled with care and consideration; how we deal with these beautiful yet incredibly powerful parts of us will determine our happiness and fulfillment in this realm, and open us to the next. Absorbing ourselves in them is failing; releasing ourselves by observing them is succeeding.

Let me now relate how all of this was so beautifully illustrated to me by my first abbé, Abbé Paul.

He called it the lesson of the Three Stems.

The Three Stems

One who performs his duty without attachment, surrendering the results unto the Supreme Lord, is unaffected by sinful action, as the lotus is untouched by water.
　　　　　　　　　　　　　　　　—Bhagavad Gita, 5:10

In the aftermath of Elena, I knew I had to go back to "ground zero" to rebuild my life of Spirit. I was out of practice dealing with fierce, unrelenting temptation, and it showed. I had passed other tests in the abbey, such as one meets on a daily basis, but I had not met one of this force. When it arrived, I was brought low. I never really thought that I would so selfishly deflect the love of God. I was ashamed. That incident served to be the cathartic moment that burst the bubble of my smugness. Two steps forward, one step backward; or, in my case, one forward, two backward. Now it was back to work for me and here is how I began reconstructing my spiritual life using a method of thinking about things that Abbé Paul taught me.

Abbé Paul, my first abbé, was a remarkable man. He was (I should say is — I feel his presence always) that rare and memorable mélange of wit and sincerity, erudition, the common touch, spiritual depth, and goodness. There was always a twinkle in his eye and an ever-present sense of humor.

I felt his benevolent influence from our very first meeting when I was just a timid "recruit." I became a novice under Abbé Paul's leadership, so I had frequent contact with him for the first years of my time at Kervennec. In fact, we would meet daily the first couple of years. I soon started looking more and more forward to those times alone with him. I saw in him so many of the qualities and personal characteristics that I myself hoped to develop and nurture in my life. He put me on the road to that end. What remains with me are many memories, but what always springs to mind first in my memory is his sense of fun and humor. That is one quality that I still seek in my assessment of anyone purporting to be a true man of Spirit, beyond, of course, the sense of holiness I feel around him. The spiritual man must be by definition a happy man, or the Spirit means too little in his life. No true believer in the Good News could not at source be happy! In Abbé Paul's case, that happiness so evident of his convictions was magnified by his natural gregariousness; it only added to all of his other qualities of genuineness, goodness, and holiness.

He took an interest in all that was around him, especially his brother monks. He loved his flock. The warmth and affection exuding from him gathered us in like a big, snug blanket, enfolding us. The saddest moment in my life, rivaling even the news of my parents' deaths, was the sudden passing of Abbé Paul. It was on a spring night almost eighteen years ago. Abbé Paul was only sixty-three years old and showed no sign of decline or ill health. It just happened — one day my mentor was there and the next day gone — without warning. I still feel the pain when reminded of that moment, as I am each April 2. "Abbé" means

"Father" — representing the father of the abbey and the Christ amongst us, and that is the word perfectly attributable to him for me. I miss him with all of the feeling I reserve for my own father; in truth, I miss him more.

We have been examining the connections between emotions and spirit. There was a certain moment with Abbé that I particularly cherish around that subject. I was taught a lesson that day that I have never forgotten. It was during an afternoon walk that the two of us had by the sea around my second year at Kervennec. He used to take his brother monks aside for conversation and instruction, keenly interested always in the spiritual well-being of his charges. He would oftentimes do this with a walk on the beach along the Atlantic. He used to say that it was fitting to talk of God there by the majesty of His ocean. He said that it helped give a true perspective to us humans of who and what we are and especially Who God is. The ocean was but a tiny speck in His universe. It helped one imagine the Greatness of the Supreme Being. One could never be reminded of that enough, Abbé Paul used to say.

That particular day the two of us were scheduled for a one-hour walk by the sea. Abbé Paul would always keep an appointment, so the walks by the sea were kept, rain or shine. That day, I remember, was blustery, with a constant westerly wind gusting off of the Atlantic. But it was clear and sunny and the tide was in retreat when we arrived by car at the beach.

Abbé Paul had this endearing habit of putting his

arm around the shoulders of those whom he was teaching as he would walk with them. This day was no exception, and with an arm on my shoulder we started out at a leisurely pace. We would walk about five meters away from the lunge of the sea, which was then being dragged reluctantly back by the forces of the moon and sun.

"So, my boy, how are you finding things now at Kervennec? You've been here, what, all of two years?" Abbé often used the appellation "my boy" for those he particularly favored.

I was still a little nervous at being the sole recipient of this great man's attention and I hesitated a moment before responding, unsure of how to put my feelings into the words that best conveyed them. In this case, I had to express a certain sense of discomfort.

"Père Abbé," I began, "I sometimes feel some things that I am not so sure what to do with. These are things that I feel deep inside me. I am a little embarrassed and frustrated by them."

I felt silly at how inadequate my explanation was and I could barely look at Abbé Paul while speaking…but I went on, bravely.

"These things have nothing to do with abbey life in general. I am sure of that. I really feel I am called to be here and I like it. The things I am talking about — feelings, really — have been with me a long time and the abbey is a help, not a hindrance, to my recognition of them. I appreciate that, I really do. It's just that I'm annoyed at myself for having to continue to battle feelings that, to me, feel like they should have disappeared years ago.

"This must sound like a silly thing amidst all the other opportunities I have and the beauty of my surroundings here, not to mention how many other more serious problems there are in the world! It is embarrassing to me. I wonder, too, if I am squandering precious moments of God's gift of life to me.

"Abbé Paul, the best way I can summarize my condition, my feelings, is with the word frustration. I am frustrated on the one hand with what little progress I feel that I have made on the spiritual path in this life, especially my life at Kervennec; and, I am also disappointed that that frustration is compounded by my overly emotional response to it, especially my lack of patience, which I know plainly has always been a problem for me."

My explanation to Abbé Paul went on. "I seem to get into a vicious circle of emotions — first frustration, then self-condemnation, more impatience, and then anger. When that anger bubbles to the surface, I know that I am lost and I feel like I have regressed all the way back to my teenage years. I become ashamed. The frustration mounts and I begin to think, What's the use? It takes a long time to pull myself out of this vortex of emotion — time that I feel is wasted and empty."

Abbé Paul chuckled a little. I had steeled myself for the worst and didn't expect that.

"Jean, you sound like a carbon copy of me about thirty years ago. I am chuckling not at you and what concerns you, but at the vision of myself truly agonizing over the fact that in my mind no 'progress' toward perfection was being made. I thought I was just treading water, stuck in one place. No one could have convinced me otherwise, except my own abbé, Abbé Robert. What a man he was, Jean! Maybe what he told me will help you."

I was so relieved after hearing Abbé Paul's words, knowing that I was not the first nor would I be the last to feel little progress was being made, which was at the heart of my own complaint. It became a lot easier for me to disgorge all that was troubling me. As I then told abbé, I knew I learned more about my feelings every time I tried to explain them. I've used that technique a lot since then. Writing helps, too, that way.

Abbé Paul squeezed my shoulder with a firm hand and then released me as we walked along. After several more paces, he stopped and turned to me and said, "Jean, have you ever seen the picture or heard the story of the three stems and had the symbolism explained to you? It is also sometimes called the three paths."

I couldn't think of anything except for some vague reference to Buddhism. "No, Abbé, nothing rings a bell like that. Is it a Buddhist reference?"

"I can't say if it is or isn't a Buddhist reference. I have only known it as it was offered to me by Abbé Robert, and I can't tell you where he first heard it articulated. I do know that the concepts and processes connected with it are universal and beneficial to anyone regardless of any belief that one may hold.

"I think its story might help you. Would you like

me to explain it to you as I understand it?"

"Yes, Père Abbé, please, if you think it may be helpful," I said. "I'd very much appreciate learning all I could of it."

"Very well, I'll explain it as Abbé Robert explained it to me when I was a young monk about your age. It has been so useful and helpful for me these many years. You, Jean, have great potential; and if I can help you in any special way, I shall."

I loved hearing those words from my abbé, although they also scared me a little bit. I, who at that moment felt like a first-grader at catechism, having great potential — it was hard to contemplate. I even remember feeling embarrassed and the shade of red I turned must have indicated that clearly. None of that bothered Abbé Paul.

"Jean, Abbé Robert explained it to me this way. He called it the 'three stems' and you'll soon see why. I believe, however, it could also be called the three 'paths' or 'ways' or however else it would resonate with you. That will be up to you."

Abbé Paul took the stick he was accustomed to carrying on walks and began to draw something in the sand. First he drew a horizontal line. That, he explained to me, represented the soil, the earth. He then drew two smaller-looking "stems" that came out of the soil, rising up and curving away from the soil on either end of the line, the right stem being longer. That was then followed by a third, rather long stem rising from the middle of the horizontal line and topped with a large flower. Above the three stems he drew a representation of the sun, adding many small vertical lines or marks descending from above, to the right of the sun towards the plants, which he indicated represented rain. Below the soil line, he drew several more short lines beneath each stem, which he indicated were roots, the longest being under the center stem. The drawing was rudimentary but served its purpose.

"Jean, here are the stems of three plants, and below, the roots. The plants represent man, rooted in the essence of his material creation in the earth. Who knows the extent of his depths? Above, of course, is Father Sun with Mother Rain, sustaining man in his existence. Now I will name each stem. On the left, this small stem is called 'emotional.' Here in the center, the long one with the blossom, we'll call this one 'spiritual.' And over here on the right, the one of medium length, we'll name that one 'grounded.' Now, you're going to ask, what does this have to do with your problem as you described it to me? Let me tell you what this little illustration did for me all those years ago after I first saw it drawn out for me. I must say that Abbé Robert was a much better artist than I am, but I think this will help you all the same," said Abbé Paul with a twinkle in his eye. "Now I will explain their significance."

I took a hard look at the illustration, quickly memorizing the names and positions of each stem and of the sun and rain, curious as to what Abbé Paul would say about each.

"Most of us, most of mankind, nourish this stem, the emotional." Abbé Paul was pointing to the shortest stem on the left. "We have been brought up surrounded by others exhibiting various emotional states of mind and nourishing them. We are encouraged even by our own nature to live in this superficial state. Most of us grow into adults staying in that spot unwittingly. The problem is that our growth becomes stunted if this is all that we nourish — that little stem will never mature and blossom and reach its full potential without the discovery and nourishment of other aspects of self. Its roots are shallow.

"On the right we see a longer stem, though still without a blossom. This, the grounded stem, is a much sturdier and hardier stem, rising higher than the emotional stem, though it is still limited in its prospects for growth. Some people are able to eschew living the emotional side of themselves enough to nourish the grounded. That is an accomplishment, and these humans are practical, strong, and can be counted on. They endure, but ultimately they, too, wither before they are able to produce a flower.

"Lastly, and most importantly here in the center, is the spiritual stem rising up to a much greater height. This stem is crowned with a magnificent blossom, a joy to see and to be around, emitting a most pleasing fragrance, with all delighting in its beauty. The spiritual person is like that flower, something and someone to admire, to be close to, and to delight in. That person is deeply rooted in his or her essence, strong and grounded, yet flexible, healthy, and still growing; and, as Christ has told us, able to reproduce and give back a hundredfold. He or she is reaching for his or her Supreme Creator and Nourisher, Divine Father/Mother, which is shown here in my much-less-than-gifted attempt at drawing by this representation of the sun and the rain."

Abbé Paul continued.

"After I had been taught to understand how most of us were brought up nourishing just our emotions, Abbé Robert took me to the next step. He told me that we always have a choice — we can live in whatever world we choose. That is the gift of being human. It also means that we can participate in any of the three worldviews illustrated by these three stems. Most of us start our growth as the stem of emotion. The first step to master is being conscious that we are potentially fractured into these three parts. Next, it is up to us to decide where we are at any given moment in relation to them, and thirdly, to decide where it is we wish to be in that moment and those moments to follow. Deciding where we want to be at any time, what we wish to nourish is always our own decision. The final step is to develop the tools we need to be where we wish to be, and to stay there.

"As I said, most of us are nourishing our stem of emotion and don't realize it. As each day passes — some would say as each lifetime passes — the person looks for happiness by nourishing emotions, which cleverly imply some good thing coming or some satisfaction arriving that is not, however, in its power to give. With negative emotions surrounding us, we can remain mired in hatred, anger, or jealousy, which can attract us in a perverse way but that will only let us down in the end. Inevitably, when one follows and nourishes this path, it proves to be a road to unhappiness at worst, or a cul-de-sac at best. The same with the so-called "positive" emotions.

"Let me show you what I mean. The emotion of romantic love is so often characterized as an ideal in our world today. On the surface, at the emotional level, it often has a pull that is not to be denied, especially for the young. Love is real. But the romantic emotional side of it, as shown in our consuming passion of one for the other, is not. It sprouts quickly and grows, but if not nourished by something more than emotion, it dies.

"Or take anger. It is and always has been a human epidemic. Anger is an emotional response to not getting what one wants. We get satisfaction in the short term from invoking it, as if we can then somehow force the result to go our way. Ultimately, we achieve nothing, except doing unhealthy things to our souls, not to mention our bodies. Jealousy, hatred, envy — in fact, all of the so-called 'seven deadly sins' — they all pull us in with a false hope that they will make us happy, and thus we nourish them. It is not within their power, however, to do so. It is within their power to inevitably hurt or even crush us, however. The same sorry end results with the emotions attached to worry and anxiety. Somehow we believe those emotions will help us through a difficult situation, and we nourish them, when they do nothing but exacerbate the situation.

"There are those who, after catching themselves nourishing their emotional stem, regain their footing

— or, in this case, strengthen their roots by centering and grounding themselves. They begin to nourish that part of themselves that promotes balance and equilibrium. They are able for the most part to leave their emotions alone, to see more clearly, to act with equanimity and to experience life in a deeper and more 'rational' way. Some of these people can grow to great heights. Grounding provides a clearer view, a respite from the emotional, but it is not enough in and of itself. It has the great advantage of taking us away from the irrational and harmful emotional state and providing us with a quiet place to consider and appreciate the present in a constructive way. But we will never reach the heights ordained for us by our Creator by remaining only grounded. It serves only as a launching pad to those much greater heights, those to be obtained within the spiritual self, which is mankind's third state, or stem.

"There is a part of all of us that can see beyond the immediate, beyond what the sensual world shows us. It is the great bringer of perspective and thus of Truth. It sees and rejoices with a consciousness not troubled with the vanities, irrationality, and emotions of daily life. This is represented by that third stem — that of Spirit. It brings us the gift of direct connection with God. It brings us joy in abundance and also brings the Peace of God 'which surpasseth all Understanding.' It gives us vision, the vision of who we truly are in all of our true spiritual Glory. This vision is Awareness.

"I am sure that you have experienced that gift before, Jean. Like all of us who seek, this moment of

God-realization can visit us when we are least expecting it, brought on by a loving act or a sight of natural beauty or the innocence of a child or in the act of meditation. It often comes in softly, staying but for an instant; but, its effects can last a lifetime. Those effects are life changing. To live in that state, the state of God-connection, is the goal of each of us in the monastery, the first and last step towards sanctity in this world. The middle stem, that of spirituality, represents the highest flowering of the human condition, where we truly share God's image and likeness and where the rich living of our life blossoms and then spreads its good on any fertile ground around it. Thus, we never die; the good we have engendered goes on generation after generation. Even in the Dark Ages, Jean, the light never went out — Goodness remained. Those who lived in the Spirit kept it alight and were the guardians of untold riches for the world, the kinds of riches that we in the monastic tradition hope always to possess and to continue to donate to mankind.

"Where are you as we look at this plant representing our humanness? If you can come to see that there is a choice, you are on the way to fulfillment. If you see that you are nourishing only the emotional, for example, perhaps worry or dissatisfaction, you can choose to change that and that change will be good for you. Work to become aware. Awareness is the key to spiritual advancement, and only advancing in the Spirit can give us true satisfaction."

I certainly recognized myself in this parable of

life. It was clear and empowering. I remember trying to let it all soak in. It was so simply illustrated, yet what that illustration showed would be life changing for me. I was very comforted to see that there might be a way out, and I decided then and there to take it.

"Abbé, this is a wonderful example for me to look at and apply to my own situation. There is no question that I have been nourishing unawares the emotional stem. I guess I'm surprised since here I am, a 'man of God' trying hard to please Him and make myself the best I can be spiritually."

"Don't be in the least put off by this," said Abbé Paul seriously. "There is not one saint in God's great universe who has not gone through the same experiences and then the same awakening. You are on the spiritual path. You are advancing and will continue to do so. Your questioning readily shows that.

"Does this all make sense to you, Jean?"

I looked him in the eyes and nodded. I understood. Never had so much been imparted to me in such a few short minutes. I remember feeling empowered to make the changes I needed to make in outlook and habit right then and there. I knew that I would succeed. The teacher had indeed come when the student was ready.

I also remember then telling him, "Abbé, I don't know what to say. It is you who have said so much so simply and so eloquently.

"I have some work to do as a result of those words. I see where I want to go — where I need to go — much more clearly and I've started to feel the door of my imprisonment by my emotions opening. For that

I can only thank you a hundred times over. You have shone a light on the path that saves me from having to stay within those prison walls with no clue how to escape, and I will do what I need to do to get out."

Abbé Paul then took me by the shoulder again and we began to walk back. He turned to me and said simply, "Jean, I know you will. I know in my heart that you are that kind of priest, that kind of man. Take care now that you stop and regard sometimes during your day and check and see which stem you are nourishing. If it is the emotional stem, step back, ground yourself, and then move on to the spiritual stem. Sink those spiritual roots deep and grow that blossom to its highest height. Nothing can upset you, Jean, nothing can stop you if you do that. May God bless you."

We shortly found ourselves back at the car and we took the five-minute ride back to the monastery in silence. Then we each went our separate ways, preparing for Vespers. Going back to my cell, I felt closer to God than ever before and vowed then and there to continue on that path, to grow my stem of spirituality for the rest of my life.

I knew I had made a giant detour with my actions in the orchard with Elena. It was time to find my way back. One of the things that I took away from that day with Abbé Paul is that we all need to be patient with ourselves. Time and patience and effort will bring us where we want to go. I kept that uppermost in my mind as I looked to bring myself back to a spiritual state. I hope his parable for life helps you, too, in your thinking and your Awareness.

I would need all of the patience and emotional control — and help from Divine Father/Mother — that I could get as a result of my actions for the trials to come. I had been my own worst enemy. I had forgotten my life lessons like the Three Stems for a time and let my emotions hold sway, to my sorrow and shame.

I would need to answer for that — and my indiscretion.

Part Four

Repercussions and Change...

The Aftermath

And Adam said, I heard thy voice in the garden, and I was afraid, because I was naked; and I hid myself.
—Genesis 3:10

Three days had passed since Elena's visit, and they were the three most difficult days of my life. What I had done had gone against the very heart of my religious interdictions. Me, a monk, kissing and fondling a woman — at the monastery! What a fall from grace, if grace had ever been there from the start. Frail humanity — didn't I epitomize it? Man of Discernment — hah! I felt like finding a cave and staying there for as long as necessary to hide until I could find some peace and move forward.

I had not heard from Elena, but I had posted my own letter to her the day after our episode. I was hungry for news and for some kind of contact with her. I so hoped that it would eventually come, but I saw clearly why it might never come. I couldn't believe that it had been only three days. To me, it had seemed like weeks. My mind was supercharged with emotion. Everything around me seemed to me to move so slowly, like I was seeing everything moving under water. I only calmed a bit when I finally, consciously, sat down and thought about things and realized that it was, at least, not unusual to have not heard anything from her. After all, it had only been three days, and who could blame her if she did not resume contact with me? Then it would all start again. I had trouble looking at myself in the mirror. My shame was complete.

What would other monks see in me now — anything different? My relations with the other monks had not been the same. I was defensive, as if my guilt were blaring from the monastery loudspeakers. I tried to put on a brave and "normal" face for the others, while covering up the shame that was so evident to me. It had not occurred to me to think that it might not be so apparent to the others. Close friends like Brothers Herman and Luc could see a difference in me, I could tell, especially with my lack of joviality, but they were used to a little of the ups and downs with me and thankfully left me alone. I felt like keeping my distance and I remained guarded and kept my interactions to a minimum with my brothers. I was not scheduled for work in the shop that week, and that helped. I spent an inordinate amount of my free time in my cell, and much more than usual outside in the fresh air. For the most part, this worked to help me maintain some balance.

I continued to ruminate over the events of that day. Not permitting Elena to kiss me, and not returning her affection so adamantly, difficult as that would have been both theoretically and practically, would have been the only right course of action. There was no rationalization possible for what had happened. I did keep alive a faint hope that there might come an "aha!" moment, a discovery of some little detail that I had not seen before that would be the key to unlocking the prison cell of my disappointment, which had become my new emotional home. It was dwelling on those details where I spent most of my time. My mind returned again and again to the scene, to each word that had been spoken, each gesture, each facial expression as I could remember them. I was very active in those considerations during my long walks on the monastery grounds, where it was conducive to thinking.

But in the end, all of that theorizing was in vain and of no consequence. The damage had been done and no amount of theorizing or "what ifs" would bring back my state of innocence or make things more palatable. I was just looking for something, anything, that would lessen the guilt I felt and was unable to discharge.

My relationship with God was still another embarrassment. Can you imagine the way I felt? A monk, caught in a ridiculous loop of temporal emotions, consumed by a creature of the Divine instead of the Divine Itself, a failure as an example to men of the way of Spirit and of the Man of Discernment — what was I to say to Divine Mother? The truth was I didn't want to pray just then. I just wanted to hide from God. In my mix of guilt and embarrassment, I felt retreat the best policy. So I went back into my cave whenever the opportunity afforded in my structured day, to lick my wounds. How feeble that all seems now. My God was not a friend in Whom I could confide at that point. God was the One that I wanted to avoid. I truly felt like Adam wanting to secret himself when he had been found out — embarrassed and guilt-ridden. Intellectually, perhaps it was silly.

I am a human being, a million miles from being a perfect creature of God. As a human — no more and no less — I am bound to make mistakes. To see how I attempted to turn and hide from the One Who has sustained me always, my Father/Mother, shames me as much as my silly act in the garden. What a gift to have such a Supporter and Helpmate! I wasn't the first to fall in a garden, and our Merciful God understands.

That wasn't on my mind then. Perhaps I had become complacent during those twenty years, thinking that my battles with passions — the extreme expression of emotion — were over. Vigilance had been lacking, and I fell at the first assault. It had been impossible in my weakness, or in my turning a blind or overly fastidious eye to things, to evacuate myself from my dungeon of emotion. I was so caught up emotionally and so desperate to think that somehow I was not "guilty as charged," that my deeper self never got a chance to make itself felt, nor act, nor allow my self-perception to open up, not to mention offering self-forgiveness, so important.

I mentioned I had written Elena. "She would have had the letter by now," I thought. I had my doubts whether or not it would make any difference, and was pretty sure at that moment that I would never see her again. I couldn't blame her.

Here is what I had written:

Dear Elena,

What thoughts you may have at this moment, I cannot know. If they involve any sense or feeling of guilt for what transpired yesterday at the monastery, please know that they are badly misplaced. Your efforts to tell me that you cared for me as a friend became entangled with normal flesh and blood reactions. That is all that it was. It was I who could have, and should have, backed away as those emotions began to show; but, I did not, and that has nothing to do with you. Nothing at all. I was caught up in the moment, in my own emotions, and I should have done better. But I didn't.

I know you for the wonderful and caring woman that you are. I know that you would never do anything to hurt anybody if you could help it. I didn't help you out there in the orchard, and that indiscretion was a result of my own weakness and failure to act. You were doing nothing more than being your natural, openhearted self.

I value your friendship in so many ways — I will not let anything that happened damage it or end it on my part. I could not. It would not only be unnecessary, it would be horribly unjust. We are friends, forever, and nothing will change my sentiments about that. What is really important to me is that we talk about things and keep up our communication in any form that you would like. Writing to you is a good thing for me right now. I can express myself easier, put my thoughts in a logical order, and free myself from those emotions arising that can trouble my clarity of thinking; it helps me avoid any misstatements that might end up giving the wrong impression. Naturally, to see you again someday would be my hope, but I fear at present that may not be something you would like. But what I want to assure you is that there need not be any long-term repercussions for us in terms of our friendship. I mean that and sincerely believe it. I so hope that you do, too.

Please write to me soonest. I want very much to hear from you and to know that you are all right and that we are all right in our friendship. We have so much to offer each other in that regard, and it is and will always remain very precious to me. Please forgive me if I have caused you any pain — it was unintentional and I deplore my conduct in this affair. Know that you remain in my thoughts and prayers, and that I want to hear from you as soon as you can write to me.

God bless you.

Jean

It was a relief to feel I could communicate with her once again, even if it were a one-sided affair. Shortly before Vespers that day, I received a knock on my door. I was sitting in my chair when I saw an envelope being slid underneath the door, and I eagerly jumped up to retrieve it. I saw immediately whom it was from, and I rejoiced. I think I even blessed whoever had delivered it to me, sight unseen. It seems our letters had crossed. I remember going over to my bed and eagerly tearing open the envelope. I was so excited, so hungry for contact from her.

Dear Father Jean,

It will not be easy to write this letter. Not because I do not want to. On the contrary, I want more than anything to communicate with you, to apologize to you, to say how much your friendship means to me. That part is easy. But it is how to frame my words, my emotions, my state of mind after what I did to you — to us — yesterday at the abbey, that is the difficult part. I have no excuses, and I will not try to invent any. You would see through them anyway, and especially through my own misbelief in them. I suppose that I could say that I got carried away — I guess that part is obvious. I said things and did things that I never should have — and never in my wildest dreams thought that I would do. In so doing, I may not only have compromised you in the abbey, which is damning enough, but I may have compromised our friendship — something that would cause me far greater pain than I can tell you. I fear that having done both might be too much for me to bear. I know that this letter will be about friendship, our friendship. That is what counts for me. That is all that is within my power to try and salvage.

When we first met those few months ago after an absence of twenty-plus years, I was in a world of my own. I was treating patients almost every day, learning more about myself, engaged in my spiritual journey, and creating my art and not worrying or caring about others for the most part. It's not that I was selfish. I was in a stage of life that demanded I do what I was doing, but the universe has a way of telling you when that stage is over. That was part of what happened when you came into my life again after all of those years. But because of you, and your goodness and kindness, you showed me another side of life, your side, a side that was nonjudgmental, which was concerned every minute of every day with what I was just getting to know and love about life — spirituality — and how a person, even a place, could be full of unconditional love.

Your friendship has been a type that I have never known with anyone else — also unconditional, looking for the best in people, and kind — before and during your abbey days. With my unlucky history with men, which I haven't told you so much about, it was kind of hard to imagine. But, believe me, I have learned now that there are people like you, and institutions like the beautiful Abbey of Kervennec, that live exactly as I have described and that view life in a healthy, balanced, generous fashion. I quickly got to love coming to see you there — with both you and the abbey itself making my world a happier and more enlightened place. Now I feel that I have perverted it, thrown it all away, and I can't forgive myself or punish myself enough for that.

I know just what you would say: "C'mon, Elena, don't take it so hard, don't take things so seriously. Nobody's perfect — not even me!" That would be just like you. I try and imagine what constructive thing you would say to me right now, and then to do what I have imagined you would say, but it doesn't work. It's too hard and I'm too sad. In fact, I am inconsolable. I will say my prayers tonight, of that you can be sure; but, I don't have the faith that you do and I don't know if I will even be able to finish them. But, I will try.

All I really want, Jean, is for you to say that you forgive me, and that our friendship will continue. Maybe it will have to change, but that I could take. To not have it anymore is not something I could easily deal with.

Will you write to me — please? Tell me how I can start to make amends. I will do whatever you say. You will always have a piece of my heart.
Yours,
Elena
P.S. I wasn't sure enough about myself and what I said in this to send it right away. I hope and pray you will understand. Sorry.

I was one giant mass of emotion as I read through it. I was trying not to skip ahead to draw any conclusions. Each line hit home with me — I could hear her speaking to me with that soft voice. I would be remiss not to tell you that tears flooded my eyes as I read her remorse, her assumption of guilt, her generosity of spirit. Her assumption of responsibility for all that had happened was what I did not want to hear. It worried me and preyed upon me. What continued to upset me all the more, of course, was the fact that I was the one who could have prevented it; I, the priest, was the one who should have been the "gatekeeper." Now it was horrible for me to think that she was suffering so, when so many things pointed to me and my lack of planning and control. She was ready to assume all, as if I were free of any wrongdoing or omissions. I knew that I would have to straighten that out with her.

I remember how I read the letter again. I was focusing more on the first part, and it was there that I brightened a little. Friendship. It was the very theme of my letter to her, and, as I reread Elena's, the theme of hers. "I know that this letter will be about friendship, our friendship. That is what counts for me." I was very moved by that — and made happier by it. What perhaps I feared most I needn't have feared at all. With Elena, our friendship was assured, despite everything. Things would be all right that way, at least. That eased my mind considerably.

I then reread the part where she asked for my forgiveness. Tears welled again as I felt so angry at myself for this whole affair. I realized, however, that that was not going to get me too far. I went back to my training, my breathing, trying to calm myself. That helped — it slowed down my mental wheels. I finally started to relax.

Then, I did something I hadn't done for the better part of three days: I prayed. I prayed to God for guidance and asked for His forgiveness. I prayed deeply and long and when I was finished, when I had risen from my dais, I felt a lightness that I was at a loss to understand. I looked up at the crucifix adorning the plain wall of my cell. Often before I had seen it as something a bit macabre, a bit unreal — just the Son of God being brutally treated, and we constantly reminding ourselves of that fact, but never the Resurrection and His return to life. But now it appeared somehow different. Some of the pain and guilt associated with that symbol seemed to have been lifted from it now as I gazed. I actually felt at ease looking at it. It seemed now like a loving, giving symbol. I had no desire to run and hide from it, from God. Something had changed. It was like something had entered me. It was peace, certainly, but it was that special all-consuming peace brought on as a gift from

God. I recognized it. It was grace, the free and undeserved gift from Above, that showed me that I was not estranged from the One I loved most. I was forgiven for my very human faults. I wasn't to judge and it was only for me now to make sure Elena knew that she was not to judge.

I knew then what I must do. I quickly got a sheet of stationery from my desk and then sat and wrote the following:

Dearest Elena,

Your letter arrived this afternoon at the perfect time for me. How happy it made me to see it under my door, the one thing I had most hoped to see. I was at my wit's end these last three days, afraid that you would continue to hold on to the guilt and sadness that you showed at our last parting. I can only say you mustn't. I explained my feelings about that as well as I could in my last letter, which by now I hope you have received.

Now I feel that I need to tell you this: our friendship will always remain intact. Fret no more about it. I was so delighted as I read your letter that you feel the same. I was worried about that — it would have scarred me deeply had you called it quits and left me alone. I already cannot stand that you have taken on so much of this as your responsibility, that you have somehow attached it all to your behavior. Please, I ask you from the bottom of my heart to put that notion out of your head forever. You must let blame go and let me deal with my own inadequacies, so obvious, which our Father in Heaven knows well. I can only say that He has forgiven me, and that that forgiveness cannot be complete until you forgive yourself and stop judging. That will complete the circle of wholeness that we need to reestablish within ourselves, with each other and with God.

God bless you.

Jean

When I had finished it and then reread it, I felt satisfied that the letter was clear about what I had meant to say. I wanted to waste no time in getting it to her. I felt confident that she and I could work things out. I felt a renewed strength, and with a little burst of energy, I left my room, said my prayers as I walked, and posted the letter myself. God's grace and her letter of committed friendship had loosed me from my emotional prison and all of those chains with which I had fettered myself. I wished nothing but the very same now for Elena.

Things were looking up. God is great.

The Challenge of Repentance

*Upon what meat doth this our Caesar feed, that he is grown so
great?*
— William Shakespeare, Julius Caesar

New Year's Day had come and gone some weeks
before. It had been cold and rainy. I wasn't surprised
about that — it always seems to be that way on the
first of January in Brittany. I remember as a child
wanting it to be nice so I could enjoy my school
vacation outside, playing with my friends and doing all
the things I liked to think about doing while stuck in
school. I was often disappointed. As I got older, the
weather mattered much less and I began to think more
about the idea of new beginnings. I find it emotionally
satisfying, this opportunity offered by a New Year. It is
a time of renewal as I look to evaluate my life and
jettison non-useful things, like outmoded beliefs and
habits. It's a rare chance in life when one gets to start
over, and even if it is only figurative, my mind
resonates with the idea and I try to take advantage of it.
I see the New Year as a psychological springboard to
better things ahead, to a time of progress in the
perfecting of my earthly man via a growing and
maturing spirituality. On New Year's Day this year, I
wanted it to literally be a "restart" — at least as much
as possible. I found myself becoming excited again,
looking forward to that new start.

We don't formally celebrate Christmas or the New

Year in the abbey or treat them any differently than any other feast day. We do not do gift exchanges or observe the traditional customs that most of the Christian world does. Sometimes I miss that a little but our services are so beautiful here at the celebration of Christ's birth and my brothers make such a wonderful family, that it isn't really difficult. I had spent the last few days of this Christmas season coming to terms with myself and my behavior, just allowing myself time to heal. Emotionally, I knew it would take some time. My spiritual healing was nearly complete. The final act would be the confession of my transgression before my abbé and my God. I had started already with God — we were on good terms — but I knew I had to confess to my earthly Father to finish my rehabilitation and I was prepared to do that. I was beginning to feel a lot like my old self.

As for Elena, she had written back so positively after she had received my second letter, so relations with her had been reestablished for good. We have continued our written exchanges over the intervening time. In our writing, the affection has remained apparent even in our mostly newsy letters, and I have appreciated that. She is still like a happy ray of sunshine that I can conjure at will, a ray that can only be imparted by a most intimate friend — that kind of friend that one could see infrequently and still pick up right where one had left off. It has worked well. We have only occasionally touched on our deeper feelings after those first few letters that we exchanged. Shortly thereafter she became busily engaged in her project for the sisters at the Abbey of St. Michel, and I, as you will see, was soon otherwise very occupied myself!

The installation of the interim abbé had taken the men's attention away somewhat from the sorrow they felt at the loss of Abbé Rénard from the monastery. The liturgical distractions of the Christmas season had also helped in this regard. The three-month interim term of the abbé was now well underway, and adjustments had begun in earnest. It was the routine and a method of rule that could possibly last the lifetime of Abbé Guinot. I could see that the abbey wasn't too much concerned with that — yet. The men longed to get back to a routine. It wouldn't be the same atmosphere in many ways, some subtle, some not so subtle like his outreach idea, but it would be a routine and for now that sufficed.

It had proven to be a rather difficult time for the new abbé, and not an easy transition. To be fair, it had all come about very unexpectedly, and very unusually, and that would make the task more challenging for any incoming abbé, but Abbé Guinot brought a reserve to the post and a personality that was not easy to decipher. He was not at all gregarious and sometimes found it difficult to communicate in everyday parlance. He was certainly intelligent, but had this air of arrogance and impatience that does sometimes arrive with intelligent men. Abbé Guinot also had what one could only term a moody personality — not a problem for the most part when one was but a monk, but a potential issue for the head of an abbey. In fact, this personality defect created tension immediately. Little by little, the feeling grew that one had to walk on eggshells around him to assure a "normal" response. Much care was taken by the monks in this early period to not ruffle his feathers.

While the conclusion of the prior year had surely been a draining and unhappy one for the abbey, for me it was all of that multiplied many times over. I had nearly lost my best friend on earth, to be sure; but to my shame, I had lost my connection for a time to my greatest Friend, my true Soul Mate, my Source. What emptiness had taken hold of me! I could never again tolerate such a separation. Now that I had gotten through the worst of that experience, I wished to formally make things right. It was time to confess.

As you may recall, my own relationship with Guinot had never been what I would call comfortable. He was one of the few with whom my personality just did not mesh. He had seen me as a monk who lacked discipline and respect for the Church and its Law, as I have written. He also thought that I was not as dedicated to the demands of solitary life as I should be. He had more or less told me so on one occasion after his installation. I was too social, not serious enough, and not an intellectual. This viewpoint gave Abbé Guinot some sort of internal permission to view me with only a modicum of respect. I saw that as arrogant. His severity also irritated me. Prior, we had always been civil one to another in the daily course of events. But now, in the few conversations we had managed, Guinot's demeanor had become very brusque, a clear dislike visible in his eyes. I wasn't imagining it.

I would ask myself, why couldn't he show just a spark of happiness? Had he bought completely into the old line that our earth was just a Vale of Tears, and that somehow it was not "monklike" to smile or have a sense of humor? What I eventually saw as time passed was that Guinot had such a poor opinion of himself that he by nature had to put down others whom he saw as threatening. It could have been that my easy style and rapport with the other monks threatened him. In that regard, I was all that he was not. I continued to try very hard to love my brother.

You can imagine how the thought of confessing to Abbé Guinot was very distasteful to me. However, I used it as a goad to develop those two most difficult of virtues, love of neighbor and humility. As challenging and repugnant as it might have been to me on many levels, I was ready to confess. I knew that that experience, if I handled it in a Christlike fashion, would make me a better human, and I meant to get it done right. I was most sincere in that belief. My opportunity to accomplish this was to arrive much quicker, and on terms much different, than I had expected. This is what happened.

As I passed through to the residence during the last week of January, I saw Abbé Guinot at the other end of the hall. As I approached abbé, I saw him eyeing me. I must say that for a time my guilt had made me suspicious of people and events everywhere around me. He was talking to someone at the time. I was preparing to greet him, trying now not to think so much of my guilt, but to think positively, of better times to come. Then, suddenly, I had second thoughts. I saw who our acting abbé was talking to. It was none other than Father Michel, the priest who had been in the orchard that day with Elena, and there was no mistaking that Father Michel was also now looking at me in an uncharacteristic and rather unpleasant fashion. I had little doubt about the subject of their conversation and I felt a hot flash of anger rise within me as I regarded Father Michel. Abbé Guinot also now presented the same icy stare. I lowered my gaze. I felt ashamed all over again. I nodded to both men and passed by. My heart was racing. I walked on more rapidly, feeling their cold stares, my emotions of shame and anger raging, all the while thinking how difficult it would be to love these two men, and then praying for help. Punishment — perhaps it had begun in earnest.

A few days later, prior to Vespers, I again passed Abbé Guinot. This time as we passed the abbé looked at me very severely and said that he wanted to talk to me, and would I accompany him to his office? I had no choice and followed the little way to the abbé's room. I was asked to sit down. Abbé then started to speak.

"Father Moreau, what I have to say to you is grave. It is about an incident witnessed by one of our brother monks some weeks ago in the orchard and recently related to me. As your spiritual leader, it is incumbent upon me to take you aside and hear your side of things and if necessary, your confession. I am your spiritual Father and it is up to me to lose no one in this community to mortal sin."

I swallowed hard. This was it. I had no choice but to hear the abbé out.

"Any interaction with a woman poses issues for a monk. Women occupy a place that is hardly suitable for monks. We must never descend to cultivate a female relationship — we have a higher calling. The Scriptures have made it clear that Jesus chose men as his disciples, not women. He did not marry or have interactions with women except with those who were related to his friends, like Lazarus, or those who needed his forgiveness to serve as an example to all men and women, as in the case of Mary Magdalene. His own mother was conceived without sin and remained a virgin, showing us God's example of the ideal feminine personage."

I found myself recoiling at this theology and its condescending nature, and my anger again was building deep inside of me. I was still working hard to see my brother, now my Father, as another expression of God, deserving of my patience and love, even though in error. I can tell you that it wasn't working very well.

"Your actions in the orchard," Guinot continued, "were anything but Christlike with regard to relations with a woman. In fact, they were reprehensible. Know that as your earthly Father I must tell you that neither I nor this community can or will tolerate such behavior." Abbé tried his hardest to look as severe as possible and then added, slowly, "I am not certain that you are cut out to be one of us. You will have to show me a lot in the coming months to make me see that indeed you belong here with us."

I sat in stunned disbelief.

Then Guinot added, "Is there anything you wish to say to me about this? If not, I will consider the subject closed after today but I will be watching you closely.

"I am ready to hear your confession."

I was thunderstruck by this commentary. Not cut out to be a monk? After over twenty years of living it every day and loving it? Who was this man to say this? What gall! Yes, I was guilty of going too far with Elena. That much was sure. And I had paid for it dearly in pain and suffering and guilt. I was putting that behind me and was starting to feel all right again. But this accusation, and by someone who in my mind spoke spiritual nonsense and gave only lip service to the true Christlike spirit, was almost too much. I couldn't respond right away with all of this circulating in my head. Coming months? His term had barely six weeks to go. Nothing was assured. My anger had risen to the point that it became really difficult for me to speak. I tried to gather myself and slow my breathing. I looked the abbé in the eye with a regard that he could readily understand — hardly a look of love but of challenge. He looked back and would not budge. He couldn't afford to not engage and win this battle with me, even if I were fighting it with one hand tied behind my back. Not only was I ever conscious of my need to feel and display only Christian charity, but with himself as abbé, I was required to give complete obedience to my "opponent."

Finally, I did speak, slowly.

"Père Abbé, I did transgress. It was not premeditated by any means. The woman to whom you are referring is one of my dearest friends in life. I do not condone anything that occurred but I do respect very much this woman and all the gifts she possesses and the charity for others she carries within her. Know, however, that I accept all of the blame."

I hesitated before going on. The next exercise in humility was going to be the most difficult thing I had perhaps ever done. I steeled myself and began.

"I confess to you, Père Abbé, and to Almighty God, that I did sin with the woman in the orchard, and that I am heartily sorry. I throw myself upon God's mercy and the mercy of my Father and ask for forgiveness from both from the bottom of my soul."

I had thought hard about my confession during this past week in order to complete my rehabilitation, and was about to do it anyway when all of this happened. I can tell you that I meant every word of my confession. With it done, I thought I might feel better, relieved to have told all in this setting. But there was no relief. There was just that steady anger in dealing with this man, despite all. I was disappointed; this was not the response I wanted from myself. That made me angrier still. I wanted to be truly humble, and I wanted my emotions to reflect that. I wished to remain focused on my sin and the wrong I had done and to learn from it. I felt I was willing to accept whatever was coming to me from my community and from my God. But in the end, it simply wasn't in me to do that. With God I had found peace, but with this man I was angry, and could do no better. I had to think of the office and not the man, and that was the best that I could do.

After I had thus humbled myself, Abbé Guinot looked momentarily satisfied, both in my confession and in my acceptance and understanding of our positions. He then continued.

"Father Moreau, I absolve you of your sin in the name of the Father, and of the Son, and of the Holy Spirit. I will consider this episode closed. But I warn you that I will be observing your behavior with a vigor that I believe is necessary and insist that you now consider yourself duly warned. You are on probation with me and this community. We will review your situation in six months' time. You may go now — and sin no more," Abbé added, with what I could only consider a supreme arrogance. I stood and bowed to the abbé and took my leave.

Probation! Who was this man?! I felt violated, but I was bound to follow the abbé's dictates. That such a man could judge me! There was no wiggle room in the *Rule of St. Benedict*, however. Abbé's word is final — he is the Christ figure in the abbey. That was what he was trained to do. I had had by the grace of God three wonderful abbés, at least in comparison to this man. I could not gainsay the abbé, nor did I have the right, no matter who that abbé may be. But somehow, it wasn't right — it wasn't proper for him to put me on probation after so many years of service and excellence in the community. I knew this in my own heart. I was positive that that this could not possibly be what God wanted.

I walked back outside into the winter sunshine. Usually after confession, as I mentioned, there was lightness of spirit, a happy connection with life and all that goes with it. Not today. This confession had been draining, humiliating, damning, and provoking. I had no choice but to confess. It had been my will and my command as I saw God's law. But, to have been "sent to the office" and chastised before confessing had hardly been in the script. My anger was deep – it was my Achilles' heel and I knew it. Anger. So prevalent in the world, as it has always been. What a test of Christian generosity of spirit had been placed in front of me. And to review my case in six months — the arrogance of the man to assume he would be abbé even two months from now!

One thing was for certain in my mind. I remember writing and telling myself over and over again: I will not be defeated by these events. I will bear them as the Christ would bear them, and in the end, I will triumph. This is my vow.

There was, however, something that was beginning to creep into my thinking about all of my resentment at the attitude of the abbé. That something was telling me not to be so colored by the character and personality of the abbé as by a true consideration of the thing that I had done and its ramifications. Was it okay what I had done? No. Did I deserve reprimand? Yes. Did I deserve to be "watched with vigor" and put on probation? I hesitated there. At first, naturally, I fought the idea. But doubt persisted and more questions surfaced. Do I deserve probation for my actions? What would you have done in the abbé's shoes? Was I not guilty now of viewing my own case as a "special case"? Why was I so special? Was it Jean Moreau showing the arrogance, really? I might have done the same thing, given the same lecture, but not the same probation, of that I was convinced.

I slowly walked back to my cell considering all of this. I wanted to speak to someone about it, to gain some perspective. I thought immediately of Elena, but that was out of the question. Besides, this development would only make her feel worse. I then thought of others in the abbey to whom I could speak. Brother Luc was my friend, as was Brother Herman, but these were not the right men with whom to discuss this kind of affair. I could only think of one other that I might discuss it with — Father François, who happened now to also be the man just under Guinot. Abbé Rénard had appointed him as sous-prieur — the number three at Kervennec. Now he had moved up to prieur. He knew me as well as anyone else in the abbey. He had always been more than fair and generous with his time, and in his assessment of others. We had been close in a way that neither of us may have considered openly, but I knew he had a special regard for me, just as I did for him. I decided that I would speak with him right away and went to see if I could find him at the shop.

When I arrived there, Father François was behind the counter speaking with an older couple, who were in the process of selecting a book. Father always had time for the many questions posed by visitors and was not hesitant to give his opinion, if asked, about most things, books in particular. I knew this wasn't the moment and I stayed out of sight. Soon, however, the transaction with the couple had finished and for the moment Father was free. He looked up and saw me.

"Can't stay away, Jean?" Father joked.

"I was hoping for a promotion, or at least a raise, if I came during my off-hours. I am trying to impress you, Father," I responded, in jest.

"You'll have to do better than that!" Father François retorted.

I walked up to the counter and smiled.

"Father, I have something that I need to talk to you about — not about work, but something personal that is on my mind. Would you have time to chat sometime soon?"

"I'm certainly always available for you, Jean. If you are free, we close in…" Father François regarded his watch, "eight and one-half minutes. Would that be soon enough for you?"

I laughed. "Of course, Father. I'll wait by the foyer."

Father François smiled and started to cash out the register. I went outside and looked around. It wasn't a bad day — lots of sun and the temperature might hit an unseasonable ten degrees Celsius. I thought that it would be nice if we could talk outside. After a few minutes, I went back inside. Father François was ready for closing and was looking for his keys to the shop.

"How's the weather out, Jean? Should we just have a turn or two in the garden?"

"I think so, Father. That would be nice."

We headed out at a fairly brisk pace. When we reached the garden, Father François looked over at me expectantly, and I began, rather formally at first.

"Father, what I am about to reveal to you saddens and embarrasses me considerably. I am at a dead end in my thinking, and I respect your wisdom and thank you in advance for agreeing to hear me, especially on such short notice."

Father François nodded and looked at me and said, "Jean, I have always liked and even admired you in so many ways. You bring a freshness to everything and to everyone that you encounter, and I'm not just talking about those you meet in the shop. You have a very positive influence on people and, in saying that, on the abbey. It is rare to find men as humble and agreeable, and intelligent, I might add, in any setting, much less an abbey. I've never had occasion to share my opinion of you like this, but I always have felt it best to be direct, and especially to tell someone to his face the things one appreciates about him and not to wait for the eulogy!"

I laughed nervously. I had not expected this from Father François. It would make it that much harder to tell him what I had to say. As kind as these words were, they burned a little. At any other time in my life at the abbey, I would have loved hearing Father's sentiments, those very words. Now, they mattered little and perhaps even rang false. I still had a tendency then to judge myself and not to let self-criticism go easily.

I had no choice, of course, but to go on and say what I wanted and needed to say. I settled in and began.

"Father, not too long ago I renewed a contact with a woman that I had known in university. She was a good friend then and we were extremely close, but we had lost contact over the years. She appeared one day at the abbey some months ago and we reconnected. We found that we got on very well together, just like old times, only this time it seemed different. I suppose it might have been because we were more mature and better able to appreciate the qualities of the other person — I am not sure. That's how I felt anyway — that I appreciated her and her many qualities more than ever. We wrote back and forth and she visited several times, and I enjoyed every bit of it. She is not a religious person, but is certainly a person of Spirit — she is a practitioner of applied kinesiology and is an artist. We are sort of on the same wavelength."

I stopped for a moment to focus on the coming few sentences. Even speaking to a friend and mentor like Father François, it would prove difficult to explain what had happened with Elena. I was ready to go on and I cleared my throat.

"Father, one day some weeks ago, she and I found ourselves in a compromising position. I didn't control things when I should have. What I mean is, we kissed and embraced passionately and I could have prevented it — but I didn't. She has suffered many pangs of remorse, but I have always felt it was something that I could and should have prevented from happening. I didn't and now we all are paying for it. It happened before we knew it. I do have feelings for her, but I would never leave the abbey. This is my home."

I stopped, looking ashamedly but hopefully at Father François. Father was gentle in his return gaze but silent. I could see that he knew that I wasn't finished. He waited until I was ready to speak again, not saying anything.

"Father, all of that, unsavory as it is, is one thing. There is another. I have confessed to Abbé Guinot." I stopped again as I saw a reaction from Father François.

"Abbé Guinot?" he said, tensely. "You should have come to me first. And what in heaven's name did he say?"

"I wish I had thought of that, Father. I was so confused. But as it turned out, it was he who approached me. He accused me of forgetting who I was, saying that I have been a poor monk and am perhaps not cut out to be in the abbey, and that I was now on probation. Somehow, he already knew about it."

"And you have no idea how?"

"Yes, I have an idea. Father Michel was in the orchard at the same time, unbeknownst to us until later. I saw him and abbé talking and staring at me not long ago — I am sure it was he."

Father François was quick to respond and did so in an agitated fashion.

"That rigid old fuddy-duddy! He is the perfect lapdog of Guinot. And I am being charitable with that opinion. Probation! Those two — those attitudes — perfect for each other and exactly what the abbey does not need. How Abbé Rénard could have seconded

Guinot I know not. I am privy to so much as sous-prieur, and I have never figured that out. He is a disaster waiting to happen. He never discussed this with me, either, his prieur…

"Look, Jean, you need say no more about this to me now. I can see your sorrow and I can understand the circumstance. I know it will not happen again. To accuse you of not being cut out to be a monk — why, that is preposterous. I mean what I say that this man, and his institution of probation for you, was way of out of line."

François stopped a moment to collect his thoughts.

"There is nothing really to do for the moment but to wait and see if it escalates. I don't know that he has the stomach for it, but power can change a man overnight. I've already seen him having a very bad start with the men, and as he goes, so goes Kervennec. This disturbs me no end.

"Know one thing, Jean," Father François continued. "You have a friend and supporter in me. Come to me if you feel you are being picked on or treated in any way unfairly. It is important that you know you have a friend at this time, and support and friendship I can offer you in plenty. We won't let the likes of him get the better of you." Father said that last sentence with great emotion.

I was overwhelmed. I said a silent prayer of thanks that this man saw me for who I really am and that he was available to support me. This would be a moment that I would always cherish, a moment of true friendship. He was full of kindness and strength and cared about me. With his compassionate nature, he would make a great abbé.

I felt a tremendous weight thrown off of my shoulders. I stopped back at the church to say my thanks after I left Father François. I recall having had a strange feeling, a feeling that things were going to be fine, yes; but something else came to me, an intuition, that there were big changes coming. Was it for me or for the abbey — or both? I didn't know, but I silently assented, and promised to welcome and support anything Divine Father/Mother would send me as I knew that it would be for the best. And as is so common in life, I realized once again that though I had sinned, though something unthinkable had happened, with true contrition and hard work, I, like David of old, could learn a great lesson, and from that lesson attain a greater love and appreciation for my God. I knew already that my relationship with the Divine Creator would come back sweeter and stronger than ever.

My gratitude was without bounds.

Abbey Life Becomes More Difficult

In a hierarchy every employee tends to rise to his or her level of incompetence.
—*Laurence J. Peter,* The "Peter Principle"

It was mid-February and spring was approaching. I had been in the shop all afternoon with not much happening. I took my break and I decided to go outside and breathe the soft air of the new season and take a walk in the wooded area behind the monastery.

I was feeling a little more lethargic than usual. Spring fever? I started thinking about personal rhythms, cycles. Everything has its rhythms: the tides and the seasons, the moon and the stars, life and death, and Life again. We humans have ours, be they physical, mental, or emotional. I do believe thoughts can have their cycles, too. I had just been through one…an obsession, with Elena.

But here is the strange part: these thoughts, often tied to some emotion, can dominate our minds during waking hours at any given point in our lives, but then they pass, and long after we no longer recall what those thoughts were that had enveloped our consciousness so. For example, if I could go back in time, I would be amazed at any given point to see what issue was seriously on my mind, now long forgotten. For any one of us it can be, for example, a worry or a fear (Can I get through to my next exam? Do I have a certain disease? Will my brother get through his divorce OK? etc.) or anger (My pay raise should have been more! The neighbor's new dog is driving me nuts! My new car has a dent in it! etc.).

Yet, if we could summon up any given moment in the past, very few of us could recall in advance the trifling or even the serious fears or angers that occupied much of our conscious thinking at that time. This process and its result is a message: all things are transitory, and there is very little that should disturb, or is worth disturbing, our tranquility. As we dwell on the negative particularly, we lose our sense of mindfulness, and that is precious time lost. What we must do is to take notice of the whole process consciously, know and realize what we are thinking about and feeling, and have a plan to exit a cycle of negativity when we recognize it. That practice may involve breathing, meditation, or relaxation of some kind. On the metaphysical level, it calls for a trust in the universe, Providence, God, or Whatever you wish to name it, that all is for our good. I am sure this is why saints are happy people; they realize what is important and what is not, and what is real and what is not. And as for the cycles themselves, might it not be also true they are with us in the spiritual side of our makeup? Times of clarity, times of obscurity — times when God is close, times when He has turned His face from us — tests of faith?

That day was beautiful and perfect for these thoughts as the late afternoon sun softened things. As I walked further, I also saw Father Maurice walking in the distance and gave him a discreet wave. The question of our new abbé, Abbé Guinot, then entered my mind, as it often did at this period. A very angry man was now in charge. How many of the monks were feeling and thinking the same things as I was? I was keenly interested in how they felt about the new abbé more than two months into his "reign." I already had a good idea of the answer some would give.

If Abbé Rénard showed considerable improvement and had the strength to resume his duties, he would return, of course; but it didn't appear now that that was going to happen. In fact, it was nearly a certainty, and the question of Guinot's leadership had now become a more urgent one. The end of the three-month period was approaching and it had become evident that there was a problem. Guinot's tone of communication with the monks had become even more abrupt and aggressive. Innocent comments, questions, and even pleasantries as they were attempted were greeted with moodiness, silence, or outbursts. Comments were now exchanged among my brothers in the abbey, and even some of our many lay workers were upset with the way things were going. The atmosphere was slowly being poisoned and it was beginning to take its toll on the community.

For the first few weeks under Abbé Guinot's direction, things in the abbey had run along without major problems — our cycle of prayer, work, and meditation ran as usual, though some found the abbé's manner changed. But, at the second chapter meeting, about six weeks into his term, some real cracks had begun to show. Abbé Guinot's responses to questions or comments were harshly critical and "overly intense," as one monk would describe it later to me.

At about the same time, there had occurred one incident that came as the final straw for me, personally, in my attempts at a loving relationship with Abbé Guinot. I had also been charged by him with chairing a committee to consider repairs to the stained glass windows in the church. He insisted the report to the chapter be ready and presented within ninety days. There was a great deal to do in that time, and considering the normal responsibilities and time constraints of the monastic life, this would involve a sacrifice of time for many and extra work for the monks involved that would not be inconsiderable. Architects, specialists, and possibly even restorers would have to be contacted. A general understanding of the whole process would have to be gained and discussions on each step of the process would need to be made. Budgets would need to be put together from a bidding process yet to be determined. All of this was being asked of the committee members. Elena's help was out of the question. I had thought at the time that ninety days was squeezing it very tightly, and especially aggressive given Abbé Guinot's interim status — there was still no certainty that he would even be abbé in ninety days. When I asked the abbé if there were any compelling reasons why it all had to be done so quickly, he exploded in a fit of anger, saying in effect, it was he who made the decisions, that he didn't need or expect any questioning by his underling monks, and that I was to get on with it!

My initial reaction had been one of great surprise, followed quickly by anger at the response and treatment I had received. After I calmed myself (which was necessary a lot those days) I wondered what had touched off this rude and curious behavior. I found myself replaying the conversation in my mind to look for clues, but there clearly were none. There was nothing extraordinary either in my question or in the way that I had framed it. The same phrase always came back to me: this is not a well man.

I'd had discussions with others in the monastery around this time. Many brought similar stories of erratic and indefensible behavior. The abbé had already gotten out of touch and out of step with the men. I couldn't help but wonder if Abbé Guinot, with his increasingly apparent insecurity, had not been pressing others in order to be able to demonstrate quickly his adroit and progressive leadership skills, which could then justify his lifelong election. It was a most difficult situation. One of our own had been appointed and entrusted with the duty of guiding us spiritually and leading us in the very important daily work required to manage the physical running of the abbey. The man in charge was not well in mind or spirit. A continuing situation of abject failure on both counts was unacceptable and could be dangerous to the very existence of the monastery in the long run.

What were we to do? It was a troubling question, and a troubling time.

Two Camps

I give you a new commandment: love one another...by this love you have for one another, everyone will know that you are my disciples.

– Jesus, John 13:34,35

One thing seemed very clear to me at that point: Abbé Guinot would have to change his way of presiding over the abbey or he would have to go at the end of his three months — for the good of the community.

It would be a painful and divisive, not to mention complicated, process to get this done if Abbé Guinot did not offer his resignation. It would be painful because none of us wanted to turn on one of our "own"; divisive because of the fact that the issue was pregnant with the potential for problems resulting from strong and opposing opinions of what should be done, and again complicated because no one knew what we would "do" with an ex-abbé. How do we treat an ex-Father of a monastery?

I quickly found myself in the middle of it all, with two camps forming, one very "pro-Guinot," the other most definitively "anti-Guinot." It was the beginning of a hectic time for me as I was being lobbied by both sides, those who would retain Abbé Guinot, and those who wanted him to go. New and different pressures were exerting themselves. I was of a certain age and a "moderate" in terms of personality. It was known Guinot and I didn't get along particularly well (though to his credit the probation and affair were not public knowledge). My support was being sought by both camps, however, despite that fact. Every vote would matter.

Looking back now, I see my life at that time as full of opportunities for personal growth: Guinot's ascension was now at the fore, on the heels of my affair with Elena where I had been pushed and pulled and bloodied. Everything decided to happen to me in a single nine-month period after a serene twenty-plus years at Kervennec. But, isn't that the way life often works? "When it rains, it pours." Out of nowhere, it seems, we are confronted with a series of problems and challenges, often of a type we could not have envisaged. My father always told me it's the one you don't see coming that brings the knockout. After that barrage, I tended to agree; but I was still on my feet, though staggered and sometimes a bit groggy.

As I said, I believed at the time that I had a pretty good notion of how I was thought of personally in the abbey. I knew from my closest friends that I had the reputation of being coolheaded and thoughtful, a person without emotional responses to people and situations. I was known to speak my mind without being overly aggressive and without fear or second-guessing. I was also known to possess a good sense of humor, which seems to put people at ease. Thank goodness! It has saved me many times in relationships and from sinking into some low places mentally and emotionally. Humor at the right time so often helps us cut through to the truth. It diffuses tensions and gives perspective, particularly in charged situations.

There was nothing formal yet, but two groups were coalescing around the topic of Guinot and occasionally I saw one or two of the monks that I knew felt strongly one way or the other eying me. I knew that some brothers would come to me — for advice on what to do, or to tell me how to think, or even to want me to take a leading role, perhaps to help organize or lead a group with its own idea of how best to move forward. I labored with the idea that I should have any particular involvement in this, other than to have my own opinion. I have to admit that at the time I still felt that I was too young a monk and too inexperienced, not yet cut out for the leadership role required to direct a group. After all, some of the men at Kervennec had been monks for the whole time that I had been alive. In the back recesses of my mind, there was also the idea that I wanted to avoid any hint of anything that might look like retribution for the obvious dislike of me by the abbé, if I were to come public with my anti-Guinot views. I knew that it would be so easy for others to judge me and my views as a thinly concealed retaliation for his general posture towards me and one or two others. I decided that I would take my time and see what developed.

I found, however, that I wouldn't have that luxury. Things were moving forward very quickly. Both camps, pro-Guinot and anti-Guinot, came to me separately to discuss their positions and to enlist my support. Father Vincent, a priest of about sixty years of age, was the first to come to me, in late February.

There was to be a chapter meeting that evening, and Father Vincent had passed a note to me that day asking if we could speak privately just before that meeting. As it promised to be a nice evening and we could be undisturbed, we agreed to get together and walk a bit on the grounds before the meeting. Father Vincent was waiting for me by the garden entrance and spoke first.

"Good evening, Father Jean, it was good of you to take a few moments to see me."

He took my hand and flashed a wide, friendly grin.

"Father Vincent, I am happy to meet you. I hope I can be of help in some way."

"Believe me, so do I," smiled Vincent.

"You know how long I have been here at this Abbey?" Father Vincent paused as he took me then by the arm, thoughtfully guiding me toward the garden. I knew that he didn't expect an answer. "Almost forty years. I love this place. It is my home, my calling."

He paused, choosing his words. "I've never really wanted anything like power or authority here; but, a number of the priests and brothers, and you can probably guess which ones, have come to me to ask me to take the lead for them in a situation that has been begging for a response. I'm talking about their unhappiness with the direction of Abbé Guinot. I think you may have guessed already that many of us have been greatly disappointed in his leadership of the abbey. I also want to emphasize that the men that I have come to represent, however reluctantly on my part, are Godly men, unaccustomed to conflict, suffering at the thought of, at least in their minds, 'plotting' as it were against the one who is head of our institution, the one they themselves call abbé. I am sure you know that, too. But their fears revolving around the abbey's future are very real and take precedence. We need strong, considered leadership, and the men I represent do not think that Abbé Guinot can give it to them or to the abbey. They are talking amongst themselves about what strong measures might need to be taken to ensure the growth and continued stability of our great abbey, particularly because they had no say in the elevation of this man. It really means only one thing. It's not a good sign."

Father Vincent looked somber and his fatigue was now apparent as I looked him in the face. I could sense the personal suffering the man had been through. Here was a man accustomed to neither leadership nor conflict. He was a monk trying to do his best at the request of others still less capable. I was not surprised, of course, when the issue of dissatisfaction with the abbé was raised by a group, though I did not expect Father Vincent to be the point person for that group. Nevertheless, I found myself admiring him for taking on a role so foreign to his nature and I remember marveling how stealthily life and its problems can still reach and touch men even in a small and inconsequential byway like Kervennec, cosseted from the world.

I responded to him.

"I know how difficult this is for you to come to me today representing some of our brothers in the abbey. I know it is not your style, but I also know that you are a good man and a fair man and believe profoundly in what the men must feel and in everything that you have said.

"As perhaps you can imagine, I, too, have given this situation, this problem — and I use that word purposely — much private thought. Abbé Guinot and I have had some difficulties in meshing our personalities. But I accept him, for the tenure of his interim, as my Father here at the abbey."

I wasn't sure that I should have said the following, but I did.

"I have come to some conclusions that may be close to those arrived at by you and the monks you represent. Certainly the abbey can little afford the continued kind of leadership he is displaying. I have held on to, and still cling to the hope that either Abbé Guinot will make the comportmental changes needed to do this job, or realize that this is not a good match for him and his personal skills and offer to resign at the end of his interim period. However, in truth, I don't have much hope that either of these things will come to pass. I am sure that he will serve his full appointment and then run for reelection. But, I will leave the door open for change."

Father Vincent seemed to be encouraged by my words reflecting his and his group's views. There came a marked curl of Father Vincent's bottom lip. He then again spoke to me.

"Jean, how can we see our way through this? Is it our role to question our own leader? Are we stepping well beyond our rights here, to consider for even a moment measures to help prevent his election when the time comes? Some of the men want him to go now, even before that election. But he is our Christ figure here."

I remember Vincent's imploring face that demonstrated clearly the personal agony of his situation. His look was that of a man who clearly would have liked to get back to what he knew and loved — the routine of a monk living in an abbey, dedicating himself and his time to his personal growth and service to his community. Character was being formed in a reluctant man. This situation was now part and parcel of the personal growth of Father Vincent, among others, all of us, really, if the truth be told.

"Father Vincent," I began in response, "we need to give this further prayer and reflection. There is yet more to be said and considered about what we both realize is a major issue. We have to think and act carefully. I would not favor anything radical. We will have a chance to resolve it all."

Then I told him, "I will tell you, though, how sacred I find the trust that you have placed in me by coming to me today. And there is nothing that could cause me to violate that trust in any way. Why don't we plan to talk in a few days' time? I'll let you know a good time to meet. God bless you, Vincent."

I left to go back to my room to pray over this issue. I knew what at that moment I would like to see done, but I had also promised myself that I would continue to pray and make no quick decision. It was clear that the only way to properly dismiss him from office would be at the election at the end of his three month term, difficult as it might be to imagine a sufficient number of monks turning against their Father. I also would not consider any radical action ahead of that election, as I knew a few might have wished.

I also vowed to listen to what the other camp might say, led, I suspected, by Father Martin, should they also come to me. They would obviously have much different feelings about this issue. Again, I didn't have to wait long. In fact, I had just turned to go back through the church when there appeared Father Martin, right on cue. He was a portly figure, about fifty years old. He smiled and gestured that he'd like to speak to me. I thought to myself that this was as good a time as any, fresh as I was from discussions with the other "camp" and with my mind fully trained on the subject.

"Good afternoon, Father," I said, wanting to show some enthusiasm as we touched the sides of our foreheads in the Benedictine way.

"Good afternoon, Jean," said Father Martin. "Do you have a minute?" he continued.

"I do, Father Martin. How can I be of help?" I asked.

"Well," said Martin, "it's a bit of a sensitive subject. I'm sure I can trust you to hold confidential the things I am about to say."

"Yes, Father. You can be sure of our discussions remaining private."

Father Martin nodded and directed me to another

stone bench, this time not far from the cloister. We sat down. Father Martin, leaning a bit forward, his forearms resting on his thighs, began to speak softly. His hands were in constant motion, gesturing, his eyes fixed on the garden.

"I know you may have heard rumblings from some of the brothers regarding their discomfort with our abbé's leadership. In fact, I noticed you just now having a conversation with Father Vincent. He is normally a mild-mannered man, but I have seen him uncommonly animated about this topic, and I think I know his feelings, which, I must say, are probably much different from my own."

Father Martin stopped a moment to glance at me looking for a clue as to my sentiments, but I left my face unexpressive and he continued.

"In fact, there are a number of our brothers, and not a small number, who would agree with my sentiments, my own feelings on the matter."

"And what are your sentiments, Father Martin?" I inquired.

"I'll get to that, Jean. I first wanted to seek out your thoughts on the matter, to see if you are 'friend or foe,'" Father Martin said, half smiling.

"Well, I'm trying not to be a foe to anyone, but I have to say that while I have thoughts on the matter I am still in reflection. Can you let me in on your thoughts?"

"Spoken like a true politician, Jean! Have you ever thought of running for office?" Father Martin teased.

"I do enough penance already," I retorted, with a little laugh.

"Well, then, to answer your question," Father Martin continued, "my feelings are clear. I will tell you that I have known Abbé Guinot for over twenty years. Like you, I assume, I have seen a drastic change in him these last two-plus months. We all have even if some don't want to admit it. These changes have been difficult for us to accept, especially his new autocratic manner, but, to tell you the truth, few of us can really understand what he has had to deal with in his position on a daily basis. I will be the first to admit that in the past others have handled the change, and the position, much more adroitly, but, alas, we're all different…"

Father Martin stopped for a moment. He then peered at me intently, looking, I thought, for sympathy. Finding none, he continued, "I know there is a faction that would terminate Pierre's mandate as abbé at the end of his interim. They would have him replaced, and none of us knows who would assume that role, but that is not the point.

"Jean, this is our brother. We both know he is trying his hardest. We promised our allegiance to him, even though only as interim abbé. To me, that is hugely important. One can even say, and in fact we do say, that we are guided by the Spirit in such things. It's true, we didn't actively vote for him as he was already our prieur, but the Spirit's guidance was certainly still there. Given that dimension, how can we fight against or terminate the tenure of the man who is as our Father in the abbey?"

I nodded as if to say Father Martin had a point.

He continued, this time with his emotion apparent.

"Who knows what would happen to Pierre if this dissent takes him out of office, what effect it would have on his already volatile nature. I'm afraid it would send him on a downward spiral from which he might never recover."

I remember the strong admiration I felt for Father Martin rise within me as I considered his words and their meaning. It showed me the pure generosity of spirit existing within him and the group of monks that he represented. It was plain to see that he was full of love and respect for Abbé Guinot, though perhaps more as a man and fellow monk than as abbé. That such love existed in this small world of Kervennec, as I knew that it did exist, was and is a thing of beauty to me. It makes me feel thankful to God for creating men with such caring in their souls. Among all of the strong emotions to which this situation ended up giving rise, perhaps the strongest was my pride in my band of brothers.

"Father Martin, your words have not betrayed you. You have spoken plainly and openly and affectionately, and for that I thank you. You have also given me much to pray and think about. Father Vincent did indeed speak to me about Abbé Guinot, with his concerns. He is also thinking of the greater good of the abbey as we head into the future. The question remains on what we all do in two weeks' time at the end of his mandate.

"Give me another week to reflect, Martin. In the

meantime, I will serve, if chosen by you and Father Vincent, to become an 'arbiter' of sorts, to help us as a community come to a happy resolution of things. If that suits, I will be happy to meet with you and with any other party with another point of view."

Father Martin nodded, smiled, and took me by the hand, clasping it firmly.

"Thank you, Jean."

As I watched him walk away, his steps were perhaps a little lighter.

Once in a while — sometimes after a moment like this, with things confided — when I am given a chance to speak from the heart or to listen to someone else do the same, or when I have attempted to do the noblest thing, I can feel something like a "super-consciousness" come over me. It is a feeling of deep tranquility and peace, a feeling as if the approval of the universe had been stamped upon me. There is the notion, too, that I can grow in wisdom and absorb so much when I feel this way. It's a feeling of being "elevated," greatly heightened in sensitivity, on top of the world — literally — in my view of all that is around me. It is as if I could gaze over all that there was to see, and to see it all as it really is, sometimes even to feel I know the ultimate solutions to things. It is as if my earthly man, with its loud and ubiquitous ego, has stepped aside and I am left with the Real me — the Essential me — no longer "looking through a glass darkly." It is a feeling of immense calm and vision — maybe something like what it must feel to be Divine. Yes, I think it is the Divine. It is to me none other than the Higher Self, the point of human connection with the Divine. It is proof to me that Goodness, the consummate essence of God, can be its own reward; and, at the end of all of these magical feelings, there is one other thing that stands out plainly and seductively before me and fills me with joy, and that is that it is Real. There is nothing overlaid on the experience, no layers of confusion to cut through, nothing false about it. These feelings, these energies that pervade my soul at those times, they are an intimate part of my makeup — as real as anything material or sensual. It is the manifestation within us of a power, a power for good that reigns supreme when we let it, when ego is set aside. We share that power for good with our Creator.

I got to my room and I remember just kind of collapsing into my chair. I was exhilarated, but at the same time I was tired. For all of the emotional drain of that time, however, I felt the glow of something within. It soothed me. Somehow it would all work out, I knew. It always does. I thought then, "What a great God we have!"

Nothing since has changed my mind.

A Meeting

But let him who is to be elected be chosen for the merit of his life and the wisdom of his doctrine, though he be the last in the community.

                         —The Rule of St. Benedict

In a little more than a week, we monks would gather again to either reelect our former prieur to the office that he currently held, that of abbé — this time for life — or to dismiss him and appoint another. It was unlike any election for abbé that I or any of the others had ever seen before. There was going to be tremendous emotion attached to this selection.

What did I really think about this whole situation? It was pretty clear. As much as I disliked the current administration's way of doing things, however, it was difficult to subject one of our own to the anguish that would accompany a defeat. I felt a physical pain when it would come to mind. I was happy that I could feel that way — there is no room for more anger and revenge in our world. We in the monastery must be the first to demonstrate that. But in the end, I thought he must go.

I had been able to grow through this episode. God puts us through what we see as nothing but a trial, in our myopic vision. But, really, trials are agents of liberation. We can use those difficulties to cleanse and purify and ultimately overcome our emotional person and look beyond this transient life to become the Man or Woman of Discernment that we were always meant to be. Admittedly, this is not an easy thing to do, but it is the only way forward.

As for the election, there was not only the issue of possibly rejecting one of our own that loomed large. There was also the unmistakable sense, for me and many others, that this election was going to be a seminal event. There was no doubt that it would pave the way to Kervennec's future. Much was riding upon the personal characteristics of the one that the brothers would choose to be their Father — his gifts, his experience, his energy, and to some extent also his age. This man's decisions could determine the course of the abbey for decades to come.

If Abbé Guinot were not to be retained, what sort of man might be selected to replace him? The election would most likely leave a younger man than our retiring Abbé Rénard at the helm. A younger man would bring some new thinking and perhaps a significant shift in attitude diffused from the top. That, in and of itself, would have a big impact. Who would I have liked to see in the role? I had my ideas — I could easily see Father François in the position: levelheaded, spiritually mature, experienced in business matters, respected. There may be two or three others qualified, but the pool of "eligibles" was not a large one from which to select a spiritual Father.

Time would tell. That time was drawing nigh, and it was on my mind continually that last week. I knew that I owed a response to each of the two factions that had come to see me a week earlier. The group led by

Father Vincent desperately wanted to see change. They wanted to be sure that Abbé Guinot would not continue as abbé. There was no animosity among these brothers towards him; on the contrary, Guinot was one of them and loved as a brother, but he had clearly gotten in over his depth, to their way of thinking. The opposing group, led by Father Martin, shared the view that as prieur, Abbé Guinot had been selected by Abbé Rénard as his second and that this had not been by chance. Abbé Rénard had been guided by Spirit to make this choice, and it was clear to them that Abbé Guinot should be allowed to continue in his role as abbé permanently, that the monastery had no right to strip him of the office. I knew, too, the one unstated fear surrounding the dismissal of brother Guinot, especially for Father Martin. It was that the current abbé was a sensitive soul, and rejection come election time might be dangerous to his mental health. While that was an extreme view, it was a view held by a few of that group in addition to Father Martin. This faction had been somewhat more aggressive in its approach to the monks, sometimes even asking those whom they felt were "undecideds" whom their preference might be. They seemed to reflect the personality of their champion.

But for me, there was just too much at stake to let this chance to replace Abbé Guinot slip away, well intentioned as he may have been. The "winner" could well preside over the abbey for another three decades. I had made my selection and was ready to cast my ballot at the upcoming election. I remember feeling strangely confident at the time that our interim abbé would not be asked to continue.

While there was no "campaigning" permitted, there was a natural tendency for those who held similar opinions to recognize one another and to form an informal group, as had come to pass. While leaving things to God, there was also an unstated view among a few of these men that it was all right to help the brothers whom they felt may not be aware of the situation's gravity, or who tried to not involve themselves in the running of the abbey, realize that it was important to understand the issues at hand. It was imperative for them to get involved, and hopefully, after they had been most cordially invited to learn more about that group's particular viewpoint, to adopt that view going forward. Few monks would give an outright opinion, though. For most of the brothers, their opinion was that it was God's work in the conclave that mattered, not anything that one may say or express beforehand; so, the faux "campaigning" tactics were not particularly important or effective.

I decided six days before election day that it was time to meet with the two group leaders, Father Vincent and Father Martin. I found myself going back and forth on whether to meet with each individually or to have them both together so that I could let them know my feelings without fostering suspicions between them. I finally did decide on the latter course and I set up a meeting for the following afternoon after None.

At the meeting, Father Martin was the first to

arrive. I had taken a little *parloir*, or meeting room, in the reception building. I thought that it would be good to arrive early, and it was a good thing I did as no sooner had I seated myself than Father Martin arrived. I just smiled as I saw my eager friend, and Father Martin wasted no time collaring me after he had taken his seat.

"Father Jean, I am eager to know if you may have made your selection for abbé. I have come early to speak to you privately in case you had any further questions about my views, or why there are so many others who have adopted them. I hope you don't think it inappropriate, but it seemed important enough that I thought I'd risk it," Father added with a wink.

I was inwardly amused at this amateur gamesmanship, and I smiled back at Father Martin. Here was a man who was cut out to represent or sell something, but he was still a bit rough around the edges. I did not for a minute doubt his sincerity, but he was as easy to read as an elementary school book.

"Father Martin, good of you to come early to tell me this and give me that opportunity. As it happens, I feel comfortable with my feelings on the subject, and if you don't mind, we'll wait for Father Vincent before we carry on much further. I hope that you understand. In fact, that may be him now."

Father Martin and I turned toward the meeting room's door. As it opened, I saw his glance meet that of his opposition, and the face of Father Vincent tense a little. He entered the room with a tight smile, and then greeted us both with a nod. He took his seat and both of my visitors immediately looked to me expectantly. I began.

"Thanks to both of you gentlemen for coming to meet with me here today, and, for agreeing to do so in each other's presence. What I have to say is for both of you and I did not want either of you to get the mistaken idea that there was anything hidden by me from either party. This way, we eliminate any opportunity for misinterpretation. Again, I appreciate your flexibility.

"To be honest, my views on this have not changed. I have made my choice, but I have decided not to reveal my preference for abbé to either of you. I see my job rather as facilitator between the two parties that you represent, if you'd like me to continue in that role. I want to reiterate to you both, however, that the *Rule* is clear about overt campaigning. We are monks and our duty is to God first and then to each other. Our duty to God tells us that we must leave it to Him to manage everything when the time for election comes. Our job is to reflect and vote honestly. He will guide us.

"But there is something else I want to tell you. I can only say that I have been so impressed by the sincerity and goodwill that you and your associates have shown and by your honesty and thoughtfulness in the positions that each of you have taken and expressed to me privately. I know it all comes from the heart. It makes me feel proud to be associated with you and I have no doubt that those good practices and intentions will lead to nothing but success as we choose our

Father.

"I hope that you don't think that I have wasted your precious time by bringing you both here today to say that I cannot commit to either point of view, but I feel strongly about that. I thought it the fairest and simplest way to have you both present to acknowledge it. Remember my offer to mediate now or in the future, no matter my personal feelings. I mean that sincerely and want to reaffirm that to both of you. I appreciate the trust that you have put in me to help and to be involved in the process. That means a lot to me, as do both of you as men and brothers. The important thing in my mind is that we keep campaigning to a minimum and maintain the high tone that we all want to see as we move to the election. Let us be true to our faith as monks, and know that it will be God's way prevailing in less than a week's time."

There was silence for several moments. Then Father Martin responded.

"Father Jean, I naturally agree that we must let God be the Arbiter. I had secretly hoped that we might count on you in the election, but I completely understand and respect the reasons that you have decided what you have decided."

Father Vincent was his usual thoughtful self and seemed somewhat ill at ease but I knew that he must be relieved that I had not pledged myself to Father Martin's faction.

"Father Jean, I am happy that there was someone like you that each of us could come to for aid and discussion. Each of the groups that we represent feels strongly about its position and I don't think it would serve any purpose to talk more about those positions now. I do think, however, that your services might be valuable after the election should we have to bring about any reconciliation. I sincerely hope that that will not be the case, but if we need to hash out issues, you are the one I would like to come to for mediation, if Father Martin would agree."

"Well spoken, Father Vincent. I concur wholeheartedly," added Father Martin.

"Thank you again, my brothers, for coming today. Please take with you my sincere love and appreciation for all you do, and may God bless us all and keep the abbey safe and viable for decades to come."

With that, I closed the meeting. I was very pleased that it had gone so well.

I went back to the church right after that to say some prayers. I started to feel a few nerves as I began my prayer when I thought about all there was at stake, but as usual, when I come to God in humility and honesty, I am quickly soothed. All was in Good Hands.

The new or returning abbé's future decisions would have a dramatic affect on the abbey, its well-being, perhaps its very existence, in what might very well be leaner years ahead. I continued to pray for that future and for wisdom in my own role in the matter, whatever it may be, and remained there a good half hour.

But little did I expect the drama that was to unfold in just a few days' time.

Prayer

I mentioned prayer at the close of the last chapter. When people ask me the best way to know God or to feel His presence or even to "ask for what I need," I give them a simple answer: Prayer. When they ask me, "What is your secret? Why are the men in this monastery as happy as they are?" I have the same response: Prayer.

Why? Because prayer is the open door to the Divine. It is the sine qua non of the spiritual life. It is heightened meditation. It is an aspect of Mindfulness and a pillar of Awareness.

It probably sounds too simple; but the Good News is that it is that simple! When you pray, you are asking your dearest Friend, your Creator, your Father/Mother for help or to give thanks or to say I'd like to do better. Why make it more complicated? You are asking the One Who is Everything to do something, and the more you ask for His intimate friendship, the closer you will be to the Source, because the Source always responds. To be intimate with that Source is to be connected to All There Is. What joy can escape you then? What knowledge, wisdom, or peace can be outside your reach when you have that Resource behind you? The answer is also simple: None. My relationship with prayer is crucial to my attempt to become the man I aspire to be.

If you don't believe it helps, or even that God exists, I challenge you to do the following. Reserve five minutes (ten is even better) each morning for seven days. Find a quiet place where you know that you will have those moments of uninterrupted time. You needn't get on your knees. Just find a comfortable chair, but don't slouch! Sit upright and relax and close your eyes. Set the timer if you wish, and…begin. Begin by being what you must always be in prayer — honest. Say to Him, or to Divine Mother, if that vision is more powerful and true for you, that you don't know if He/She is there. That you would like to know and that you will sit with an open mind. Tell God that you will still require some "proof." Let God know that you realize that that proof can come in many different forms, and ask Him to help you recognize and understand such a proof when it arrives. Realize it can come as just a sense you have inside you of a calm presence, or as a burst of joy; or it may be another thing that comes — the healing of a relationship, an intuition, a meaningful encounter, something that you read or see that suddenly strikes you, or the answer to a question or nagging doubt you may have been harboring. Very few, including the saints, have heard a loud voice, the voice of God, commanding them or showing them what to do! That is not what you are after. God resides just behind the conscious mind most of the time. Your place of quiet, the stillness that you develop, helps you to find Him, or, should I say, for Him to finally get noticed by you. He may not respond to you in a way that you expect, and He may not respond right away. But He will respond.

There are so many times that we are not listening when God is trying to get through. This technique helps solve that problem. If you find yourself staying more than five minutes in that quiet place that you have constructed, just stay there. Even if you end up not finding any evidence of the Divine in your life after that week, at least you will have found a new way to relax and add depth to your life. You will have found a secret reserve to rest and refresh your body and soul in a world that offers so little of it.

Our Creator wants to teach us that this life is not permanent. We mustn't get too involved and enmeshed in the everyday, but remember our Source. We are just here to learn. Life is only a training ground designed to find Him, to appreciate Him and the range of emotions and experiences that only life can bring. With that knowledge, we can be complete. We receive lots of "messages" to teach us this, but we often still don't listen very well, if we listen at all. The result of our inattention can be a rap on the knuckles or sometimes even a rap on the noggin…St. Paul got knocked off his horse! Unfortunately, it is usually tragedy in our earthly lives and loves that brings us literally to our knees and we learn the hard way.

Typically, God's response, is rather subtle — we need the quiet to recognize it. When you pray, just remember to be sincere, direct, and forthright. You must be sincere in your search for God, even if your question is about His very existence — then things will flow.

Right prayer is asking for what is best for us and for the strength to recognize and utilize it, given where we are on the path to Awareness. We will get what we need when we sincerely ask. We can and should ask "not to be put to the test," as Jesus said, but ask to find our answer just the same.

Will we also get what we eventually need if we ignore the spiritual dimension? No doubt, but we may not enjoy very much the long and bumpy emotional road and occasional knock on the head that our non-attention will continue to attract until we get it right.

That is my premise and my promise for prayer and its role in our lives. All theology and catechism aside, it really is quite simple. Try it. Make some time for Him every day, as often as you wish. Do it in a quiet place and at a quiet time, if you can. Outside of those times, do it when you have a spare minute. Instead of switching on a device or the TV, think of Him and ask Him to come around and visit. You will see results in ways that can range from the subtle to the spectacular, from the merely helpful to something beyond your wildest dreams. Prayer is a call to action. And you are the beneficiary!

Election Day

There is a tide in the affairs of men, which taken at the flood, leads on to fortune…
– William Shakespeare, Julius Caesar

Election day was upon us. Curiously, there was a mood more of restraint than tension. Some things were different, there had not been the usual occasional quiet conversation after Mass between the monks, for example, but otherwise nothing was exceptional. As we were seated later that day for lunch, Abbé Guinot, as was custom, did the prayer of blessing before the meal. In it, there was no appeal to the Heavenly Father for an extra dose of *sagesse* that day. In fact, there was no mention at all of the upcoming proceedings that meant so much to the abbé's future and the future of the abbey. It would have been unusual for him to have said anything self-serving in that setting, it is true, but I still thought it laudable that the abbé did not discuss the election, maintaining a spirit of neutrality from his pulpit. When I mentioned that to some others later who were not enamored of our abbé, one sardonically said that he thought Guinot must be in denial about the whole affair.

There had been a reading at the lunch from the letters of one of the early Church Fathers; the monks listened, some more attentively than others as they took their meals, but a keen observer would have noticed that there was not much interest in what the lector had to say. Outside the refectory windows, the day was cloudy, adding to the atmosphere of restraint.

I was at my usual seat between Brother Luc and Father François. I had had an interesting conversation with Brother Luc after Mass. Luc had been my protégé. I had been in charge of his training ten years prior when he entered Kervennec. He had become head of the kitchen recently. I liked him very much. I particularly liked his sense of humor and his *joie de vivre* and we were still close and on the same wavelength about most things, not the least of which was recognizing the need for new leadership.

Luc had been busy the night before. He told me about a little adventure he had had. He had heard about a sort of informal caucus scheduled for a meeting room at the welcome center after the recitation of Compline, our last Office of the day. It was being organized by Father Martin. Father Martin knew that any vote to effectively remove the abbé would be very close, and he wanted to waste no opportunity to "unofficially" swing the undecided among the men towards support for Guinot. He had some hopes, evidently, of meeting with some of these men. He knew that campaigning was certainly not permitted. He must have known he was walking that line precariously. I had not heard about it, but then it had been arranged in private conversations and I would not have been the first one on his list asked to attend. He knew how I would feel about it. Brother Luc, however, had ventured to the center to see if Father Martin were indeed there and meeting with anyone. Luc found the whole idea grating and unacceptable. He had in the back of his mind a plan to stop any "meeting" type assembly led by Father Martin.

Luc told me that as he neared the room, Father Martin had caught sight of him. He was under no illusions as to why Luc was there, and Luc said he was laughing inside at the thought of Father Martin secretly fighting the uncharitable thoughts he no doubt would have had about Luc, a mere brother, coming to spy on him, an ordained priest. Luc reported the following conversation, with some added commentary as he related it.

"Good evening, Brother Luc," said Father Martin. ("In as cheery a tone as he could muster," added Luc.)

"Good evening, Father Martin. It's getting a bit late…"

"Lots to think about, Brother. What brings you out so late?"

Luc hadn't been pleased at the special emphasis Father had used on the word "brother."

"Oh, I couldn't sleep and saw the light on," Luc had responded. ("I crossed my fingers behind my cassock and asked for forgiveness in advance.")

There was a moment of silence between them. Father Martin then put down his pen.

"Big day tomorrow, Luc. How do you think it will go?"

Luc said that he responded with, "It will go as God wills it to go, no doubt. Each left to his own conscience, the best thing will happen. Me, I'm more concerned about what to prepare for lunch. The men will be hungry," trying only slightly to lower the tension between them.

"And God's will shall bring an end to the reign of our Père Abbé, no doubt you think," responded Father Martin, not enjoying the frivolity, according to Luc.

"Well, Father, I try hard not to render judgment on matters such as these, but to trust God in all things and leave the judgment to Him. I find it the right course of action for me and would strongly suggest it would be proper for all of the brothers, and priests, in the community."

Luc admitted he feared a certain edge had appeared in his voice and countenance, especially when he said the word "priests," though he said that he was trying hard not to leave the side of charity.

With irritation in his voice evident, Father Martin replied, "You speak wisely, Brother. No one could argue that judgment should remain with our Almighty Father, particularly on the subject of intention and purity of heart. One could argue, however, that in matters of intellectual and practical judgment, there is room for those with more experience in worldly things to come to the aid of others less experienced, who perhaps might be subject to some confusion in their consideration of these things."

Luc said that he looked at his brother intently. He admitted to me at that moment that he disliked Father Martin, but found he could not question his motives, as he and I knew that he certainly was not lobbying for the job himself. He had neither the temperament nor the stomach for it. He had a conviction, certainly, that no community should consider what amounted to a "recall" election for any sitting abbé, period. The job should be the interim abbé's to keep, apparently, even though it not yet been voted on by the community nor given in perpetuity. Luc told me at this point, put off by the arrogance and aggressiveness of the man, that he decided to terminate the impromptu meeting.

"I don't have any doubts that our great God has taken all of that into consideration amongst His many other duties, and is quite capable of helping those of whom you speak as they ask for guidance in prayer. As I said before, I am content to leave it in His almighty hands. I hope you agree. With that thought, I'll bid you a good night, Father. It will be much better for all of us to have a good restful sleep, yes?"

Father had smiled politely at his philosophical foe and nodded so as to bid him good night. Luc then left, happy in the knowledge that no one had showed up at Father's rather ill-conceived rendezvous.

As lunch finished, I was feeling uneasy. This abbey and its community was my home and, in many ways, my life. Never had I seen the community so divided. There was no use in kidding myself that all would be the same in a few hours' time. The effects of this election would certainly linger for a considerable time — measured in years if not in decades. Leadership here, as in any earthly institution, is critical. Given the power of the office of abbé, especially in a community of modest size like Kervennec, the abbey was especially susceptible to the character, experience, and sanctity of its leader.

Our situation also posed a very unique side issue. The community was being asked to, in effect, pass judgment on our acting abbé — not just our leader, but the man who, according to Benedict, is our "Father," as his title implied. This complicated the typical strain of an election in a significant way. This unavoidable fact had the potential to create almost irreparable rifts in the community unless the right person took charge and made the canny moves necessary to achieve accord and to move everyone forward.

I had thought and prayed about my own choice for abbé. Once it had become clear that Abbé Rénard could not come back to resume his duties, I had begun my considerations, and having had some time to reflect had made it somewhat clearer for me. I preferred to go with a younger monk, perhaps one five to ten years my senior. I reasoned that that relative youth bade well for long-term continuity in directing and planning for the future, provided, of course, that that youth was combined with the requisite experience and personality. I also believed strongly that such a man must not be seen as extreme in any way, whether in personality, viewpoint, or religious ardor. It would be a time for healing in the abbey and all of those attributes, combined with an intrinsic ability to lead, particularly in consensus, were crucial.

I believed that the best choice was Father François. He had been appointed sous-prieur by Abbé Rénard, and it had been a good choice. He was younger, but not too young. He was not a man of extremes in any way. He had had much work experience in the abbey, managing a few smaller projects. He had also helped manage the reconstruction of the monastery hotel and done so in an exemplary fashion. Perhaps most importantly, he liked seeking consensus on decisions. I was confident that that characteristic in particular would remain an important part of François' approach, particularly in any decision that involved a change of routine for the abbey. He would be a good abbé.

There were large obstacles to overcome for the pro-Guinot faction. These included his stiff and increasingly autocratic manner, his lack of good humor, and his opinionated, arrogant style. Still he was acting abbé, a huge advantage. This was a unique election in a very unique circumstance. There was no way to know in which direction the monks would go, but there was one thing that was sure: If Abbé Guinot did not prevail on the first ballot, when all of his supporters would be sure to come forward, then he would not win and a change would be forthcoming.

It would be a difficult afternoon for some, but I started to feel better. I had done all that I could in preparation. I had again reviewed things in my mind to my satisfaction, but also felt deep in my heart that any verdict reached would be God's will. That verdict might really test the abbey if the ancien régime prevailed, but that would be up to the residents to work through. If it turned out that a new abbé was elected, it opened other avenues forward for the abbey, and that would be welcomed as God's will, too. The next few hours would tell the story.

The election was to be held in the chapter room and it had been called for four thirty that afternoon. After lunch, I took a breath of fresh air and was feeling, rather surprisingly, both calm and increasingly upbeat about it. There were few of the creeping worries or apprehensions about the course of the abbey now. It was certainly true that I continued to have great trepidations about continuing with Abbé Guinot; but, once again, my faith came to my aid as I knew God would have a plan for the abbey that resulted in ultimate good. It truly was in God's hands, and where better could it rest?

I began to wonder what Father François might be feeling. I thought that François must have had an inkling that he would be a contender. I wondered if certain ideas of reform or change for the future direction for the monastery might not even now be working their way through his thoughts. I tried to put myself in that position just for fun. I'd never given it any thought. Only one monk had come to me to suggest to me that I might make a great abbé, and that was Brother Herman. But Herman had said that since the first month of his arrival. I knew that I couldn't take this loveable man too seriously on that score. He was good but tended to be very emotional, and partisan, and sometimes he wore those emotions on his sleeve.

I did notice that Brother Luc was starting to let his emotions show. After lunch outside, he could not help but comment to me how Abbé Guinot definitely had had a more distracted look and clearly seemed ill at ease. What was almost comical to him, he said, was the way the abbé seemed to sense he was not looking imperial enough and could be seen, if regarded carefully, to consciously modify his "look" from time to time. I found that description of his demeanor a bit extreme, but emotions were running high. Luc then told me that he had found himself uttering a silent prayer that this man not be returned to office each time he saw his look.

As the afternoon progressed, the monks occupied the time in their usual fashion with work, private prayer, and rest before the chapter meeting. I found the time passing slowly. I was not on duty at the shop. I tried doing some reading and then tried to nap. I was able to do that for about twenty minutes and felt refreshed afterward. It was about three o'clock when I decided to take another walk in the free time remaining, and I headed for the area near the rear of the church that the creek ran through. There is a nice path there for strolling up and down. I had taken Elena's most recent letter received earlier in the week with me to read again. She was full of support and confidence that the best would work out. She wished me good thoughts and reminded me not to get too emotional about any of it. I appreciated that!

I like walking along that path in any season, looking at the various plants that sprout in the summer and at the beautiful age-old trees that crowd the creek's banks, but I especially enjoy spring and autumn there. Winter, too, with its dramatic look of starkness, gives it an expression that I find lovely. I also knew that my chances of meeting fellow monks were slimmer here than in the gardens. I didn't really feel like seeing or speaking to others at that point, but preferred to be alone with nature and my thoughts.

Having nearly finished my first "tour," I began to hear voices approaching. Looking up, I saw Father Martin and Abbé Guinot coming my way at about the same time that they noticed me. They were most assuredly not two I particularly wanted to see; however, I proffered a big smile when the pair came near.

Abbé Guinot was the first to speak, looking tense. "Hello, Father Moreau."

"Hello, Père Abbé. I hope you are well. Hello, Father."

Abbé Guinot gave a strange smile but said nothing more. There continued an awkward pause until the abbé spoke again.

"Well, Father, this is the day the abbey has been waiting for. No doubt some will be cheered by the opportunity for change."

I found the comment provocative but I didn't let the tone of it bother me.

"Père Abbé, it is indeed an important day for us. No doubt it will deeply affect each member of our community. I rest assured, though, that God's hand will direct us. I prefer to let His Providence and not my opinions rule the…"

"Come now, Father Jean, it has been clear since our first meeting that you hardly embrace the status quo," interrupted Father Martin, emboldened in the abbé's presence.

I tensed as I heard those words. Abbé had no comment or visible reaction to his colleague's outburst and did nothing to quiet or censor him. I took two deep breaths and then replied.

"It is true, Father, that you came to me some time ago to ask my thoughts and elicit my support for Abbé Guinot's election."

I was happy to be able to address the question directly, though I was still angry at the impertinence of the man, and I continued.

"It is God's hand that will be guiding each man's careful reflection on the matter, including my own. I will only make up my mind fully when my ballot is in my hand."

Abbé Guinot then turned to Father Martin after I spoke. He saw there was no point in continuing this conversation and abbé's look made Father Martin see clearly that it was over. Father Martin, realizing that he had been foolish and not wishing to let the situation become complicated, nodded to me and said, in a complete about-face, "Thank you, Father, for your well-considered thoughts. We look forward to seeing you later at the chapter meeting."

With that Father Martin guided Abbé Guinot past me and they continued to walk. My eyes followed them as they departed. My head was swimming as I gazed at the pair. How much on the one hand I detested this man as abbé. That emotion was hard to ignore or redirect, even though I was grateful he had terminated Father Martin's attack. I still thought him a weak and vain little creature, completely changed since he took office. On the other hand, I knew he was a child of God and that the Godlike qualities of the abbé were also there, and I would see them beneath the surface if I were generous enough in spirit. I had to resist the urge to pass judgment. I certainly had room for improvement on that score.

I know that all men possess God's Spirit deeply. Some have hidden it well beneath a veneer, blinding them to all but sensory perception; they have yet to peel back that layer of delusion to discover their real and unique God-connected selves. That is why they, and all of us for that matter, are here in these bodies. We are here to discover that truth, that Spirit, and see it for its real beauty. There is an effort to be made to get to that truth before it is ultimately revealed to us. There are lifetimes to live, much experience to gain, good decisions to be made, emotions to deconstruct, and love to be given and received. Then, and only then, will we understand creation in all of its subtlety, depth, and mystery.

I had come to learn that this is the way of things. I also had begun to see how hard or perhaps impossible it would have been to accomplish this without the aid of a body and an earthly home. God's plan is indeed perfect, and man's job is just to complete the exercise and eventually return home in his wisdom to abide in eternal bliss with his Creator.

Three thirty — I remember the bell tolling the hour. I thought it best to return to my cell for prayer and final preparation prior to the meeting. I continued on the path along the creek until I reached the end. I then turned back toward the partial cloister and continued on to my room, ruminating on the importance of living in the "present moment." It was a conscious thought. I stopped for a moment to concentrate on the awareness of that thought. I began to hear my inner voice tell me about another thing. It was telling me that it is man's tendency to pin exaggerated importance on certain moments that we perceive as critical, spending valuable time anticipating those moments even when we cannot possibly know an outcome. It's a mistake because isn't it true that all present time and each present moment is as pregnant with possibility as any other, every moment full of God's promise and richness, each moment a miracle in itself? Yes, of course it is true. Living in anticipation or fear or excitement causes us to lose that perspective. Each moment lived in mindful Awareness can show us another truth, and eventually the sum of those truths teaches us the wisdom that will set us free.

I remember feeling at that point a surge of positive energy flow through me. My search for mindfulness at that moment had been a God-connected thought. I began to feel a real sense of contentment. The simple ideas that come like this one had come, all of these little truths and realizations, become significant refinements in our view of the world and of the Creator. These refinements are small progressions, evolutionary "tweaks" in the apprehension of Awareness. They often bring a change in outlook, but much more to the point, this kind of refinement brings growth. That is how we arrive at Truth.

I remember then feeling suddenly excited, very much alive to all that was going on inside of me. I passed Brother Herman and gave him an uncharacteristic and enthusiastic slap on the back. Brother Herman stopped in his tracks, a look of incredulity passing over him. I didn't speak to him but went right into the church. I passed through it and got back to my cell very much ready for whatever God had in store for my abbey, this place that I love. As I allowed the thoughts to come, I found myself suddenly very optimistic after having had those many days of concern. I was really enjoying the feeling. It felt like I was experiencing life deeply, garnering all I could with each moment.

I remained in my room, continuing to enjoy the feeling, until the bells started sounding. Fifteen minutes to go. I picked up my copy of the Psalms and left my room, deciding to arrive at the chapter room as early as possible. I was full of anticipation. I would go and soak in the moment and have a chance for a few last prayers. How quickly our emotions, not to mention our lives, can change!

The Moment Arrives

Whate'er we leave to God, God does, and blesses us…
— Henry David Thoreau, "Inspiration"

I had been seated in the chapter room for about ten minutes, sitting quietly with eyes closed and feeling very peaceful and content, when I started to hear my brother monks arrive in numbers. I left that moment of quiet and opened my eyes. I watched each monk arrive, silently, alone or with one or two others. I felt my heart swell in my bosom — I loved these men, not just as reflections of my Heavenly Father, but as a family, my family, with whom I was committed to dwell for the remainder of my days on this earth. At that moment, I felt nothing but gratitude to be in their company and to be where I was stationed in life. Later, I would think back on how remarkably calm I had felt on the eve of the monastery's decision. Maybe my faith was finally maturing. I was comfortable relying on divine Father/Mother God, our true Confidante and Hope. What a comfort to be able to weather such an emotional event in this fashion!

I had taken my seat in the second row of chairs, just about dead center. All thirty-eight brothers in total were expected to attend, and that was the number that did in fact arrive. All of the monks were present just prior to four-thirty, with Abbé Guinot having arrived alone and seating himself in the abbé's chair in front. The room was very still after the last monk had seated himself. It befitted the occasion.

Abbé's stick sounded exactly at four thirty and there was a general rustling. All eyes were now fixed on him. He began with a prayer.

"In the name of the Father, and of the Son, and of the Holy Spirit, let us pray. Father in heaven, we come today into Your presence, a family of men attempting to live as You will us to live, following the example of Your Son and our Savior, Jesus Christ. You have blessed us with health and material goods and this opportunity to serve You in community as Your servant Benedict directed us fifteen centuries ago. Come to us today with Your Holy Spirit, in Your tender mercy, and guide us in our choice of abbé. We thank You and ask You to bless us. This we pray through Jesus Christ, Your Son, who lives and reigns forever and ever. In the name of the Father, and of the Son, and of the Holy Spirit. Amen."

With that, we were seated and all was silent again. To be honest, I had not expected so graceful a prayer from Abbé Guinot. I was impressed by its humble spirit and tone and felt it boded well for what was about to take place, but I was not so confident that that tone would mark the abbé's manner should the vote go against him. I was disappointed to feel that way, and I attempted to bat the thought away.

The business part of the meeting was now getting underway. Abbé Guinot moved to make an introduction. In any election for abbé, an observer from the congregation to which the abbey belongs is always present. This observer was also seated in front at the table with the abbé.

"My fellow priests and brothers, here to assist us today in our election process is Father Michel Durandy from the Abbey of Solesmes. Please welcome and attend to him and to any requests he may have as if he were the Christ come amongst us."

With that, Father Durandy stood, smiled, and began.

"My brothers, the reason for our coming together today is well understood. It is important now to tend to our business at hand, the selection of abbé, and I would like us to take up that issue immediately. I will ask Brother Luc to distribute ballots to each of you. Remember, a two-thirds majority is required for election to the position of abbé. If there is no such majority on the first ballot, a second will commence after a period of reflection. The election process will continue until a brother is ultimately selected.

"Brother Luc, you may start passing out the ballots. My fellow monks, when you are finished, please hold your ballot and deposit it in the urn Brother Luc will bring to you. Thank you and may God bless us all today."

At the conclusion of these words, Father Durandy reseated himself. Abbé Guinot then stepped down and moved to a seat among his brothers. He took his ballot in turn and made his selection. The balloting went quickly. Father Durandy presently indicated to Luc that he should start the collection of the ballots. Luc passed among the monks with the urn, into which each monk placed his ballot. I had written on my ballot the name of Father François, as I had felt guided to do, and I quietly put the ballot in the urn as Luc passed. There was inevitably some tension in the air, and while I continued to feel calm, there was just a little of the nervousness of anticipation starting to creep in.

Luc brought the urn back to the table to the two monks, Fathers Martin and Vincent, who had been selected to tally and verify the vote. They had been the first to place their ballots into the urn. These two clerics began counting under the watchful eye of Father Durandy. The latter would verify that the election had been conducted in the proper spirit and in accordance with the rules associated with abbé elections. It was also to Father Durandy to announce the results after receiving the tally submitted by the two resident monks.

Father Durandy rose to give the results of the voting. "My brothers, after tabulating your votes, I find we do not have a two-thirds majority. The votes are as follows."

Father Guillaume rose and walked over to an easel upon which lay a large pad of paper, and prepared to write the results of the first ballot upon it as Father Durandy announced them.

Father Durandy disclosed the results.

"Father Pierre Guinot, fifteen votes. Father François Le Gall, fourteen votes. Father Jean Moreau, nine votes.

Did I hear that correctly? Nine votes for me? I was absolutely stunned by what I heard and now saw. There was my name listed in the top three vote-getters.

How incredible to me…nine votes! Never in my wildest thoughts had I considered myself "abbé material"! I became very self conscious. Like a little child, I suddenly felt that everyone was looking at me. My head was swimming. But nine brothers had cast their ballots with my name on them. Almost one-fourth of my fellow monks had thought that I, Jean Moreau, would make a good leader — no, not just a leader, a "Father" to them. And at my age. I couldn't possibly take on a role like that, could I? My thoughts continued to race. I must, if by some miracle I were to prevail on another ballot…but, my goodness!

But now, just as importantly, I knew as did the whole community that there was no chance that Abbé Guinot would win reelection. His strength lay in the first ballot, that was sure. Change was coming. Even with that realization, I was sitting nearly paralyzed and could do nothing but start my deep breathing. The other monks were mostly still looking at the tally and analyzing it and what it might mean to them, and thinking already of their next ballot. Finally, I started to calm a bit, and looked at the tally again. As I began to reason more clearly after my first few moments of surprise and confusion, I had to believe now that Father François was the clear favorite

Father Durandy again began to speak.

"My brothers, there before you is the tally from the first ballot. I ask you to take time to reflect and search within your hearts for what you perceive is the will of the Spirit, He that guides you and all of us in this process, during the upcoming break for reflection.

"I will, however, ask any of those whose names appear in front of us to speak to us before we break if he wishes to remove himself from further consideration for this high office and its grave responsibilities. Please speak now before we pause."

There was the rustle of a cassock just behind me, and Father François stood looking pale and distracted.

"My brother monks of Kervennec, the honor you have bestowed on me by even considering me for this most high office is something for which I am truly grateful — and surprised. But I find in my heart of hearts that I am unable to accept the position under any circumstances. I do not have the will or wisdom or constitution to be your abbé, and it is with regret that I must withdraw my name."

With that, he sat immediately.

The atmosphere in the room that had been deathly still suddenly became more charged. Now the relief felt by the monks of having cast the first ballot, me included, had been replaced very quickly by the idea that a runoff between two decidedly different personalities was the inevitable prospect for the next ballot; that is, if both candidates should choose to run. Of Abbé Guinot's intent there could be no doubt. Clearly, all knew that he wanted the job. I glanced at him. He had taken his seat as a regular brother monk for the election, sans regalia, just to the left of me, one row ahead in the front. I couldn't help but notice that he appeared smaller to me. His look was now impassive. But I also noticed something else — how many eyes were now catching mine as I lifted my gaze.

I felt again as if there were a spotlight directly over my head, like a ringmaster at the circus, as if I were the room's center of attention with all waiting upon my next word and my next move. Like an electric shock, it came to me that it was I, and I alone, who represented the best hope — now, in fact, the only hope — of moving Abbé Guinot out of the position for which he was so clearly ill-suited. Again, that thought that another few years under his rule would most probably bring disaster to Kervennec raced through my mind. I needed to accept the possibility that only I could prevent that. God's will for the abbey was being expressed in this and every election, this I firmly believed. Incredibly, I was now clearly a part of that expression. I had vowed to let the Spirit be the final Arbiter of the election process, and now I would remain true to that vow, even though it might affect my life in untold ways.

I was under no illusions about the demands, the difficulties, and ultimately the responsibilities of the position; but, since I felt so strongly that it was the will of God being expressed in this forum, I felt I must do nothing to detract from or thwart that expression. My mind was made up. I found myself rising to my feet. The monks perceptibly leaned forward in their chairs as I rose. I could feel the tension — perhaps I was rising to reject the office? The monks were still not sure of my course of action. I knew I needed to speak and clarify my intent. These were my brothers. So much was hanging in the balance for the men and they would also hang on my every word.

I wanted to look at each of them as their faces all turned to me. I wanted to look at each in tenderness. I knew that among them many already were asking me to become their earthly Abba, their Father. As in a dream, all at once those faces appeared to me like the faces of children, looks imploring, eyes wide open and attentive. I remember a wave of gratitude sweeping over me. I was at peace with what was about to happen.

I looked up at Father Durandy for a moment before speaking. I was gathering my energy, the positive energy that was being sent unconditionally my way by many of my brothers. Sweeping the room with my gaze I began to speak.

"My dear and esteemed brothers, your confidence in me has astonished and all but overwhelmed me. Those who know me well know that I firmly believe that the Spirit moves in these assemblies and that I must accept completely and irrefutably any result that it brings. Therefore, I humbly announce that I would be Abbé of Kervennec, without hesitancy, should you confer the position upon me."

At that moment, I suddenly found myself overwhelmed with emotion. It was the speaking of those words aloud, "Abbé of Kervennec," that did it. I knew at that point that there might be very little now that lay between me and that exalted office — and responsibility. From that moment on, each time there has been any reference to the word abbé in any forum or even in private address, the word "responsibility" has quickly followed in my mind. It all started with that utterance, as I accepted the sudden and unexpected realization that I could hold that office.

I seated myself and continued to think a minute about what I had just said to all. My mind was still flooded with emotion. I had spoken words that were in no way premeditated, words that were inspired from I knew not where. Yet they were my words, and I wholeheartedly believed and embraced them. I had meant what I had said. God would speak in this conclave. If He spoke in such a manner as to ordain me abbé, I would accept it without reservation, despite the fact that being abbé had hardly been a part of my design for my life at Kervennec.

After some moments, I began to feel more my normal self once more. I thought more about this strange course of events. It is mine and all of humanity's daily call to listen, to process, and then to act on God's word as each understands it. How the Heavenly Father can move mysteriously! Intuitively, I knew that I was being called. There is certainly one other thing I did already know then: if I act contrary to my intuition, no matter how outlandish or contrary to my own perception of things it might appear to be, if I do not do what the Spirit is telling me, there will be problems. Like Noah and the prophets before, though on a much smaller scale, I needed to follow through…to answer the Father's call as I understood it, even if I could not find an explanation for it. It was hardly decided for me to be abbé, however. Those who voted for Father François might not see me as their ideal champion. All this passed through my head very quickly.

Father Durandy then rose to address the assembly. He appeared almost somber now, aware that a major change may be coming for the abbey. He spoke.

"We shall go to a second ballot to decide among the remaining candidates. We will do so after time is taken for further reflection and meditation. I bid you not to speak on the subject to one another in this intervening twenty minutes, and to trust in God and use this time to clear your mind of any questions, any doubts, or any prejudices that it may harbor. Without any further remarks, we stand adjourned for twenty minutes. God bless you."

Most of the assembly quickly stood up after these words of dismissal. I remember the rattle of chairs being moved and the sound of rustling clothing and shoes tapping the floor hitting me like a cold rain, jolting me. I quickly and quietly left the room and hurried back to my cell. There I went right to my dais, looked at the Christ above it, and I began to pray. This is what I recall saying:

"Lord, what You have done for Your humble monk! Should this office come to me, please give me the strength, the courage, and the wisdom to fulfill the office as it should rightly be filled: in a Christlike way, and in the spirit of Your servant Benedict. I will have much to learn and quickly. But with You on my side, how can I fail?"

After some moments of silence, I slowly walked back to the chapter room. It was funny; as I entered the room again, I sensed a distinct difference in the energy pervading it. Whereas before it had had an air of heaviness and thickness, the atmosphere now seemed perceptibly lighter — a remarkable shift. There was still the quiet, and perhaps it was just me, but I sensed a calm that I had not sensed before the first vote.

Nearly all of the other monks had already returned before me, ready for the second round of voting. Father Durandy entered the room along with Fathers Vincent and Martin, and they proceeded immediately to the front of the room where the two resident priests again took their seats at the table. Father Durandy remained standing and, when the assembly was complete, tapped the table with a stick, easily gathering the attention of all of us to signal that the chapter meeting was about to reconvene.

"My brothers in Christ, we will now vote a second time for one of you to become the Abbé of Kervennec. If one of you should receive the necessary two-thirds of the votes, twenty-six or more in this case, then the abbey will have elected its new Father. I inform you, however, that should no one receive the necessary number, we will proceed after a short adjournment to a third ballot. Should we still not have a brother monk obtaining the requisite number of votes after the third ballot, the balloting will continue to a fourth round, with the modification that a simple majority will carry the day.

"With that, I will leave you to vote with clarity of thought and inspiration, perceiving as you will God's plan for the future of Kervennec. Thank you and God bless you all. Brother Luc, will you please pass the ballots?"

Father Durandy then took his seat and Brother Luc again began the distribution of the blank ballots. He then returned to the front of the room to wait after casting his own ballot, holding the urn into which the other completed ballots would be deposited. I cast a quick glance across the room; the rest of the monks were seated ahead of me. I was again in a bit of a daze. Could I lead these men? Could I be their spiritual Father?

The voting on this occasion went even quicker and Luc saw that he could begin the collection immediately. After retrieving the ballots of Fathers Vincent and Martin, he proceeded across the first row of chairs. The priests and brothers seated along that row quickly in turn deposited their ballots as Luc passed. When Luc came to Father Guinot, the latter hesitated a moment before offering his ballot. He stared at the urn and didn't move. Then there was an almost imperceptible glance by Guinot in my direction as he finally placed his ballot in the urn. I noticed that Luc nodded to Guinot as if to acknowledge the moment before continuing down the front row to finish collecting the ballots.

When Luc arrived at the beginning of the second row, things went swiftly again. He then came to me, seated alone in the last row. He seemed to know instinctively that he should discreetly slow his progress to let me, his brother and good friend, collect myself. Luc turned away and nonchalantly began pushing the ballots already deposited further into the urn to gain some time. I felt I was in another world, far way, suspended in a bright and airy place — my head felt so very light. I could not concentrate. I felt absent in a sense, yet very present as I considered what was about to occur. Luc told me later that I seemed like one in a trance as I slowly and mechanically tried to offer my ballot.

Then, Luc did something that only a close friend can do. He had sensed the time was right to bring me back to the present. It was time for a potential future abbé to take charge. Ever so gently, without anyone noticing, the rotund brother and chef de cuisine stepped heavily on my left foot! There was no expression on his face, just a subtle twinkle in his eye that I instantly recognized for what it was. I snapped out of my trance and, a split second after that ponderous load had been removed from my foot, I looked and felt like the old me. He was telling me I was ready for the next "step," whatever it may be! I was confident again. It was as if the power of the Spirit, which I had summoned to help me, had arrived via Brother Luc.

Luc brought the urn to Father Durandy. The latter in turn regarded its contents for a moment and then passed it to Fathers Vincent and Martin for the final tally. The room seemed expectant, but not so terribly tense, as each monk awaited the results in his own fashion. Many were visibly praying in their silence, some with their lips moving, eyes shut. Father Guinot remained alone with his thoughts, his hands on his thighs, his gaze cast downwards.

The two priests finished tallying the ballots. There were two piles in front of them. One was significantly larger than the other. When each pile had been straightened, Father Vincent leaned over to say something to Father Martin and the latter nodded assent. Then the two looked at Father Durandy and nodded as if to say that their work was finished. Father Durandy then leaned over the table and called the two priests once more into parlay. It was a very short meeting and Father Durandy wrote something on a sheet of paper and then stood and turned to the waiting monks. He adjusted his glasses as he regarded the paper one more time before speaking. He straightened himself for the solemnity of the moment. Father Guillaume resumed his post at the easel.

"My brothers in Christ, I hold the results of the second ballot in my hands. Thank you for your inspired actions today as you looked into your hearts with love and gratitude to vote for your next Father. This will be the final ballot. You have selected your new abbé. Here is the result of the voting. Father Pierre Guinot, ten votes. Father Jean Moreau, twenty-eight votes."

It was as if the room immediately exhaled. It all came home to me in a rush and after a moment of intense internal and emotional joy, I erupted into a broad smile and greeted my brothers who were now applauding with a simple wave. Instead of feeling stunned or speechless, remarkably I was feeling eager to assume my new duties. I felt one thing even more than that — gratitude; I, the lowly servant, had been lifted up. I was bursting with joy.

Father Durandy came to where I was now standing.

"Father, now Abbé-elect Moreau, let me offer my congratulations. Yours will be an important and challenging task, but I am sure you will achieve all that you attempt. I ask the Holy Spirit to always be at your side in your new responsibilities."

I, Abbé-elect Moreau, could only nod my thanks with a large smile, taking his hand of congratulations.

Father Durandy returned to the front, tapped his stick and said, "My brothers, our work here is finished. The chapter meeting is adjourned."

The excitement in the room did not diminish. Monks around the room continued smiling and nodding at me. For me, the moment had arrived, the moment for which deep within me I knew I was ready. The joy and excitement continued to flow over me at this fait accompli. I was unruffled. God had chosen me and I would not disappoint my greatest Love. Even at that moment I had begun thinking of all there was to do. I felt the energy rise within me as I stood and received those visual well wishes from my group of brothers. How I loved these men!

The monks continued chatting amongst themselves as I gathered my prayer book. Father Durandy made his way over to me again before leaving. He gently put his hand on my shoulder and smiled broadly.

"Congratulations, my friend, and best of luck as you assume your duties. No doubt we will meet again."

I proffered my thanks and then I started making my way across the room. As I moved slowly among the men, I thought of something. There was a duty for me to perform and I didn't want to forget to do it or let the moment pass. I sought out Father Guinot and found him near the door chatting quietly with two brother priests. He saw me coming over and turned to greet me. His eyes told the story. His disappointment was great and I could only imagine how he felt. He looked very tired. I knew that he was trying to shrug off his feelings of personal devastation and abandonment as best he could. His attempt was falling short, and who could blame him, but he was able to summon a tense smile. There was little else that he had the power to do.

"Congratulations, Abbé Moreau."

"Thank you, Father Guinot. I appreciate that very much," I responded, aware of the tension in the air.

"I only hope that I can count on your help in making this transition. I will need all of that that I can get, Father," I said, as I looked to find reconciliation with my brother priest.

"Abbé Moreau, you can be assured that I will do what I can in that regard," said Father Guinot as he turned away quickly and prepared to leave the room. That was his signal that the conversation was over. As I turned to leave I felt a tap on my shoulder. It was Father François. His huge grin lit up his face.

"Jean, I mean Abbé, I couldn't be more delighted! It was my fervent hope when I declined to run for this sacred position that you would pick up that mantle. And now, with God's help, you have!"

I looked at that broad smile and knew that his tribute was heartfelt. What a good abbé he would have made had he seized the moment; but François felt his limitations keenly and I respected him for that, most certainly.

"I think I'm only at the very beginning of realizing what a task it will be. You, Father François, will be very important to me as I get my feet wet, and I will count on you for advice and sagesse. I know you possess it — and there is no doubt that I will need it!"

Father François' grin grew broader.

"You humble me, Jean. I am only too happy to call you 'Abbé.'"

I remember how I felt a tingle run up my spine. "Abbé" — the power of the word and the power it signified gripped me like a vise. It was I, Jean Moreau, the simple kid from Brest, who had never in his life thought of leading and directing a monastery and the great and holy men who resided there, who was to be their spiritual Father. These men would now be depending upon me, my judgment, my wisdom, and my adeptness at ministering to their needs both material and spiritual. "I am to be that man!" said the voice inside of me.

Brother Herman approached me, his usual winning smile now absent. He didn't have to say anything. I saw in Herman's eyes, however, a look that I had never seen in them before. This friend whom I loved was now standing quietly in front of me, saying nothing but expressing everything with his gentle and sincere look.

"Abbé Jean, my friend, what can I say to you to express my feelings of joy…and love? You are to be my Father. How joyful I feel! How lucky! Oh, such progress we are going to make!"

Brother Herman could no longer control his emotions and wrapped his arms around me in a loving embrace. I stood there, receiving that love, and returned to him the monastic salute of our foreheads gently touching, humbled by this expression of genuine feeling and joy. I didn't have words. It was just a time to let the emotions flow and to allow them to take their course. It was a rare moment, a precious opportunity for both of us and for the monks in general to open our hearts and emote. Mine was full to bursting. I fully realized again how God had been so good to me, not just for choosing me as abbé — such a blessing of trust and responsibility — but in leading me to this special place where I can share life and get to know Him with these men I loved.

All of the monks had made their way over to me to acknowledge and congratulate me before departing, and then it was over, and I stood alone in the empty chapter room. I felt a new sensation. It was now all coming down on me. My shoulders felt the invisible mantle of responsibility that was now mine. I was ready. It was a solemn moment.

Suddenly, the door opened and I snapped to attention. In came Brother Luc, looking embarrassed for a moment as he strode over to the head table still strewn with the second ballot results.

"I'm sorry, Father Jean…I mean, Père Abbé, but

in the excitement I forgot to collect these for the archives. Sorry for having disturbed you."

Oh my dear Luc! I walked over to my friend and former protégé and, looking him in the face and without saying a word, took the young brother in my arms and gave him a hug that lasted for two minutes. When we finally held each other at arm's length, there were tears running down Luc's cheeks, and one or two down mine. Nothing was said. Both of us were beaming despite the tears, and both of us understood each other in that unique way that only a close friendship can make possible

"Luc, thanks for stepping on my toes…"

He gave an undisguised chuckle and made his way out with the spent ballots and the urn, and again I was alone. I felt a calm descend over me as I stood in the empty room, alone. Then, I felt the growing excitement return. Maybe it was the friend's embrace, maybe it was my unconscious coming to terms with what had happened this day — I wasn't sure — but my zest for the job in all of its potential and opportunity came roaring through me like a torrent. I felt energized, and I liked the feeling.

I looked around one last time to savor the moment and the atmosphere of this life-changing event. Never would anything in my life be the same again. A new vista had opened to me, so vast and pregnant with promise that I could see nothing in it that resembled anything that had come before. I was ready — and I knew it.

I turned to leave and entered the corridor. The air

in the passage was fresh. I closed the door to the chapter room — and opened the door to the newest and greatest chapter in my life.

A Ceremony

Pride makes us artificial and humility makes us real.
— *Thomas Merton,* No Man is An Island

The day arrived for my formal installation. As Abbé-elect, I was already abbé "in fact," but this ceremony would mark that elevation officially and publically and give my brother monks their opportunity to pledge obedience and fidelity to their new Father.

This was not the first permanent abbé installation for most of the monks — all but three had been here since the election of Abbé Rénard seven years prior, and, of course, all had been at the interim abbé's installation. An installation is always a very powerful and meaningful moment for each monk, and above all, a personal one. Its vows and significance for a monk cannot be overestimated. The installation brings in the man who is to be one's new Father, the one whose word and judgment were to be final — mentor, guide, and shepherd for the rest of one's, or the abbé's, life.

I was busy preparing myself in the church that morning in the small sacristy situated adjacent to the altar. I was dressing for the first time as abbé and I remember I was ready to place around my neck the abbé's cross signifying my place, the symbol of my authority. It was a large and beautiful cross with a silver finish. As I hung the cross upon my chest, I expected to feel something different; but, there was no bolt of lightning or anything else appreciable, no zap of energy or feeling of power or even of humility as I stood there with it on. As I walked across the room to retrieve a book that I used for meditation, I caught a glimpse of myself passing in front of a mirror. It was then that it happened. I was caught completely unprepared for my image as abbé. I was virtually arrested in full stride. I stood there, looking back at the man I had always known, but there was now a difference. The cross dominated the image and made the man look small. The cross was everything, not just the symbol of the ancient sacrifice of God for man — for the cross I now wore had a profound history all its own. This cross was the same as those worn by abbés around the world; but, even more significant to me, it was the cross worn by so many great men and saints of history, themselves abbés — from Benedict to Bernard of Clairvaux to my own wonderful abbés — and now it was coming to me.

How was I to feel? Who was I to now be wearing this symbol of recognition, this outward sign of personal power but also of the terrible responsibility that all abbés carry, charged as they are with so many souls and their salvation? These thoughts came crashing down on me like a great burden that was now mine to bear. I started to feel weak and was almost unable to stand. Then I found a kneeler and, placing my elbows upon it with my head in my hands, I began to implore the Ancient One to give me the strength to move forward and to do this job to the best of my ability. I prayed fervently and almost to the point of tears. I knew that I was God's choice, but I was frightened. Now it was all up to me...with His help.

As my prayers continued, the terror died down. I raised my face to a crucifix on the wall above me. I felt stronger, yet still very weak. I remember resting in that position for some time, exhausted, too tired to pray or to think. I heard the bells calling the men to worship. I stood, not knowing where to go or what to do for that moment, but I knew I must move. I must do something. Slowly, I walked over to retrieve the remainder of my vestments, and as I did so, I passed the mirror once more. Again I was surprised at what I saw. This time I saw something completely different. I saw a man that was purged of any pride. I saw myself, drained and subject to human weakness, but marvelous all the same, full of possibilities. God's child. I felt relieved, gathering to myself a renewed energy. I began to see myself as who I had become. A Shepherd to a flock, the leader of the Abbé of Kervennec. Everything seemed to fall into place in that moment — I felt free of fears and full of truth. In that split second, I had become reassured and confident of my role and how to play it. "Maybe it was a little miracle," I thought to myself, or maybe it had been God's way of showing me who and what I really was and upon Whom I must depend. It didn't matter. I knew one thing. I was completely ready now to become the Abbé of Kervennec. With eagerness I finished dressing and in a few moments I had taken my place with the men in the corridor, awaiting our entrance into the church.

The day was a beautiful one and light was flooding down through the church windows from a radiant sun. The bells of the abbey continued their pealing. This is always a joyous moment in an abbey's history and it is good to express it. A new Father was here and it was now time to celebrate him and one's faithfulness to him and to God. As each monk found his accustomed spot, a hymn was raised with the accompaniment of the organ as a joyful prelude to the ceremony.

I entered and looked around. This was my day, yes, yet it was also the Church's day, Kervennec's day, the continuation of a grand tradition, the affirmation of the relevance of one of its oldest and most venerable institutions. Yes, I was to become abbé, but I was only one such man in a long line stretching back into the mists of time. There would be many more after me, God willing, more men entrusted with a community of souls carrying out the Word as given them from their Father in heaven as they understood it, nothing more and nothing less. I vowed to myself to be true to that tradition and that task given me. It was an environment at once solemn and radiant. My joy was complete.

The ceremony passed with chant and tradition. At the end, it was time for each monk to profess his joy and his obedience to the new abbé, his "Abba-Father" for the rest of his or his abbé's life. The first to greet me was Father Joseph, the doyen of the abbey, now in his eighty-seventh year. With some difficulty, but with a big smile on his face, Father Joseph knelt, clasped my hands, and pledged his obedience. He slowly rose and gave me a kiss on the cheek and whispered the word "congratulations" in my ear; then, with a slightly faltering step, he moved on. Each monk continued in this fashion and I often felt overwhelmed by the emotions summoned up and expressed by my brothers during the ceremony. They were so supportive. As each passed, I felt myself growing stronger and stronger in my new role as their leader. My view of myself was changing rapidly from Jean Moreau, simple monk, to Abbé Jean Moreau, monk and Father of the abbey. I acknowledged that change interiorly, fully open to and appreciative of it. I was settling in.

I looked down the line of monks yet to pledge. I saw Father Guinot just behind Father Maurice. I felt a little signal of alarm rise in me, which I quickly put aside. I nurtured whatever feelings of compassion I could summon as I considered what it must be like for Father Guinot at this moment. Had our positions not been exactly reversed not so long ago? Was this not the man who had justly lectured me about my lack of propriety, but who had also unjustly lambasted me on my unsuitability to carry on as a monk? Was this not the man who had put me on probation? Was this not the same man that I had come to despise in his role as temporary abbé, just a few weeks before? These questions raced through my head, yet at the same time I felt my compassion mount. How strange, I remember thinking, to feel such conflicting messages simultaneously. There I was in all my humanness. The human condition offers us emotion after emotion but always gives us choices with those emotions. I as a man had the choice to be mean-spirited or soft and compassionate, a little lesser than the angels. All of that passed through my mind in those split seconds.

Father Maurice whispered his congratulations in my ear and then moved on. I was brought back to the present moment by this contact and I smiled and touched Maurice affectionately as he departed. Father Guinot approached slowly, keeping his head down until the last moment, when his eyes met mine ever so briefly. Strangely, it was a moment that I both dreaded and welcomed, not unlike other moments that can be fraught with fear. We are being offered a chance put things behind us and to grow in strength and wisdom. It was the right time to face those fears. And there was one more thing: I was being given a chance to cultivate compassion. I felt myself brace instinctively as Father Guinot approached to kneel in front of me. The moment was expectant; it was silent, and then seemed motionless.

Father Guinot's eyes slowly met mine a second time, but only briefly. They were not the happy, congratulatory eyes of those who had come before. There clearly was a great sadness in them, a disappointment that could not be disguised. It was up to me to see the true man, not just a man's unavoidable emotional reaction to a tremendously difficult moment springing forth uncontrollably from those eyes.

It seemed laborious for Father Guinot to lift his hands to meet mine. I wondered later if his movement was really that slow or if it was only in my imagination that it was so. His hands eventually met mine. They were cold and clammy. That wasn't a surprise to me. I felt him now in all of his humanity. I was his Father, and all my attention and efforts with him must be to bring the prodigal, if he was one, back to God. I would try to the nth degree.

I brought my other hand over to wrap around my charge's. His head fell. I prayed silently in my head that no residue of malice remain between us. I had no consciousness any longer of our relative positions a month ago, no remnants of guilt or shame from what I had confessed to this man. Father Guinot could not raise his head again to look at me. It was as if a power had constrained him, making it impossible for him to do what was expected.

My heart started to feel warmer as I waited, watching him. It was a feeling that I had experienced with children and even with my parents as they grew older. I saw Father Guinot as a child at that moment and that instinctively made me want to reach out to help him. I was internally repeating my prayers for conciliation. There was no sort of satisfaction for me to take from this situation. I found myself hoping that my erstwhile abbé could raise himself to the levels of charity and humility necessary to move on. We were under no time pressure. I was prepared to wait until that happened, hopefully this very day, at this very moment.

Father Guinot again raised his head, eyeing me. He seemed to steel himself as he attempted to speak. Slowly, very quietly, he did so.

"I pledge to you…" he paused and continued,

"Abbé Father…my…obedience."

There was nothing more. As he stood to move

away, his eyes averting my gaze, no further words were proffered. It was finished. The next monk, Brother Benoît, was now approaching. Like that, the moment had passed. I felt a heaviness in my heart, but I could no longer afford to dwell upon it. I had done my best and attempted to approach the situation with a clean slate and a loving heart. It was up to God now to help effect a true conciliation on the part of Father Guinot. I fervently hoped that with God's help Father Guinot could do it.

Shortly after, I had finished with the last brother and the ceremony was finished. Thirty-seven men had promised to obey and follow the dictates handed down by the new Abbé Moreau. There were only the last hymns to be sung before the procession would file out of the church, ready to continue the monastic day.

With that procession finished, I returned my vestments to their hangers and walked out alone. There were many new duties needing my attention, but they could wait. I needed now to go back to my beloved gardens for that breath of air, that salve that only nature could provide and that I craved. As I walked slowly down the garden paths, I found myself running my fingers over my abbé's cross, rubbing it gently as if to imbue myself with its power. No particular thoughts were with me — it was a quiet time. I walked a long time. The words "it's lonely at the top" came to me. They had new meaning.

I realized that I would have to pace myself and get to know my new role and its responsibilities over time, and, most importantly, to not begin judging myself in measuring my performance. Trusting all in God was the solution. It would all transpire as it should. I remember pausing one more moment to gaze out at all before me before going to my new office to begin the administration of the abbey. As I stood there, looking out over the orchards still dormant from winter, I thought of all of the other abbés before me who had taken these paths or had these thoughts. It gave me a sense of comfort to know that I was not the only one to ever carry this burden, not the only one to have just started in this pivotal role of leadership. As the others had done it, I would do it, in the very best way possible given my talents and given the challenges posed by my weaknesses. It would be all right.

I was glad to have this time alone after the grandeur and emotion of the ceremony. Right then, though, I knew that I could use a friendly voice and a reaffirming word before I got down to business. I knew where to go. I headed for the abbey shop which had just reopened. I knew that some time spent with Father François would be time well spent indeed for me. He would know what to say — and especially what not to say — and take my mind off the rigors of the job ahead for a little while.

It was a day that is now etched in memory. It was a life-changing event. We all have them. It was up to me to make the most of this God-given opportunity. I chuckled as I thought about it, looked up to heaven and winked, and said, "Thanks a lot!"

I smiled all the way to the shop and Father François.

Elena Comes to See Me

As I have written, Elena and I have stayed the good close friends we have always been. We have substituted letter writing for visits. We just write about feelings and whatever might currently be on our minds. Often it involves things spiritual, new ways we are looking at things or new books or ideas we have encountered that impressed one of us. Her search has continued, and I have been very happy discussing all of these things with her as well as reminiscing about our younger days and our life at university, but I haven't written any more of what has been happening here in the abbey, not even telling her about my elevation. It has probably just been a defensive reaction on my part from our past, but she respects it. She has never pushed the subject of the goings-on here, knowing perhaps intuitively it was just no longer something that I wanted to discuss.

Life and relationships are full of change and ours was about to change again. One day, very recently, she decided to pay me a visit. Why did she come? She described it as "one more piece of business to attend to." Never had I been far from her mind, she told me. Now she needed to see me and she had decided that "no matter what, it would be today, out of the blue with no warning." That way, she said, "You couldn't reject my overtures for a visit!" (Not that I would have now). With that, she had jumped in her car and driven the short distance to Kervennec.

She arrived before Vespers that day. The shop and welcome center were still open. She told me that she had hurried out of her car, and at reception had asked if she could speak to Father Jean Moreau. Father Guillaume had given her a rather queer look but took further information.

"Whom should I say is calling?" After she told him her name, she said that he said nothing other than for her to sit in the reception area and that he would see what he could do.

Father Guillaume then disappeared but returned very quickly, asking her to follow. She told me she was a bit surprised at this as Father began leading her into an area not usually open to any but the monks. They walked a short way down a corridor and stopped in front of a door marked "Abbé." She thought this more curious still.

After a quiet knock and my acknowledgment to enter, I saw the door open. I watched with amusement as the blood drained from her face. I stood there with a huge smile, saying nothing, happiness written all over me.

"Hi, Elena. Nice of you to come!" I said, laughing out loud.

Elena had put her hand over her open mouth, incredulous. She told me it hit her all at once. She thought, "Jean the abbé! Could it be or was this another of Jean's jokes?!" She could see in an instant, however, it was no joke. I was wearing the cross of office. Father Jean Moreau was now Abbé Jean Moreau.

We stood there just a few seconds and then we embraced. I pulled her away to arm's length and looked at her again. "My friend!" was all I could think — and say. I really loved seeing her again — I had missed her so. Here she was standing before me, looking the same, radiating still that soft energy. She had nothing but compliments for me, telling me how happy she was, how surprised she was, how I deserved the office, how strange life was, and so on. I took it all in happily.

We talked and talked and sometimes we would stop and she would just look at me in wonder. I asked her to stay until after Vespers so that we could speak more. She was more than happy to do so. She attended the Office and she told me how "her heart was full" as she saw me lead the men in and out of the service. Happily, I can say that the singing had never been lovelier. Afterwards, we talked away the hour until dinner. Elena told me some really good news, too. She told me that her windows had been installed for the nuns at the Abbey of St. Michel, and that they were delighted, so complimentary. I was very pleased for her but had to kid her and said, "My best friend, soon to be a nun at St. Michel!" I well remember how those words kept racing through my mind for a minute.

She peered at me with a look of curiosity and sweetness. I could tell she had more to say.

"Maybe you know already, Abbé Jean...that's the

piece of business I wanted to discuss…"

"Know what, my great friend?"

With a slight hesitation and with a little smile creeping over her face, she replied, "I'm thinking of entering the novitiate next month — at St. Michel."

Now it was my turn. I was speechless. I sat there with my mouth agape, overcome with joy. My best friend…someday, perhaps, a nun at St. Michel! All that I could think was, "Is it possible?"

I put my hand on hers and gazed at her, a huge smile crossing my face. It was all that I felt like doing. I felt this queer mixture of astonishment, pride, and real happiness flooding through me.

Finally, I found some words.

"What a fantastic story, Elena. It would be a fairy-tale ending," I told her.

Slowly having turned it over in her mind, she then said something quite prescient.

"Jean, it wouldn't be over…it would be just the beginning…"

The Other Things Have Come

But seek ye first the kingdom of God, and his righteousness; and all these things shall be added unto you.
— Jesus, Matthew 6:33

As I finish this volume, it seems as if winter has returned to my Brittany, though we are in April. Looking outside, I see a wall of gray clouds, creating a somber background for the bushes and trees sporting their first spring leaves and newly opened branches. The sky is filled with mist from horizon to zenith, and they, trying to acknowledge the dim light permitted them through the overcast. In a pensive mood like mine today, I am finding it hard to believe it has been over a year since I was invested with the singular responsibility of abbé. How much change a year or two can bring.

I remember when these damp and cold spring days could be a heavy and emotional time for me. Being young, I had no practice in Awareness. I got caught up in the somberness around me. Having aged now and learned, everything has changed. In my internal life I am now hardly affected by things brought to me from the exterior world, and I am ever thankful for this. I know that I have found my truth in Awareness and the spiritual life, and that I have grown in Spirit and I praise my Divine Mother for this precious gift.

In those early days here, my friends would write to me or visit and ask how I could give up so much to be in this little place called Kervennec. They were, of course, talking about giving up the things and experiences that are accepted as the pleasures of this world for a life of near solitude or boredom. I smile a little at that misunderstanding of how life is here. It has been for me nothing more than the exchange of some of the pleasures of the temporary for the joy of the eternal. A greater mismatch I could not postulate. I rejoice every day in seeing the bigger picture. Little things help make that happen.

I have in my room, above my dais, a little plaque that was given to me by my great-aunt Marie. It is a block of wood, resembling a rectangle of tree bark, on which are hand painted the following words:

Seek first the Kingdom of God,
and all things will be given you.

This simple little piece of craft art with its rendering of Matthew 6:33 has accompanied me most of my adult life. Like many objects that we gather and keep as a remembrance of a happy or meaningful person or event, it has become a "part of the furniture," visible but not very often "seen." Still, every so often I notice it. And when I do, the meaning of this special verse and the memory of the rare and loving woman who gave it to me reveal themselves again and delight my consciousness anew. I think again, too, of Whom it was that first uttered those words, and the love that He possessed for all of us.

This phrase, in its simplicity, summarizes the

whole Truth for me. This little plank of verse on a tree's bark has encapsulated what I have tried to do faithfully these twenty-plus years. It describes what has been my one desire, my life's mission. The accomplishment of my mission to know who I am has been achieved by coming to understand that one simple phrase. I am continuing in my development, of course. My opus, my great work, this life that is even now still unfolding season after season and year after year, has yet some things to accomplish. On balance, it has been overall a tremendously satisfying voyage for me.

Today, on this bleak day in late spring, it is one of those times that I, Abbé Jean Moreau, a priest and monk for life, have taken the time to see and appreciate anew what these words are telling me here in my little corner of France. I have sought the Spirit, my God, first, and now it is true, all things have been given me. All the other things have come. My heart is full.

May Kervennec and monastic communities everywhere, of every religious denomination, continue to prosper!

Now I will end this part of the story of my life to date. There is more to tell, as in many ways I have only scratched the surface of what has happened to me personally, and I will do so, but that will have to wait for another volume. For now, I want to finish this part of my story by expressing my dream for all mankind: that each person in this world finds life "and finds it abundantly," as Jesus has promised us. And, in the end, isn't it all about what Lao Tzu told us those many centuries ago?

> *Simplicity, patience, compassion.*
> *These three are your greatest treasures.*
> *Simple in actions and thoughts,*
> *you return to the source of being.*
> *Patient with both friends and enemies,*
> *you accord with the way things are.*
> *Compassionate toward yourself,*
> *you reconcile all beings in the world.*

The End

Afterword

Releasing the True Self

When I let go of what I am, I become what I might be.
                    — Lao Tzu, Tao Te Ching

When we come to know ourselves, our true origins and our place in Creation, we become Aware. As I have attempted to demonstrate, Awareness is about Waking Up. It is a crucial moment. Waking up starts with questioning. The essential question is "Who am I?" It is the beginning of the "beginning" — the point of embarkation for the greatest voyage of our lives. It matters not how the awakening comes, whether as a growing sense of intuition, a terrible dissatisfaction with things, an encounter with the Higher Self, or in any other way, offbeat or not. It only matters that we do awaken. Liberation comes first in the mind.

To find that true self in awakening we must begin by removing the false images that we have of ourselves. It is a major work. We know our true self is not defined by our gender, our race, our ethnicity, our talents, our roles, or our place in society — none of these describes the true self. No, we are sons and daughters of the Creator, endowed with rich faculties of perception, capable of receiving Enlightenment, heirs to a universe of extraordinary consequence with unimaginable complexities and dimensions. In short, we are beyond space and time.

We are, too, as fully human beings in the world, vessels of great intellect and equally gifted in the expression of the arts — we are passionate. But sometimes we have trouble seeing beyond that intellect, or passion. There are times when it is our own hesitancy or lack of confidence that would hold us back. If we fail to act, to take that step, we remain at the unconscious level frustrated and certainly dissatisfied, and we continue to be disconnected from our Source. We must not let that happen.

We will find that Awareness ultimately brings us our Truth, the only answer that will satisfy. When Pontius Pilate asked Jesus, "What is Truth?" Jesus didn't answer. Why not? Truth is unexplainable, and deeply interior, yet, it is universal. One knows it when one experiences it, but it defies ordinary explanation. It is about experiencing, albeit on levels we must search to find and get to know. In Truth, we find our true selves.

"Wake up, sleeper, rise from the dead, and Christ will shine on you," it is said in Ephesians 5:14. Your knowledge of self, of how things really work, gives you a perspective that is unbeatable. You know your Source. You are awake, aware. You know your rightful place, and old, limiting ideas have no power over you. You have claimed your power, and released your true self.

Bravo! Peace be unto you, and to God be the glory!

. Thank You!
Your Thoughts, Please!

Can you take a minute to share your thoughts about this book?

In your Amazon account or account where you purchased the book, open the book's display page and give it a star rating and/or post your review.

Writers depend upon reviews — and word-of-mouth recommendations — and yours would be appreciated!

If you enjoyed it, please share the book with friends and social media.

Thanks *so* much!

www.clarkeide.com

IF you enjoyed *A Monks Way,* the first volume in the *Abbey Chronicles Trilogy,* you will love these intriguing follow-ups in the series: Volume Two, *To Everything A Season,* and Volume Three, *Life & Love.*

As these suspenseful stories unfold, it becomes evident how Jean Moreau, this man of spirit, continues to think outside the box, fully encountering his humanity and all of its challenges. Jean invites the reader to look at life's problems and the spiritual life in new ways…his ideas about life, love, and traditional religion will often surprise…but they will offer the reader pathways to Awareness, the key to happiness.

Find the next volume in the series, *To Everything A Season*, by following this link to Amazon, or purchase it wherever good books are sold:

https://www.amazon.com/dp/1944030050

Jean Moreau's New Series

Jean Moreau's Little Books of Wisdom series is now available in eBook and paperback versions. In each booklet in the series, Jean presents a Virtue or quality that enlightened people can cultivate daily in order to live happier, more satisfying lives for themselves and others.

With useful commentary and easy exercises, these books are designed as a short read, organized in a helpful way so that you can continue to refer to them from time to time for helpful insights and reminders.

Find the first in the series by following this link to Amazon, or buy it wherever good books are sold:

https://www.amazon.com/dp/1944030115

Acknowledgements

There are many whom I would like to thank for the help and generosity with time and advice each has given as I undertook this book about my favorite fictional monk, Jean Moreau. It starts with the one nearest and dearest to me, my wife, Agnes, one of the kindest and most genuine human beings I have ever met. She is my greatest gift.

So very important has been the advice gratefully received from those who have agreed to read my drafts and provide helpful comments. These have included Mary Maxwell, the well-known humorist and YouTube star, for her insights and advice; Paul Eide, social media wizard; super copy editor, Califia Suntree; and, spiritual Coach and noted Author on EFT, Tessa Cason. A special wink also to Phyllis Firak-Mitz for her unique perspective. Finally, thank you Frieda, Betty, and Kristi, for translating my mumbles and rapid-fire speech to the written word.

I would certainly be remiss not to thank wholeheartedly Père Abbé Philippe Piron and Fathers Benoit and François of the Abbey of St. Anne of Kergonan in Brittany for their hospitality and generous help in answering my many questions and granting me an in-depth look at the workings of a great French abbey.

And, I have Abbé Jean Moreau himself to acknowledge. Something remarkable happened to me during the writing of this book. Halfway through its creation, I decided one day to visit one of my favorite abbeys in Brittany. A few ruined structures are all that remains of a huge and vital community of monks that once numbered in the hundreds. The abbey had controlled vast reaches of land for over six hundred years until events of the French Revolution forced the eviction of the monks at the end of the eighteenth century. On this occasion I took the time to examine the dilapidated ancient church, dark, barren, and musty, devoid of furniture, altar, and statuary, save for a small statue mounted high on the wall in a dark recess of the nave. Intrigued, I walked up to it, and translating as much Latin as I could, I saw it paid tribute to an abbot who had ruled for many years and done great things for the abbey in the seventeenth century. *What stopped me in my tracks and buoyed me with a sense of destiny was his name — Jean Moreau!* I was stunned. Maybe this Jean Moreau was helping me give life to "my" Jean Moreau, modern day French Benedictine monk. Such "coincidences," or synchronicities, if one remains open to them, are at the heart of much of Jean's beliefs and philosophy of life — and of Spirit.

September 2018
Punta del Este, Uruguay
Saint-Goazec, France

About the Author

Clark Eide is a retired entrepreneur, now writer, radio host and narrator, sharing time in France, Uruguay and the United States. A native of the United States, his study of things spiritual has taken him around the world - from the USA to London, from France to Australia, and Ireland to India. He is a member of the College of Psychic Studies in London, and currently supports the Self-Realization Fellowship of Paramahansa Yogananda in Los Angeles. He has spent time at Plum Village, home of the late famed author and Buddhist monk, Thich Nhat Hanh, and was present at the Dalai Lama's visit at Plouray, Brittany, experiencing at arm's length his extraordinary presence. He has been a long-time student of Transcendental Meditation, and has met with Indian pundits both in situ and in the USA on practical matters and astrology. He continues to be a student of alternative therapies such as Healing Touch, massage, hypnotherapy and EFT, and has studied with yoga masters in Australia, Ireland and Uruguay. He is a graduate of the University of Notre Dame.

These encounters and experiences have taught him that spirituality is about one thing only — direct connection to the Divine — as a part of or independent of an organized religion. The author hopes that this story of Jean Moreau will prove a useful tool in illustrating the importance of Awareness, the most critical step to that direct connection, a true path to life's meaning and spiritual contentment.

You can contact him by visiting **www.clarkeide.com**. or use the QR code for his website below.

Notes

www.ingramcontent.com/pod-product-compliance
Lightning Source LLC
Chambersburg PA
CBHW032106180726
48284CB00002B/476